JOURNEY TOWARD HEALING

BY

JEAN JEFFERS

Omega One Press
Cincinnati Ohio

OMEGA Press
Cincinnati Ohio

I dedicate this book to my friend, Michael Logsdon, who has been a faith-filled and loyal companion. And to my family members who supported me through this project.

Acknowledgments

I would like to say thank you to the many individuals who assisted in putting this book together. Their help and moral support were invaluable. Without them, I could not have written this novel.

Foremost, I thank the members of my Writer's Support Group who listened to the scenes and critiqued them.

The readers were a great help. Topsy Miller, Mary Lou Weber and Cathy Helmick worked tirelessly to read the manuscript. Their encouragement gave me the impetus to continue in those difficult moments when I was tempted to drop the project.

Particularly helpful were my friends Cathy Helmick and Mike for their willingness to do whatever I needed for them to do. And a thank you to Cathy Fyock, The Business Book Strategist, for her suggestions.

Special thanks go to Wendy Beckman, who is the leader of the Writer's Group, for her direction and support. She met with me for a working brunch once a month and answered all my questions. A special thanks to A. G. Billig for her timely advice.

Thank you to Mary Lee Starke, my spiritual companion, who allowed me to read a chapter a week to her in our sessions together.

Thank you to Ed Gutfreund for his support and morale building.

Thank you to Nick Caya, for his time, his answer to my many questions, and his patience with a very challenged tech user.

Thank you to Nelly Murarui for her art work for the cover.

Thank you to my sisters: Linda Jeffers, Mary Carrico and Joyce Woodward, for their financial contribution in getting this book published. I could not have done it without each of you.

I would like to thank Steve Alcorn for helping me develop the novel as a mystery story in his course, Writing Fiction Like A Pro on ed2go.

Thank you to Eva Shaw, my writing mentor/teacher for so

many years, for her inspiration, love, and support.

Thank you to my friend and companion, Mike Logsdon, who patiently lived with me during the writing of this novel.

Benedicta clutched the phone in her hand, as if tightening her hold could help her understand. "You can't do this to me and I won't let you hurt my sister. I'll call the police. I'll hunt you down. Some way, I'll get you." Benedicta noted a quiver in her voice and she choked on her promise, as she met the words of the threatening assailant with her own. Her words went unheard. The line was dead.

This call had been coming numerous times over the course of several months, and she was no closer to knowing the nature of the threat or who the culprit was. The calls, the messages, were weird, and because of its threat, she was disturbed.

I can't think of that right now, I must get downtown to see Mother Margaret Mary. I have an appointment to see her.

Getting her keys to the car, Benedicta made her way to her bright red Toyota and drove the expressway to Seventh St., where she parked the car.

"It isn't supposed to be this way." Benedicta talked to herself as she walked along Seventh St. toward Sycamore. "Brie isn't supposed to be sick, is she? People don't just get sick and not get better, do they? I mean, Brie could find help, couldn't she? She could be healed, she could return to health." And then her mind reverted to the upset of this morning, "And who keeps calling me?" she asked aloud. No easy answers to these questions came to mind.

I must meet with Mother Margaret Mary, thought Benedicta. Mother Margaret Mary had been her sounding board, her support, her confidant, and novice mistress when she had been in the convent these past three years. Benedicta thought back to her last meeting with the mother superior, the occasion of leaving the order for an extended absence. The leave-taking had not gone well. Mother had been gracious, but mother disapproved, Benedicta was sure of it. How would this meeting go? Benedicta was uncertain and unnerved.

The hard part is, I don't even know if I want to leave. We've been through all of this, she tightened her grip on the umbrella in her hand. She shook her head as if to let go of the doubts that assailed her.

Hastening her step and bracing her umbrella against the pelting rain and wind, her heels clicked on the wet sidewalk, sounding a rhythm, matching, it seemed, the beat of her heart. Her mind swirled with what her mom called "ruminations." Her thoughts returned to her sister, as a passing car sent a spray of cold water toward her. *Never mind that Brie had reasons for her angst. It is all about the fire, isn't it?*

Bong, Bong, Bong, the clock in the steeple chimed 3 p.m. The church was hushed and wrapped in shadows. The only light came in muted rays through the stained-glass windows along a side wall, where the pale glow of afternoon light was wafting through the glass. A tap-tap-tap of rain drops on the panes of the glass could be heard. Huge magnificent columns lined both sides of the church, forming an archway through the pews. In front, in the sanctuary, stood an altar, an ornate twelfth century version of the table of worship.

Two smaller sets of altars stood on either side of the main altar. These smaller altars had been used for Mass back in the days when there were many priests. Now that was all changed. No more were the side altars used for Mass; they were a tradition, a place to pray.

A sacristy lamp shone above the tabernacle on one of the side altars, the lamp a symbol of God's presence. The tabernacle door was surrounded by an edge of gold trim and embossed with the figures of two angels. The fragrance of incense lingered heavy in the air.

In the rear of the church stood a statue of Saint Therese of Lisieux, the patron of the missions. The saint stood in Carmelite habit, roses in her apron, and a rose extended in her hand. This was a contemporary saint. Legend had it that when someone prayed to Saint Therese, that petitioner would receive a rose from the saint.

"My mission," she had said in her writings, "Is to make God loved—will begin after my death. I will spend heaven doing good on earth." She went on to say, "I will let fall a shower of roses." Roses have been described and experienced as Saint Therese's signature. Canonized in 1925, and because of her devotion of doing all things with love, her 'little way,' as it has been termed, she has been acclaimed "the greatest saint of modern times." She is recognized as a Doctor of the Church.

This was a favorite saint for her personal devotion. Benedicta liked to pray for that rose. More than that, she felt a quiet connection with this wonderful woman of the church. Benedicta knelt in front of the statue of the saint before she went to a bank of vigil lights. As she lit the taper, the wick sputtered, and the glass votive cup shattered. Startled, she backed away, crushed that her candle had broken.

What do I say to my mentor? That I want to leave the order permanently? Fine, if that is what is needed, I will do it. I will say it. Already she felt her defenses going up, and as had repeatedly happened, she was assailed by doubts. *Do I really want to give up a spiritual calling?* She glanced at her watch, now 3:10 p.m.

Mother is not coming. Mother doesn't want to see me. Mother doesn't like me. The thoughts wrapped about her like a too-warm shawl.

Suddenly, Benedicta was seized with choking spasms. Her hands flew to her neck. She tried to cough but was unsuccessful. Panic seized her. She looked wildly about the church but there was no one to help her. A rosary lay in the pew beside her. Instinctively, Benedicta grasped the rosary and crushed it in the palm of her hand, hurting her fingers, as she said a quick prayer. The spasms gradually subsided, no doubt because she had relaxed a bit.

She wanted this to be over. *When will Mother Margaret Mary arrive?* She squirmed in the pew restlessly. Benedicta thought about her three years in the convent, years in which she had lost confidence, becoming ever more depressed. It was clear to her she didn't belong. *Yet there had been good times,* she recollected. And then there was her sister: Brie needed Benedicta now more than ever.

She was adamant. She must leave. The depression she had experienced every day when she had been there was just now lessening. She wanted to leave, for her own health and well-being. And she would tell Mother today. It was all settled. Her plan was to end things and begin her new life, to take on the position as director of Pinecroft House of Peace. A job awaited her.

Soft footsteps could be heard, breaking her reverie. Benedicta turned and acknowledged the presence of a Carmelite nun dressed in full habit. Her white, starched wimple sat stiffly on her head, a veil partially obscuring her face.

"My child, it is good to see you." The nun put a weathered hand on Benedicta's arm. The younger woman winced, recoiled, and moved her arm before she sat back in the pew.

"Thank you for seeing me," Benedicta began politely. "Mother, I decided, just today, to accept a position as director at Pinecroft House of Peace. You know the one, a retreat center on the west side of town." Then, unsure what to say, she continued, "I was going to ask your blessing, well, that is, well, I wanted to know what you would think of my doing this–" Suddenly she could say no more. She shot a beseeching look at mother.

Mother Margaret Mary considered her for a moment, and when she spoke, her tone was sharp, questioning: "You want to leave the convent? You want to leave for good, don't you? Has the last six months taught you anything?"

"It has been quite an experience," Benedicta said, and flustered, she hastened to add, her voice rising with emotion, "I have felt so conflicted about leaving, you know? I was fearful about what I would find—" her words trailed off again, and she was lost in reverie for a moment. *It has been an ordeal,* her mind was saying, *and yet exciting at the same time. Setting up housekeeping, getting a wardrobe together, finding a job. No, it was not easy to do but I am proud of my persistence.*

Turning in the pew to face this woman of God, Benedicta's gaze held with her Mother Superior's, and the words so dreaded came out: "Mother I have decided. I have decided to leave the order, permanently.

Benedicta was not expecting the words spoken now by Mother Margaret Mary. Mother put her arm around her and said, "Benedicta, I am happy for you. I hope this brings you peace. I kind of believe it will."

The words began tumbling out then. "Mother I have missed you. I hope we may go on meeting periodically. It has not been so easy, being away."

Then she told her of the new job. "I report to the archbishop. He is quite conservative. I don't think he likes me much, at least that is my impression."

"Ah, my dear, he will get to know you."

"There are two chaplains and a cook. It seems a contentious group. Already I have been bossed by the cook, and the others are not any easier to deal with."

"You will win them over, I am sure," said Mother.

"I have found a possible friend in the massage therapist." Her face brightened, and she continued, "And then there is the lawyer," she giggled, throwing up her hands, "Already we have had an altercation."

"And how is your sister? She was unwell when last we spoke."

My sister. Benedicta leaned on the pew in front of her and cupped her face in her hands, as if to say she did not want to look at any part of life with her sister.

"She has gotten worse, Mother. I am deeply worried for her welfare. I find her crying one minute, shouting obscenities the next. She carouses at night with strange men, and then sleeps all day. She is impulsive, lacks good judgment, lies. Mother, what can I say?"

She considered her words and continued, "Brie needs more than I am able to give her. I don't know how to reach her. What is worse, I become impatient. I find myself arguing with her. Not good."

"Dealing with emotional problems in those close to us is always difficult and rarely easy," said Mother Margaret Mary tactfully.

A silence ensued. Benedicta thought, *I see this woman sitting before me, all the mentoring I have received from this nun, her unfailing support. Mother has been friend and counselor. How could I have thought Mother was criticizing me? When I took my vows, Mother was there to encourage me. When I decided on a leave from the order, Mother protected me from the whispering and gossiping of the other nuns.*

"Mother," she began at last, "it is the right decision, to leave, isn't it?"

"All things work together for those who love the Lord." Mother quoted a familiar passage from the Bible before adding, "You will find your footing. Give yourself time. Be gentle with yourself. Now, let us pray." The two knelt then, joining hands and praying the ancient prayer to Mary, the Memorare.

"Remember O most gracious virgin Mary, that never was it known, that anyone who fled to your protection, implored your help or sought youir intercession, was left unaided. Inspired by this confidence, I fly unto thee, O virgin of virgins, my Mother, to thee do I come, before thee do I stand, sinful and sorrowful. O Mother of the Word Incarnate, despise not my petition, but in thy mercy, hear and answer my prayer. Amen."

As she sat in the pew after Mother left, Benedicta felt herself flooded with doubts. *She doesn't really mean she approves. I shouldn't leave the order. What am I doing? Those are the same doubts I was having this morning. I am past that.* Her thoughts went on and on. Finding once again the rosary, Benedicta began praying, and the words of scripture seemed to speak to her: "Trust in the Lord with all your strength, on your own self rely not." *How does one do that?* she wondered.

Those words would haunt her in the days to come.

Chapter Two

The grounds are beautiful, she thought, eyeing the grove of trees and the lake from the warmth of the glass enclosed chapel. A soft snow was falling; the temperature had dipped into sub-zero weather, the coldest December she could remember. A carpet of white fluff lay over the earth and crept in curls along the sill of the window.

Pinecroft was a jewel, a snow-covered mansion set at the crest of a sloping hillside. The house was a two-story frame, with three eaves. The interior of the house was pleasant and immaculate. An entryway was bordered by a large living room. An equally large dining room stood opposite, and her small cubbyhole of an office was off the entryway in the middle. The dining room was adjoined by an eat-in kitchen, which had a large picture window with a view of a birdbath situated in a garden. This completed the first floor except for the chapel, a large room with two huge walls of glass, allowing a view of the water. The room was simply furnished, fully carpeted in champagne beige, with a small blonde table for an altar, a few kneelers and folding chairs stacked to the side, and an assortment of pillows.

The upper floor housed guest rooms and her room and a bath. The basement was fully furnished and provided space for large groups to meet as well as office space for Lulu and the chaplains.

Pinecroft House of Peace was on the property of Providence Hospital and was part of an old estate. The mansion itself was a short distance off the main road, in a grove of trees. The house was well kept. The frame façade was freshly painted. Tulip beds, now lying fallow and invisible, bushes, and shade trees bordered the place, with some newly planted trees that were set "in a memorial" for clients who had lost children or elderly parents.

Rose Marie Benedicta Malloy surveyed the interior of the house, making her way from room to room. She had been hired to oversee the running of the retreat center, to be available to take reservations for large groups and for single retreatants. She, along with the two chaplains, Beatrice Hartung and Father Joseph Gast, were responsible for counseling. It was a big job, she had to admit, and she had many concerns, but today she was delighted to be here.

No longer in the convent and wishing to forget those last tumultuous months in religious life, Benedicta had practically begged the archbishop for this assignment. Reluctantly he had acquiesced.

Now, Benedicta recalled the day almost a week before and the attitude of a certain lawyer for the archdiocese, Jude Forsythe. He had spoken to her disparagingly, upon their initial meeting at Pinecroft. The words came back like ice cold water splashed on her face. *Those words were,* she thought, *shocking, spurious, dismissive, and wholly uncalled for: "The archbishop wants a woman religious running the place."*

Benedicta had eaten a half-gallon of ice cream in reaction to those words. And she had goosebumps just thinking about her run-in with the lawyer. Thoughts now of the scene raised her hackles once again. She let the words of the incident play out moment by moment in her mind's eye.

That day, a week ago now, she stood in the entryway of the house, chatting with Sister Anne, the cook and housekeeper for Pinecroft House of Peace. She recalled the entire conversation: "I am the new director, Sister Anne. I will be bringing my things tomorrow. It is so nice to meet you. I hope we can get better acquainted soon. Today I would like to tour the facility." She went on, "I hope this is not an imposition—" Her words were interrupted by the sound of a male voice.

She heard him before she saw him. He descended the stairway from the second floor, blueprints of some sort in hand. *He seems self-assured, confidant, arrogant even*, she thought, as she watched him move down to the landing.

"No, no way," he said emphatically, dismissing the idea of her taking over the job at Pinecroft as its director. "The archbishop is not in favor of a lay woman for the position," he seemed to hiss at her. "I know he wants a woman religious. I will call his secretary, Edmund Wise, and straighten this out."

"Excuse me?" Benedicta blurted out, having difficulty keeping her emotions in check. Benedicta felt a headache coming on. She pressed her hand to her head as she remarked boldly and with something of an attitude, "I have just come from an interview with His Excellency; he not only said nothing about such a stipulation, but the Reverend Archbishop Floersh hired me for the position. I start Monday. Perhaps you may want to check this out for yourself."

Who is this man? The very idea, she thought at the time. Benedicta was irritated and barely able to repress her desire to slap this gentleman standing before her.

Benedicta remembered her initial impression of the man: He wore a dark navy suit, well-tailored with a pink pinstripe shirt and a pink and navy striped tie. She noticed he wore gold cuff links at his wrists. *He is certainly attractive, I admit, and knowing how to dress doesn't hurt either,* she recalled thinking. *Well, looks aren't everything.*

Sister Anne, Benedicta realized at that moment, appeared unruffled and indeed seemed to enjoy the skirmish being enacted before her. "Ms. Malloy," said Sister Anne, "You may want to meet Jude Forsythe, the attorney for the archdiocese. I understand the two of you will be working together quite closely, a policy book of some sort, I think?"

9

"Enchanted, I am sure," Jude said with a bow, seeming to change his tack and holding out a hand in a gesture of reconciliation. Reluctantly, Benedicta took his hand in hers, the only visible sign of a lack of acceptance being a barely disguised rolling of her eyes.

Jude headed for the door, saying as he moved, "Sister Anne, will you set Ms. Malloy straight? Such an effort would be advisable."

Benedicta's anger simmered, she was ready for a fight. Before she could mount an attack, Sister Anne, raising her hand in the air as if to ward off an assault, spoke first: "Don't worry about Jude Forsythe, if you give him a chance, he will meet you half-way." She let those words sink in before adding, "We all will."

Taking a deep breath, Benedicta considered her retort carefully: "Sister Anne, I am perfectly able to assess Mr. Forsythe's motives and choose my own response without being told what to think."

Sister Anne gasped, but recovered, and appeared to try to hide her own emotions, placing her arms over her chest. She said, "Of course you are. My job is to support you in your efforts here at Pinecroft, and I intend to do that."

Still looking angered, Benedicta swung around, moving toward the door. "I will wait until later for that tour," she said, as she retreated from the house.

Coming back to the present from her reverie, with a shaking of her head, Benedicta vowed to show this gentleman she meant business. How she would accomplish that, she wasn't quite sure. One thing she did know, she was eating to this disagreement. She had stuffed herself with a half-gallon of ice cream when she returned from seeing Jude Forsythe, and ever since, she had been eating ice cream.

The following day, Benedicta had moved her things into the mansion and set about organizing her bedroom. Now Benedicta made her way through the house until she came to the kitchen, where Sister Anne was baking bread.

Fragrant aromas wafted through the air, coming from the oven. Benedicta had felt a tension between her and this hard-working, simple woman ever since her arrival, particularly after their first encounter ended so badly. *Sister Anne seems to be a motherly sort, she is kind enough,* thought Benedicta. *Sister Anne reminds me too much of my own mother. Not that there is any similarity really. My mother rarely baked or did much in the kitchen at all. It is just the bossiness, I suppose.*

Now, Benedicta smiled tentatively at Sister Anne, saying, "That smells so good. Is it for our supper?"

"Yes, it is, indeed," said Sister Anne, appearing pleased, then added, "Are you nervous about beginning your new assignment?"

Benedicta thought a moment, then said, "No, yes, well, a little." She amended, "I am sure it will be an adjustment at first and that too, will pass."

Quickly, Sister Anne said, "You'll love it here—don't you worry about your new job." Innocent enough words but they were a source of rancor to Benedicta.

Benedicta thought about her impressions of Pinecroft thus far: A peaceful place, but one of the part-time chaplains, Beatrice Hartung had been the former director before stepping down and Benedicta felt a little ucomfortable around her. The other chaplain, Father Joseph Gast was the archbishop's cousin. *Why does he keep reminding me of that?* she wondered.

Lulu is the one bright spot in the figures at Pinecroft, she thought now. Lulu came in frequently to do massages with their clients. Completing the staff was Scotty, Scotty Betham, the maintenance man. Benedicta secretly saw him as a crotchety old geezer, though she would hate to ascribe this attitude to anyone. She had had little contact with him, but when she had bumped into him, he seemed to complain a lot. Rounding out the familiar faces was one regular visitor who had already grabbed her attention, the lawyer for the archdiocese, Jude Forsythe.

Benedicta left the kitchen and made her way through the house. Arriving at her cozy office, she looked at the small cubbyhole of a room with appreciative eyes. When coming here the day prior, she had immediately claimed the space for herself. Dragging in a secretary desk and two tall pink print wing chairs and an old ottoman, all purchased at a thrift shop, and confiscating a mahogany pie table from the basement, she had proudly arranged the room, putting a bookcase on the far wall, a picture of Pope John Paul II on the opposite one, and a pink fuzzy rug on the floor. The two chairs sat in front of her secretary with the round pie table in between. It was here she planned to do most of her work.

Benedicta glanced at herself in a mirror in the hall. Her mass of unruly blonde curls was held in place at the back of her head by a silver barrette. She wore a polyester pants-suit in grey with a pink blouse. She looked more closely at the image in the mirror. *My eyes are my best feature, she thought: blue-green and long eye lashes.*

Later that evening, after a delicious supper served by Sister Anne, Benedicta flicked on the television in the living room. Ronald Reagan had just been re-elected president. He had beaten Walter Mondale.

Ethiopia was experiencing a famine. They were hit by a drought. A million people had died. The news droned on.

Benedicta was to formally start work on Monday. She had been given a few days here already to organize and unpack. Ordinarily this would have been a great time to enjoy getting accustomed to her surroundings, but her sister had her attention. Worried, she thought of her constantly. *Brie has never been like this before. Her whole demeanor has changed. She bit my head off the other day,* thought Benedict. Brie's temper had a short fuse.

I wonder if this has something to do with the incident of the fire? Benedicta thought now. She had been pushing Brie to see a psychiatrist, to get some counseling and medication, but Brie was resisting.

Now, she picked up the phone in her office and dialed Brie's number. Benedicta had, to tell the truth, mixed feelings about her sister and her situation. She tried to feel compassionate, and sometimes she did, but more than once she found herself judgmental and even dictatorial. Brie seemed to whine a lot.

That got on her nerves, but she understood, too. At least she convinced herself she did.

The phone was ringing.

"Hello?" said Brie on the other end of the line.

"Brie, hi, how are you feeling?"

"Oh, Benedicta, I am barely hanging in. Why do I have to feel this way? I need to go to the grocery but I can't make myself get up and go. I don't have any cigarettes and I want some. It is terrible, really. Would you go get me a pack of cigarettes?" Her sister took on a pleading tone of voice.

"It is really slick outside. Can you wait until they clear the streets? Maybe in the morning I'll go for you."

"No, I can't wait. And I don't see why you can't go," she chided Benedicta as if she were the little sister. "Never mind, I'll get the man downstairs, Wooley, to go for me."

Benedicta hung up the phone feeling no less concern for her sister. She jumped when the phone rang again. She was surprised to hear the voice of Jude Forsythe.

"Is this Rose Marie Benedicta Malloy of Pinecroft House of Peace?" His voice sounded melodic and friendly.

"Yes, it is, but how did you know my full name?" She retorted and was especially business-like and firm.

"I saw your file at the Chancery the other day," he answered, bemused.

Benedicta was not sure she liked that but said nothing further. Rather, she said sharply, "What can I do for you, Mr. Forsythe?" She wanted him to come to the point.

"Oh, we are on a formal basis, now are we?" His laugh was amiable. "And I was just going to the trouble to call and see if you needed anything out there. I know you are getting snowed in."

Relenting a little, she said, "No, Jude, I think we are set for the night. But thanks, anyway."

Just then, Benedicta had an insight about this man. He had a personal interest in her. "I've got to run," she said, suddenly fearful. She didn't need the advances of Jude Forsythe in her life, but at the same time, it was intriguing. Rushing from her office, she began locking up and then headed for her room, ready to shut down emotionally. She cut off any thoughts of this man and made a mental note to distance herself from him in the future.

———————

He turned up on Sunday morning after Mass as she was putting her files together in her office. She had heard the doorbell. Sister Anne had answered. Now, he stood before her in the doorway, a pleasant smile on his face.

Benedicta found herself disgruntled by his interruption of her. With barely a civil tone of voice, she said, "Good morning, Jude, what can I do for you? I am very busy here as you are able to see."

Jude appeared not to notice her consternation. "Aren't you going to invite me in? I would like to see your office. May I come in?"

"Yes, do," she responded tersely, rising from her chair at the desk, and opening the door a bit more.

Jude entered and looked about, saying only, "Hmn, hmm."

"Well, say something, why don't you? I'll have you know I worked very hard on putting this room together, furnishing it, I mean," she said vehemently, as she realized her hands were coiled fist-like, and she had a decided kink in her neck. Visibly trying to relax, she released the tension in her hands and rubbed her neck with some instant relief.

"May I sit down?" Jude asked, as he then took a seat in one of the pink print chairs before she could respond.

Slowly lowering herself into the other wing chair, she considered how to play this. Obviously, he was undaunted by her gruff manner. She wanted him gone. Soon. He was certainly making her nervous. *Why is that?* she wondered.

"What can I do for you?" she asked once again, in a harsh and throaty tone.

"You have a talent for creativity," Jude said, ignoring her question. "You've done a great job putting together this room.

And you'll undoubtedly make a fine director," he added. "I want to apologize," he went on calmly, "for my rudeness at our first meeting. I wasn't fond of the director before you, Beatrice Hartung. I am sure you are getting to know her and may have a different impression. You see, we didn't get along. I was rather hopeful that the next director would be a gentleman, or at minimum, someone I could work with," he said, holding out his hand and looking at her in a beguiling manner.

But Benedicta was not to be won over by charm, at least she didn't want to be. On the other hand, she had to admit, she didn't know how she herself would get along with Beatrice. And this very sincere-sounding man was pressing her to accept him, warts and all.

"Humph," she said, unceremoniously, "I guess we got off to a bad start. I was quick to jump on your case. Let's see how things go, shall we?" She smiled shyly at him.

The tension in the room seemed immediately broken as they enjoyed a moment of hand-holding, the ease broken by the interruption of Sister Anne. "Sorry to intrude," the nun said, standing in the doorway. "Lunch is ready. Will you stay for lunch Mr. Forsythe?"

"Yes, please, would you like to stay?" Benedicta's voice held more of a lilt now, as she realized to her consternation, she was still holding Jude's hand. Moving quickly, shifting her position and recovering her composure, Benedicta rose, and without waiting for an answer to her question, said, "Let's go have lunch together, shall we?"

On Monday morning, Benedicta was up early, had coffee and cereal with Sister Ann and had prayer in the chapel before going to her office. Mass was at 9 a.m. Father talked about using one's talent or burying it. She hoped she was using hers. She wondered about her sister, and if she could use hers. She didn't know the answer to that.

The day was again very cold. It had stopped snowing, but more snow was expected. Benedicta noticed that the walks were icy, so she left a message for Scotty to salt them. The phone rang once while she was in her office. She thought perhaps it was her sister, but it was not. The day was off and running.

Benedicta was not used to such a flurry of activity—decisions she didn't know about had to be made. A group of ten wanted accommodations over Christmas, but she hadn't any idea if they would be open then or not. Benedicta put them off for a few days, saying that the schedule hadn't been firmed up yet. A group of nuns wanted the quarters to themselves over New Year's. She was frantic—and to top it off, Jude Forsythe came ambling in to the house, taking off his overcoat in the hall and throwing it on the tree rack, acting as if he owned the place.

Feeling lightheaded, and knowing her face was turning red, she met him at the door to her office and found herself stammering, of all things. "M-M-M- Mr. F-Forsythe, you, you aren't sup-supposed to be here. I mean," finally feeling her composure returning, "To what do we owe the pleasure of this visit?"

"I'm taking you to lunch to celebrate your first day: no ifs, ands, or buts about it." He looked hopefully at her.

"Out of the question, Mr. Forsythe." Benedicta noticed his beautiful blue eyes, the color of a translucent blue sky on a sunny day. Her composure melted once again, and her face began to redden even more.

"I can't possibly leave now! I have all this work to do, and besides—" She could think of no explanation worthy of her.

"Just an hour and a half, or one hour, no more, and I'll have you back in time to work."

Not knowing what else to do, she nodded yes, thinking it would be good to get away for a few minutes, but immediately she was sorry she had accepted.

"Get your coat and a hat," he said, "It is cold out there."

Going upstairs, she grabbed her heavy coat and gloves and put money in her purse. *You couldn't be too careful, could you?*

Oh, brother, she said to herself as they approached his car. He had a fire red sports car parked in the drive. *How very gaudy*, she thought. Never mind that her Toyota was a red one as well.

Their footsteps crunched in the snow. Suddenly Benedicta let out a gasp.

"Oh! No!! Oh, I'm, I'm f-falling." She stood precariously, tottered, and losing her balance, she went down.

Adeptly Jude caught her in mid-air, holding her in his arms. Their eyes met, their gaze held.

"There you go, missy. Be careful, or we'll both go down."

Benedicta tore away from his grasp. Flustered, awkwardly smoothing her coat, and with jerking motions, brushing snow from her gloves, she scowled. "I want you to know this is an exception to the rule. I don't generally leave in the middle of a work day. It is a bit frivolous," she said, when they were once in the car.

"So noted," he remarked.

"And don't you have more to do than barging in and bothering me?" she felt herself getting worked up once again and didn't exactly know why.

"Benedicta, I have plenty to do, but I thought time together would give us a chance to get to know each other, kind of a business lunch, so to say."

"Well, in that case, just this once, you understand."

"So noted again," he said, smiling at her.

Over lunch, and to fill in the silence, she confessed how flustered she was on this her first day of work. Jude was easy to talk to, she had to admit. *Once the defenses were down*, she thought, sipping a Coke. *Her defenses or his*, she wondered wearily, suddenly wary once more.

"I know we'll be seeing a lot of each other, and it may as well be as painless as possible, don't you think?" he said, grinning at her. And with that, she was in a huff again.

Back in the car for the return to Pinecroft, Jude said casually, "We'll have to do this again sometime. Oh, I know, I have an idea. Let's go ice skating. We have the whole afternoon ahead."

Benedicta was incredulous. She looked at him, nearly choking. When she could speak, Benedicta said, "Wh-when, now? Now!!" she replied, totally exasperated.

"Yes, let's. It will be fun. Want to?"

"But, but, I have lots to do. The time—" Her voice trailed off as he made a sharp turn. "Where, where are we going?"

"I'll show you."

He drove quietly. He was relaxed, it seemed. He looked over at her and chuckled. She gave him a wilting look.

He was headed west, out into the countryside, soon leaving the city and the main road. Benedicta said nothing further, wondering how she could quickly escape.

A turn-off led them on a winding path. The path meandered through dense woods. "Now if I can just locate it. Yes, here it is," he said, pulling up to a clearing.

"Here?" She was taken aback. "But it is a pond, a pond," she repeated.

"What an astute observation. Yes, it is a pond. It is frozen over in this cold frigid weather. I think it will hold us. Let's try skating, do you want to?" When she just looked at him in dismay, he said, "I have some skates in the trunk, we could see if they would do the job for us."

"No," was her quick response.

He grinned, that mischievous grin of his, as he assisted her to the trunk. Benedicta felt desperate. "No way am I doing this," she sputtered. They found the skates and a pair for each of them.

"Yes, let's," Jude said, as he thrust the pair of skates at her. With ice skates on, Jude said, "I'll go first, to see if it holds me. Have you skated before?"

"No, I haven't, well, years ago, but that was different." Still, it looked like fun. Putting on the skates, she took a few tentative steps out onto the ice. Benedicta slid forward, in the direction of Jude, who stood with outstretched arms, waiting to catch her.

"There, I've got you," he said.

For the next fifteen minutes they slid around, making their way to the center of the pond. Benedicta was just beginning to really enjoy herself when it happened.

Suddenly there was a sharp, scraping sound. It was unmistakable "What, what was that?" Benedicta squeezed his hand. Another noise was louder this time. A cracking sound, as the ice shifted and broke. "Oh, Jude, what do we do? The ice will not hold us. We're going to fall in. We are going to die!

Chapter Three

"Stay calm, stand still. Let me think."

Benedicta heard the words over the sounds around her, and fell quiet, trying to breathe.

"Don't just stand there, do something," she shouted into the wind.

"Now, do as I tell you. Glide slowly. There, in that direction," he pointed the way as he spoke to her. "That way, toward the edge of the pond. You're doing great, good girl."

Frantic and shaking, Benedicta skated in a small tentative motion. Her breath was coming in gasps. She let out a scream as she went.

Finally, she felt her foot on dry land. Turning around, Benedicta realized Jude was not behind her but was remaining in one spot. "What's wrong?" she shouted over the wind whistling through the trees.

"I don't know if the ice will hold me or not. Go to the car, you'll find a rope in the trunk." He added after a thought, "the keys are in the ignition."

Weighed down by her warm clothes, she made her way awkwardly through the snow, encumbered now also by ice skates. She retrieved the keys from the ignition, inserted the key in the lock, yanking up the trunk lid. Frantically she searched until she found what she was looking for. Once she spied the rope, she grabbed it. Slipping and sliding and trudging through the snow, she made her way back to the pond.

"Tie a noose in one end," he shouted.

Her gloved hands made tying a knot cumbersome. When finished, she held up the rope victoriously.

"Great, now throw it toward me if you can."

Her first attempt met with failure. The wind whipped the rope back to her. The second time it landed only a foot onto the ice. The third and fourth attempts proved no more successful.

"I guess I am going to have to make it on my own. If this doesn't work, or anything happens, go back to the car and head for the highway. Flag someone down, will you? Do you understand?" Benedicta nodded.

Jude said no more. He seemed braced for the inevitable. He took a step. A cracking sound was heard beneath his feet. Benedicta screamed. "There must be some other way," she shouted into the wind. Again, he said nothing. He took a second step and a third one. The ice, though broken, was holding so far.

Another step, he was getting close to the edge. It seemed to take forever. Finally, he reached land. He grasped Benedicta in his arms and they stood there in the wind, in the fading sunlight, snow now falling, their arms clasped around each other.

"You handled that very well. You didn't fall to pieces and that took courage," he said letting her go.

"No, you were the brave one," she was quick to say.

Back in the car, Benedicta dissolved into tears, tears she couldn't shed while he was on the torturous ice, tears of frustration she couldn't hold back any longer, mixed with tears of relief.

Jude put his arm around her, "Steady, girl," he said. "We'll stop at a roadside place somewhere and have a cup of hot chocolate to warm up."

Benedicta, bedraggled and tired, fell quiet. *It must be after five,* she thought. *It is already getting dark. And it is too late to get any work done tonight.* She made a mental note to avoid Jude in the future. *I can't be doing this on a regular basis, or else I will get no work done at all.*

They found a roadside café as they made their way back to the city.

"Would that have worked, I mean using the rope?" she asked as they sipped their hot chocolate.

"I don't know. Do you want to go back and try it again?" They laughed.

"Why didn't you go off the ice first, save yourself?"

"Well, primarily, I was concerned about you. I didn't know if it would hold me. I wanted you off first."

Her anger flared. "What possessed you to take me out to that god-forsaken spot and get me out on the ice?" Her words threatened to bring dark clouds on this already distressing day.

Looking intently into Jude's eyes, and before he could respond, she said, "Excuse me, excuse me please, the day has been a bit difficult."

"No, I'm the one who is sorry. You're right, it was a crazy notion. I just thought you needed some fun."

She was late getting home for supper. Sister Anne made no mention of the hour. At supper Benedicta was glad for the quiet and the roaring fire that Sister Anne had started in the fireplace in the living room. Sister Anne had set up a table for them there.

"Steak and baked potatoes and peas," said Sister Anne, bringing in a tray of piping hot food. "I just thought we would treat ourselves tonight. You do like steak, don't you?"

Grudgingly, Benedicta looked at the meal set before her. She wanted Sister Anne to be aware who was boss. And kindnesses like this would just cloud the issue as far as she was concerned. But she had to admit, it all looked too inviting. "Sister Anne, it is my favorite. I couldn't ask for a better meal. And that fire is wonderful," she said, wholeheartedly touched. "You know, I've been cold all day." She didn't mention her adventure on the ice.

Sitting down at the table, Sister Anne gave thanks.

Benedicta surveyed the table with its red tablecloth and matching napkins and even a floral centerpiece. "You, you've put some thought into this," said Benedicta, bursting into tears.

Sister Anne came around next to her, allowing her to cry.

After several minutes, Benedicta said, "I'm sorry." Sniff, sniff. "It was a harder day than I expected." She added, "I couldn't," sniffing as she brushed her tears away, "make decisions. I didn't know what to do. I still don't." Sniff.

Drying her eyes, she blew her nose, and admitted she felt better.

Sister Anne looked at her over her glasses, and said, "What is there to decide?" Benedicta listed the requests that had come in. Then they made the decisions together. They would be open till December 22nd, December 23rd would be a private party for staff, and a quiet supper. The staff would be off to be with family on Christmas Eve and Christmas day. She would call the group that wanted late December and offer them either before or after the holiday. And the group for January 1 could have time after New Year's.

Maybe things were going to work out after all, she mused. And maybe Sister Anne wasn't that bossy either.

––––––––––––

Tuesday and Wednesday were no better than Monday. Every day was hectic. Clients streamed in for their spiritual direction appointments. There was little time for thinking about anything else.

Yet, in those odd moments, Benedicta worried about her sister. *I must get help for her, and quickly,* thought a frantic Benedicta.

On Thursday morning, in between clients, Benedicta tried to reach Brie, but the answering machine was off and no answer. *Where could she be?* And it dawned on her, she really had not heard from Brie in days. Benedicta blamed herself for this, for neglecting to call her sister.

She was worried sick. She just had to reach her. Scary thoughts ran through her mind: *Brie lost somewhere, Brie's car broken down on the side of a lonely road, Brie overdosing.* No, she mustn't think like that. Benedicta ran to the fridge and downed a piece of pie and a glass of chocolate milk. I will not do that again, she vowed, knowing that she was eating to her feelings.

In the afternoon, she repeated the calls. Finally, there was a click on the line.

"Hello?" she heard from the other end.

"Brie, are you all right? Are you okay? Where have you been?" Her anxiety and frustration were mounting, despite reaching Brie.

"Benedicta, I am okay," her sister said with some impatience. "I went for a drive and stayed a couple of days at the old inn in Carrolton. You remember it, don't you?"

A sense of relief mixed with annoyance filled Benedicta. "Oh, honey, I'm so glad to hear your voice." She paused. "I want you to see Dr. Prescott. Promise me you will."

"I don't need a shrink." And Brie hung up quickly before Benedicta could continue.

Just then, Sister Anne burst into the room, "Benedicta, the police chief is on the phone. There is a convict who has escaped from a prison up north. They think he is hiding in the vicinity, maybe on the property. He is sending someone to scout the area." Sister Anne spit out the words with alarm.

Instinctively, Benedicta grasped her rosary in her pocket. If ever there was a time for prayer, this was such an occasion.

―――――――――――――

"Quickly, make sure the doors and windows are locked. I'll cancel this afternoon's appointments. We don't need more people to protect," she said as she rose to go to the phone. "And get hold of Scotty. Apprise him of the situation, if you would. He is somewhere on the property and will be checking in soon. Please tell him to keep a lookout. And to be careful," she added.

The afternoon was dark and windy. A winter storm was forecast for tonight. Inspector Herbert Benson Brown appeared at her door. "I have come to look for a fugitive, we will alert you when we know something," he said.

He looked about forty, thought Benedicta. She suspected he was older than he looked. He had brown hair and a kind face. His eyebrows were bushy and went down in kind of a squint, she noted. He kept putting his hands in and out of his coat pockets.

"We have the place surrounded. He is either in the neighborhood or in one of the buildings here on the property," said Inspector Brown. "We'll find him pretty quick, don't you worry." And off he went.

At 2 p.m., it began snowing. At 3 p.m., Benedicta heard what she thought were shots being fired.

Scotty reported there was no one in the buildings.

At 4 p.m., Inspector Brown returned. "He's in the vicinity somewhere. We have found his tracks. But visibility is poor. We'll get him. Yes, those were shots you heard." And he was off once more.

Finally, around 5 p.m., Inspector Brown, doing that squinting with his eyebrows again, announced to her that the crisis was over. As he put his hands in and out of his pockets, he let her know the convict was apprehended.

Benedicta sighed in relief. She watched from the living room window in the shadows of the oncoming dusk, as they led the man to the police cruiser. Just from a glance, she thought, *he looks menacing.* He had torn clothes, a big scar on the side of his face, and long unkempt hair

As the policeman guided the convict to the patrol car, suddenly the man grabbed the officer's gun, and holding the officer as a shield, he stood his ground against Inspector Brown and his team.

Benedicta watched in horrified disbelief, the scene unfolding in front of her. The light from in front of the door illuminated the men. It seemed to be happening in slow motion. The convict fired, as Inspector Brown and the others dove for cover behind the patrol car in the driveway.

"Give yourself up, you won't get away," shouted Inspector Brown. A shot rang out in response. The convict was pulling and dragging the police officer down the drive toward the roadway, his seeming exit.

As events played out, a car approached the scene on the driveway, coming from the road. It was within a few yards of the group.

The convict quickened his step, thinking he might have an escape plan. But as the car advanced and came to a stop, a police detective emerged from the car, gun in hand. The convict was between the officers behind the patrol car and the detective on the drive. Seeing he had no chance, he threw down his gun. He was then swiftly thrown to the ground and handcuffed, before being roughly put into the cruiser.

Benedicta opened the door to Inspector Brown, as he put his hands in and out of his pockets and squinting, he said in an off-hand kind of remark, "Well, we got him."

"Thank you ever so much Inspector Brown, you saved the day. May I offer you and your men a cup of tea?"

Inspector Brown declined the invitation, then turned and left. And it was all over.

Chapter Four

A week went by with relative quiet. Benedicta learned much more about her job and how to manage. Her energy level was coming back to normal; she had been so fatiqued for so long, mainly due to the depression, she believed, now she was functioning well. She was just congratulating herself on her work when the call came. The call was all Benedicta needed to be thrown into a panic. It was her sister. Brie was incoherent.

She's gone off the deep end, I swear she has. She's really flipped this time, thought Benedicta, as she raced in her car heading east to her sister's apartment in downtown Cincinnati. "I could do without this drama!" exclaimed an overwrought Benedicta. Weaving in and out of traffic, she finally pulled up in front of the Milner Hotel, a once-upscale hotel on Garfield Place in the heart of the city.

The Milner Hotel had seen better days. Now, nothing was left of its once fashionable façade. Truly the ramshackle building was a flea bag hotel. The building was secured and had been selected for her sister because it was on a bus line, had a clerk in the lobby, and offered a rent subsidy for Brie. And the place was Brie's choice of a location.

The building was situated a block from the Cathedral of St. Peter in Chains and two blocks from St. Louis Catholic Church. It was close to the Cincinnati Publc Library, where Brie thought she could spend time, though in fact, she rarely did. It was located near the theatre district, and there were a number of restaurants and shops nearby.

Entering the lobby, she nodded to the clerk, and forgetting the elevator, Benedicta bounded up the stairs. Pounding on the door of 210, she called out loudly, "Brie, Brie, let me in." No response.

Cursing herself for wasting time, she retraced her steps and hastened to the desk in the lobby. Then Benedicta's good sense kicked in—when she got to the lobby, she asked the clerk for the phone to call 911. She said into the phone, "Yes, I want to report that someone is in danger. I think she is trying to take her own life." *Why hadn't she called before?* she demanded of herself. No answer.

Asking for the key to room 210 took more time than she was expecting. "Come on, come on," she muttered to herself, until the clerk produced the key.

Why didn't she have a key to her own sister's apartment? She didn't have a key because, like herself, Brie had trust issues.

Unlocking the apartment, Benedicta entered, smelling the familiar scent of gas. Rushing to the window, she flung it open, then another. Going into the bedroom, she saw Brie, lying sprawled on the floor. As she opened the window, she heard the welcome sound of a siren.

Shaking her sister's shoulders did no good. It was then that a blessed hand grasped her arm. "Paramedics ma'am, what has happened?"

"*What has happened?*"

If only she knew the answer to that question. *I have wondered and asked myself that same question for years. Why the fire those many years ago? And what had Brie been doing? Why had her mother chosen that day to drink? Again,* she thought.

"What has happened?" The medic repeated his question, as he unpacked his gear.

Shaking her head and coming back to the present, she said, "I'm not sure. The gas was on. It can't be good. I can't, I can't wake her up."

The paramedics took over. Benedicta backed up, putting her weight against the wall, and taking a deep breath. She had been holding her breath, she realized. The scene became a blur, but she could still see the chaos and clutter existing in the apartment. *Brie is not neat,* she thought.

Why the fire when I was a child? What harm had been done? Why the panic when I think of it? What really happened to Ben?

The uniformed first responders reminded her of firefighters putting out a fire in the charred remains of the kitchen of her childhood home. The images came flooding into her awareness. She could see the scene vividly: the mess of water-logged rugs, wet furniture, debris scattered about, and the coroner wheeling out her brother on a gurney. Why, she didn't fully comprehend, she hadn't thought of that in years. *I would not let myself.*

Benedicta tried to walk, but staggered instead, from the room. She couldn't quite get it all together. *The fumes are making me dizzy,* she thought. She sat on the stairs in the hallway and began to cry. After a time, she returned to Brie's apartment, picked up the phone in the living room to call Sister Anne.

"Pinecroft House of Peace," the words were spoken calmly and in a melodious voice. She had been that calm as well, just this morning.

"Sister Anne, listen, I won't be home for a while. I have to go to the hospital with Brie. There's been an accident. I don't know how she is yet." When Benedicta rang off, she dialed a second number and waited for him to answer. She felt sure he would come. She wasn't sure, though, that this was quite appropriate behavior, but she needed someone now, and she sensed that Jude would be there for her.

"Hello," the voice of Jude Forsythe on the other end of the phone sent a jolt of electricity through her. "Jude, it is Benedicta. My sister has had an accident, could you, I mean, could you, possibly meet me at Good Samaritan hospital?"

Jude's voice was as calm as that of Sister Anne. He said into the phone, "Certainly, how bad is it?"

"I don't know yet, the paramedics are here. It is too early to know anything. Thank you so much." And she hung up.

The first responders were hauling up a stretcher. "Are you going in the ambulance?" asked the attendant.

"No, I will meet you there," she said. Her voice breaking, she asked, "Will she be all right?"

"I don't know anything conclusively yet, ma'am, but her vitals are good and that is a positive sign. She hasn't awakened though, but she is sensitive to touch. That means something."

The ambulance sped off, the siren blaring, the lights flashing. It gave Benedicta an ominous feeling. Again, she recalled that evening so long ago. It all was coming back: *the smoke, the water everywhere, her sister in tears, mom drunk. No, I will not go back there, I cannot.*

She wondered, as she drove the short distance to Good Sam: *Was it too much to call Jude to accompany her to the hospital.* She didn't feel she could do it on her own. She hadn't known Jude all that long, but she sensed something about him. *There was that anger between them, but there is something welcoming about him too. A port in a storm*, she thought now.

The truth is, dealing with such a situation like this one hurts me, thought Benedicta. *It hurts me deep down in my gut.* This afternoon's events brought back memories of Ben. She considered the past, her brother, *five years old, his body so still on that stretcher.* She shook her head to dispel the image.

Jude was waiting for Benedicta when she drove into the parking lot at Good Sam. Benedicta smiled wanly when he gave her a brief hug. *I know he is for me, I don't have to worry about that,* she thought as they made their way to the emergency department of the hospital. Entering the ER, the nurse on duty nodded when asked if Brie Malloy had arrived; she reported that Brie had awakened but was groggy. Benedicta slumped over the desk.

"Are you all right?" asked the nurse, alarmed at her demeanor.

"It's been a shock," she said, as Jude directed her to a chair.

The nurse hastened to bring her a glass of water.

Momentarily, an intern came forward, saying, "She'd like to see you, Ms. Malloy."

What do I say to my sister, what do I do? Benedicta thought now, standing a bit unsteadily. She felt her own fear at the sight of her sister, so pale, stretched out on the gurney. *Just like Ben,* came to her mind now.

"What happened, honey?" she asked, sitting down next to Brie.

"Someone was in my apartment," murmured Brie, then she fell asleep.

Benedicta looked forlorn; she glanced at Jude as she asked, "Could you go with me to her apartment for an overnight bag?"

"Of course, let's take my car," he said. Headed to Brie's to get some underwear and toilet articles, Benedicta discussed the situation with Jude.

"She thinks someone was in her apartment. Undoubtedly, she is mistaken," Benedicta said, thinking to herself, *Unless the one making threats toward us has made good on his promise of trouble.*

Brie was going to be kept in the hospital to be transferred to a psychiatric hospital in a couple of days. After delivering the bag, Jude invited Benedicta to supper, but she declined. She left him at the hospital and went back to Pinecroft.

Benedicta worried about her sister sometimes. *Well, a lot,* she thought. Today, she made her way downtown to visit once again with Mother Margaret Mary. She would talk with Mother about Brie.

The church was warm and pleasant. Workers were waxing the pews, and another group was arranging flowers on the altar.

When Mother came in, she greeted Benedicta warmly.

"Good afternoon, Mother, it was good of you to take the time to see me."

"It is always a privilege to share in your life." Mother patted her hand and smiled. "Now, please let me know, how are you doing? When last we talked, you were just getting a new job. How have you fared?"

"Mother, I am doing well. I am having to learn on the job, so to speak. It is hectic at times and is all so new. If it were not for my concern over Brie, I would be much more prepared for the work. And you know that when I was with you, I suffered from depression. That has improved, I think. I can concentrate, something I had trouble with for so long. And I am finding pleasure in simple things again. That means a lot to me.

"I feel that the depression is lifting, I felt down for so long—" her voice trailed off. Benedicta looked with a steady gaze at Mother Margaret Mary.

"That is such good news."

"Mother, I am concerned about Brie. She has just been admitted to the hospital. I'm not sure what has really transpired. We found her in her apartment; the gas was on. I don't know what to think.

"She is fragile and easily broken, you know. This is not the first time I have seen her so lost. Somehow it reminds me of the time she was fired from a job. She thought the firing was someone else's fault, just as she thinks now that someone was in her apartment," said Benedicta, smoothing her skirt, and adjusting the button on her jacket.

"She was always different from other girls her age. She has had no 'savvy' when it comes to the ways of men. She has usually shied away, but now is picking them up and taking them home, something unusual even for her." Benedicta settled in the pew and looked away from Mother.

"How do you explain this change in her behavior?" Mother asked pensively.

"I don't know. That is the thing," she said, again she changed position, crossing her legs in front of her. "Brie has never managed money very well. Now she's on disability but she has barely enough to survive, and she never tries to get a job, even a part-time one," said Benedicta, looking intently into Mother's eyes.

"Perhaps she is not up to it," suggested Mother, again patting her arm.

Sighing, Benedicta said softly, "Maybe I don't understand her and her suffering. Brie is disturbed. She has been since childhood. When Brie was about twelve years old, Mother Margaret Mary, Mom promised her a birthday party. Then Brie did some childish prank, and Mom punished her with no party. Brie was prepared to run away. It was I who soothed her, comforted her, and brought a confiscated piece of birthday cake to her room.

"When Brie was sixteen," Benedicta said and continued, "she was allowed out on an afternoon date with Johnny Logan, a boy on the block. They had taken the bus into town for a movie. The time became very late, way after dark, and no Brie.

"Mom was livid. 'I'll beat the daylights out of her,'" Mom bellowed, making a fist.

"I was," Benedicta said, more serious now, "fearful for Brie. I was afraid Mom would hurt her.

"I went and waited at the bus stop. It began to rain, to pour. Thunder roared like a lion and lightning bolts flashed. Finally, the two arrived. I secreted her into the house and up to bed." Benedicta stopped and sighed, then continued, "I was so bold as to suggest to my most unsuspecting mother that Brie had come home a long time ago, that I thought Mom knew. The ruse worked, and Brie was spared."

"So," said Mother Margaret Mary, "there is good reason for her to act out as she is now doing, wouldn't you say?"

"Yes, I suppose so. Lately, Brie is not so cooperative. She is short tempered, impatient, moody. When she gets into one of her funks, there is no talking to her. She wants my help, but she doesn't want any interference, you know?"

Mother Margaret Mary nodded her head sympathetically.

"And what is worse, I have come to believe that Brie has become secretive. She has stopped calling or coming over to visit. She doesn't share anything about herself any more, even when asked. It doesn't bode well for the girl. I wonder sometimes if she is manageable.

"One day," Benedicta went on, "I was working on my Rolodex in my office at Pinecroft, and suddenly I heard her screaming. They were screams of terror. I had heard those screams before, when she was a little girl. Brie would call out in the night, thrashing about, until I would go to her."

Benedicta pushed back a stray lock of hair from her forehead, and looked at Mother, frowning, "When I heard those screams again as I sat there, the screams were louder, closer. I just froze with fear. I jumped up and ran to the hall. I bounded up the stairs, went to the room Brie used when staying over. The screams were coming from inside. The door was locked. I rapped on the door. 'Brie, let me in, Brie.' No response other than another scream."

Benedicta continued to describe the scene. She had stood there in the hall, dumbfounded.

"There are keys in the kitchen, I'll go," whispered Sister Anne, who had joined her in the hallway. *Why was she whispering?* Benedicta wondered. Sister Anne returned with a huge ring of keys. Sorting and obtaining the right key took a bit of doing but the key was found. Sister Anne unlocked the door; it swung open with a squeak of its hinges."

"And just at that moment, I awakened," Benedicta said, throwing up her hands. "I found I was still sitting in the wing chair with the Rolodex in my lap. I had simply drifted off.

"It had been a dream, I awakened with a start," she said. She leaned forward in the pew, resting her arms on the pew in front. "Even though I was dreaming, it had happened just that way, about one month ago, the last time Brie had visited, exactly that way."

Benedicta picked up the rosary she had put in the pew, fingered it as she said, "I considered then why on earth I would have such a dream. My only answer is that it bears some insight into how Brie is behaving, how she feels." Benedicta put the rosary into her purse as she said, "I found Brie rolled up in a ball on the floor, that night a month or so ago. I think the incident must have made more of an impression on me than I realized at the time.

"Mother, was what happened at Brie's apartment the other day an accident, a suicide attempt, or did someone else actually turn on the gas? And who would that be?"

"Brie, hello honey, how's it going?" Benedicta spoke as she patted her sister's hand and brushed her cheek with a kiss. Benedicta had come today to transfer her sister to the psychiatric hospital.

The psychiatric facility was Our Lady of the Immaculate Heart Psychiatric Hospital, an older but well-maintained hospital on the edge of town. It housed the psychiatric facility for the Sisters of St. Dyphma and had an attached nursing home for aged and infirm nuns, as well as a group of apartments, for the healthy aged, right on the campus. It was on the leading edge of nursing care for psychiatric patients and care of the aged in the community and surrounding states. Locals referred to it as Our Lady's on the Hill.

"Ok, I guess," said Brie, in answer to her question. "Benie, do we have to do this, go to the psych hospital, I mean?" Brie's eyes looked big and questioning. She seemed to stare right through Benedicta, her gaze was so intense. Benedicta felt her own discomfort and sought to lighten the mood of the moment.

"Honey, it's all set. We agreed this would be the best. It's normal to have misgivings. Come on. You'll see Dr. Prescott tomorrow," she ended her statement by picking up Brie's bag and guiding her to the door.

Once in the car, Benedicta let out a sigh. *We're on our way,* she thought, *now please don't let me get lost.* Brie lapsed into a stony silence. Benedicta was relieved she didn't have to talk. "I'll visit every day, if there is anything you need, anything you want—"

"Puleese," interrupted Brie, "it is bad enough I have to go through with this." She lit a cigarette, and continued, "Please don't get dramatic on me."

The red Toyota turned into a drive and ascended a hill. Spacious grounds, bordered by pristine shrubs and trees, and a few, old well-kept buildings were in view, along with a few modern ones and an administration building and dorm buildings. Benedicta slowed the car and directed it into a parking spot. Suddenly, without warning, Brie jumped from the car, running down the hill. "I'm not doing this, you can't make me," she shouted over her shoulder as she ran.

Sighing, Benedicta backed the car out of the parking spot and headed in the direction she had seen her sister depart, but she couldn't find her. No amount of looking helped. *Where was* she? Sighing impatiently, Benedicta turned down a lane that led to a cul-de-sac. No sign of her sister. She retraced her route and tried a second street, then a third, before turning off of Culpepper and onto Chester Road.

Catching sight of Brie, she angled the car to the curb ahead of her. "Brie, please, this is not the way. You can do better than this. You can choose to help yourself here, help yourself get better. Please." Benedicta followed Brie a couple of yards further.

"I don't want to go," pleaded Brie.

"I know it is hard, I'll be with you every step of the way. You know that."

"Oh Benie," she fell on her knees in the snow and tightened her arms about her chest.

"Come on, it is the only way."

———

Potted palms greeted them in the lobby. A fountain of flowing water took up one entire wall. Bright colored plush-cushioned chairs were sprinkled throughout. A fish tank so big Benedicta was sure she had never seen one so large took up another wall.

They signed in.

"Ms. Malloy?" a voice came from a figure clad in pink.

"Yes," they answered in unison.

To cover her frustration and confusion, Benedicta spoke. "This is Brie Malloy, she is the client."

"Geez, thanks," was the retort from Brie.

The clerk in pink handed Brie a sheaf of papers. Brie glanced at them, frowning. "Do I have to sign these?" Brie asked, reading the consent to treat.

"No, you don't, but to be seen and treated, we need your permission," spoke the clerk in pink.

The pen remained poised in Brie's hand. Minutes passed, she seemed to be mustering the courage to sign. *It is so difficult for her to make this decision,* noticed Benedicta sympathetically. Beads of perspiration broke out on Brie's forehead. Her hands were wet, and she brushed them against her skirt.

"Is anything wrong? Could you just sign the paper?" asked Benedicta, interrupting Brie in her agitated state.

Brie shook her head but said nothing.

Finally, the papers were signed, the luggage was collected, and she and Brie were escorted down a very long hall to an elevator. The clerk in pink produced a key and unlocked the elevator. They arrived at the fourth floor and stood before a massive iron door. Another key was sought to unlock the door. Again, Benedicta could feel Brie's panic.

Benedicta had not been in this hospital prior to this admission but she had seen the wards of a general hospital like Good Samaritan where Brie had been up to this time. There were no iron doors or locked hallways. Sighing, she thought, *I hope this is for the best.*

Her own heart was racing. Benedicta could barely breathe. *What was on the other side of that door? What would this mean for Brie? How would Brie respond?* She wondered what was going through Brie's mind, as she stood before the locked door. Finally, the key was found. The metal clattered in the keyhole, sounding what seemed an alarm. The bolt was loosened.

Brie stood beside her. She looked ashen white and was silent. Her hands were shaking. Benedicta felt Brie tighten her hold on her arm.

The door swung open. On the left was a day room where a patient was pounding on an off-key piano. A few patients ambled about the wide hallway. Their eyes looked blank as they seemed to stare ahead at nothing. Two of the patients had on hospital gowns, which, she would learn later, meant that they were on suicide watch.

A few ladies, all in their later years, sat in chairs up against the wall. One was drooling. An attendant had a cart and was passing out orange juice. Someone was singing, another was laughing raucously.

The scene did nothing to assuage Benedicta's fear, and she looked at Brie, attempting to judge her reaction. Brie was seeming to take it all in and at the same time seemed dazed.

They were met by a figure in white. Brie was escorted away to a room and Benedicta entered the waiting area.

"Who are you? Are you a patient here, sister?" She heard a man with a raspy voice ask her. He looked scruffy. He had a bearded face, long bedraggled hair, and a rumpled shirt. Somehow, he looked out of place.

"Hello," Benedicta heard herself say. "No, I am a visitor."

"I'm Jessup. Just think of ketchup," he quipped.

"Is this a good place?" Benedicta asked, trying to make conversation.

"It's okay, I guess," he said, then ambled off, leaving her alone, much to her relief.

"This way, please," a nurse approached eventually, indicating the way to Brie's room.

It is about over for today, Benedicta thought, letting out a sigh as she greeted Brie.

Brie was sitting on the bed in a gown. She looked up with a wan smile. Benedicta thought she looked much more relaxed than when they had entered. "Come see me," was all Brie would say.

Benedicta felt herself hurrying, literally running down the corridor to the elevator. She had to get out of here. She waited at the metal door for an attendant to unlock the door. Once in the car, she banged her fists on the steering wheel in a fit of anger and outrage. "Just get me out of here. Don't let them hurt my sister. Damn it."

Her words surprised her, spoken with the same force as the fist to the steering wheel. She felt choked up. *Why did her sister have to have this illness? Why indeed have I suffered these past years with depression and distrust?* No answer came. Benedicta believed she was fortunate really, that she hadn't had to endure what Brie was going through, this coming to the hospital. Silently, her grief spent, she headed for home.

———————————

Chapter Five

"There are some very weird-looking patients here," said Brie, on Benedicta's next visit. Brie sat in a chair next to her bed, speaking quietly with Benedicta. "There is," continued Brie, "a man here who shakes all the time. It kind of makes me nervous, you know?"

Benedicta's thoughts wandered. She remembered, she had read, how only thirty or forty years prior, psych patients were kept locked up for years, left to languish in state hospitals. She had heard tales of the horrors there, of patients who were constrained to the back porches of mental hospitals where they sat rocking endlessly. Other patients, she recollected now of what she had read, stared ahead as if not seeing. Even earlier than that, back in the 1920's and 30's, patients were forced to work as almost slave labor at psychiatric state hospitals. There had been inhumane conditions, particularly in the early years, patients were literally chained to beds in poorly ventilated rooms.

Some of the treatments had been archaic and even cruel. Cold baths, wrapping in cold wet sheets, insulin therapy. Some of that had gone on as recently as the 50's and 60's.

But since that time, new advances had been made in the field. It was only in the late twentieth century that there were substantial strides in research in mental health and new drugs were marketed that allowed improvement in some of the patients' conditions. These new advances made possible an easier return to community living for some patients.

Even then, the system was far from perfect. Once in the community, some clients stopped taking their medications, others were lost in the system designed to protect them. Some lived with family, others had apartments, and a good percentage could be classified as "homeless." Many were even in jails. Most generally lacked the resources they needed to remain healthy.

She looked around at the psych patients here. Some appeared ordinary, pleasant in their dress, socializing and smiling. Many, though, were what she would consider "devastated" by their illnesses. Some of them looked disheveled and wasted in appearance, apathetic, unfocused. They would, she knew, hear voices and were disturbed by those voices, or would easily withdraw and speak to no one, or worse, grow violent and need to be restrained.

Shaking her head, she came back to the present. "You are fortunate," she said to Brie. "The drugs you receive will help you to feel better."

"I know, but—" Brie was not mollified by her sister's words. Benedicta could relate. For Benedicta had been through it herself. She had experienced an almost unrelenting depression. And her trust level was affected, she was often suspicious. She, Benedicta, had gone for psychiatric treatment, had received drugs which she had taken for some time. Since leaving the convent, the depression and distrust had subsided a little. She thought perhaps she was recovering for the first time and took her resurgence as a good sign.

Benedicta turned her attention back to her sister. *Why had Brie suffered so from emotional problems? Was it due to the past? Was it about the fire, about Ben?* Benedicta shook her head again and thought, *I won't go there today, I won't.*

The current thinking in psychiatric circles was that mental illness was largely the result of an imbalance of brain chemicals, and that getting the medicines right would help the chemistry. But she had also read that psychiatry needed much in the way of research to determine the causes of illness and ways to help. They had advanced in treatment, she was sure, but there was still a long way to go. Too much was shrouded in mystery. *It is a mystery,* thought Benedicta. *There is so little scientific knowledge in place to determine the causes of mental illness, even in modern times.*

And a social stigma exists surrounding those who require the services of a psychiatrist or seek refuge in a psych hospital. It isn't fair, and many mental health experts attempt to eliminate this scourge on their patients, but the stigma is ever present, she recollected now.

And some mental health clients are more destructive, doing acts of vandalism, destroying or defacing property. Some are violent, she thought. *Then there are those who are devastated by their illness, who will never recover fully. And so much of it is in the shadows,* she mused. *It is serious and complicated.*

Brie was speaking, "I would just like to get better."

"Work with Dr. Prescott, give him a chance. Go to Mass on Sundays, receive the sacraments. Join a support group. Keep up your prayer life. Get some exercise. Take care of yourself, really take care of yourself for a change," encouraged Benedicta, not sure herself of the truth of her words.

"It just seems my thinking is off," said Brie, persisting in her train of thought.

"Yeah, well, maybe it is." Benedicta thought of the *work done in cognitive therapy, in writing down thoughts and changing what is on your mind to something more positive. I was helped by my own efforts to change my thinking. Maybe Brie is ready for some sort of treatment like that. It is something to consider anyway.*

"What does Dr. Prescott say?" asked Benedicta.

"Oh, he doesn't say much, but he wants to observe me further before he makes a diagnosis. He says so many psychiatrists come up with a diagnosis without even knowing the patient."

Benedicta left with a heavy heart. She wanted to believe Brie could get well, could function, take care of herself and provide for herself. That she knew was a stretch.

When she returned to Pinecroft, Benedicta decided to get busy. She was in her office when the phone rang.

"Hey, Benedicta, how are you?" An effusive voice interrupted her making of a list. The voice was Jude's.

"Hello, Jude," Benedicta's mind swirled with just what to say to this man. She had depended on Jude for a little while to help her get through the upset of Brie's admission to the hospital. Her first thoughts told her to be on her guard, to be wary, but her instincts were that this was a good man. *I really would like a friend,* she admitted to herself now, *but can I trust Jude?* "I've just come back from seeing Brie at Our Lady's on the Hill. I'm a bit unnerved by the experience," added Benedicta.

"Are you Ok? Does that mean I don't stand a chance of you accepting my invitation to dinner this evening?"

"Well, I...I...I could go for a steak just now. What did you have in mind?"

"Steak it is. We'll go someplace downtown. I'll pick you up at seven sharp."

"Great," said Benedicta and signed off. She had mixed feelings about accepting the invitation tonight. *I could go for a gentleman's arm* was her thought as she mulled over her acceptance. Benedicta settled herself to finish the list at hand. She was distracted however. She considered for a moment, the episode of anger in which she and Jude had begun a friendship.

What am I getting myself into? But Benedicta's eyes twinkled and she felt a pleasant warm feeling come over her just thinking about seeing him tonight. *Well, he is an attractive man. What is wrong with* just *having dinner with him?* she asked herself.

At 6:55 p.m., the doorbell rang at Pinecroft House of Peace. Sister Anne answered the door. Benedicta came down the staircase in a less than enthusiastic mood. She had recovered from her harrowing time with Brie by taking a nap and a shower. Journaling had helped too. She couldn't quite shake this bad mood. And she did not know just what to make of this moodiness. *Is my depression returning?* she thought, as she descended the staircase.

Dressed in black dressy slacks and a crème colored turtle neck sweater, her wild hair tamed for the moment and piled up in curls on the back of her head, she approached the waiting Jude.

He was wearing a black overcoat and had on a dark well-tailored grey suit. She noticed his blue tie matched his eyes. His brown hair looked soft, and he was well groomed.

"Hi, Benedicta. Wow!!! You look amazing! Here let me help you with that jacket," he said, taking control of the outerwear.

"Jude, you'll have to excuse me, I've had a distressing week," she said, as they settled at a table in the La Normandy Restaurant. She filled him in on the happenings.

"It's okay. I do, though, have an ulterior motive in bringing you here tonight." He cleared his throat and began in earnest, "I have something to tell you, something to share that is important." Taking a quick sip of the water set before him by the waiter, he began again: "It is not something I share with everyone—" his words trailed off as he saw the look on Benedicta's face. He shifted nervously in his chair.

Benedicta's frown remained. *What was there to tell? Does he have secrets in his past? God forbid, I am not prepared for much tonight,* she thought.

Jude changed the direction of his comments and plowed on, "I am here to let you know that I want you in my life." Swallowing hard, he took a breath and would have continued but Benedicta interrupted.

"Jude, I know you want to say something, but truthfully I am on overload," she pulled her hand away from his.

"Oh," she heard him say.

"Really, I—" She began and then stopped, seeing his face. He had a hurt look about him.

There was a pause.

A long moment of silence ensued. "Let's order," he said at last, putting a noncommittal kind of expression on his face. "Maybe you'll feel better after you've eaten. I had something to talk to you about, but I can see with your sister sick, well, what a jerk I am. I thought, well—" he stopped speaking and took a sip of water from the glass in front of him again. This wasn't going as he had envisioned. "I don't know what I thought—" and his voice trailed off.

"Jude— " Her first words were halting, her eyes suddenly downcast. She said softly, "Yes, let's order, please."

The remainder of the evening was spent in polite conversation but *there was an edge of awkwardness*, she thought later. Benedicta was almost sorry she hadn't heard him out. *What did he want her to know? And why was it so difficult for her to take it in?*

Jude called early next morning and acted as if nothing were amiss. Benedicta felt caught off guard. She was waiting for the conflict of the evening before to surface once again. No mention was made of last night at all. He said he called to see if she would be willing to attend midnight Mass with him at St. Xavier Church on Christmas Eve.

Again, she hesitated. *How involved with this man do I plan to be?* In the back of her mind she had thoughts about his invitation. *What did this mean? Does this camaraderie bring us a step closer? And is that what I want?*

In the end, she agreed to be accompanied by Jude to Christmas Eve Mass.

The staff Christmas get-together on the 22nd, it is important to be prepared for it, this being my first year, thought an excited Benedicta

She had spent a good deal of time buying gifts-small ones but she had put thought into each.

For Sister Anne, Benedicta had selected a kitchen clock; for Beatrice Hartung, a picture frame for her granddaughter's photos; and Father, a new Bible. For Scotty, she had purchased a woolen scarf. She had the best gift of all for Lulu: tickets to a play Lulu was dying to see.

They sat together in the dining room. The party was slow getting started; they drank mulled wine, ate turkey sandwiches and enjoyed pumpkin pie. Once they had had their second glass of wine, the conversation flowed more easily.

"Let's sing some Christmas carols. What about it?" asked Sister Anne, putting a record on the stereo.

"Yeah," said Father Gast. "What do you have there? I like 'O Holy Night.'"

"Yes, yes, I have that one," said Sister Anne, swiftly changing records and putting his favorite on top of the stack.

"Oh, Holy Night, the stars are brightly shining—" They sang in harmony. Then, as they were more in the mood, Sister Anne changed the recording once again, and "Oh Come All Ye Faithful" was heard while they hummed along. Beatrice's choice was next, a stirring rendition of "We three Kings." And Sister Anne came in then with more mulled wine. It was becoming a merry group.

"Let's sing 'Jingle Bells,' who wants 'Jingle Bells?'" Sister Anne asked, over the sound of chatter, changing records yet again.

Lulu was quiet, seeming to take it all in. Benedicta tried to catch her eye and see if she was all right. Once she was able to connect with the massage therapist, she breathed easier, knowing that everyone was on board for a good time.

"Let's exchange our gifts now," said Sister Anne, seeming to try to run the show.

"Let's," said Beatrice, "I'll give them out, one at a time, and you can each open one in turn, and we 'll see what each received."

"Here, Benedicta, this one has your name on it," she said.

Benedicta took the wrapped gift, attempted to be neat pulling off the ribbon, but soon was tearing into the package. The gift had a card with a verse, and it was from Beatrice. It contained a Catholic missal, and a selection of holy cards.

"Oh, Bea, it is lovely, I especially like these holy cards. Where did you get such beautiful ones?"

"I sent away for them, found them in a catalogue. Do you really like them?" Beatrice smiled as she spoke, seeming pleased that she had found a satisfactory gift.

The merriment went on as the gift-giving proceeded. Benedicta received a book of meditations from Father and assured him they were just what she needed. Scotty gave her a desk organizer whereupon she 'ohhed' and 'aahed' about its intended use. Sister Anne had a clock radio for her and they shared a moment of amusement that each had purchased a clock for the other.

"What do you think that means?" asked Sister Anne, laughing.

Lulu liked her gift of theatre tickets. The gift she had for Benedicta, an off-white blouse with a pearl pin, seemed extra-special to Benedicta.

"Sister Anne, I must congratulate you on a job well done," said Benedicta as they wrapped up the supper. "Thank you ever so much."

After the party, the group straggled out, and Sister Anne left to go see her sister. Benedicta put away her gifts and was rearranging the dining room when there was a knock on the back door. Puzzled, since no one used that entrance except to get into or out of cars, she opened the door to find an unusual sight.

Jude stood grinning at her from ear to ear. And he was not alone.

"What are you doing here?" she said looking down at the sight before her. "What is that?" she exclaimed.

On a leash, was a long haired shaggy, reddish brown Labrador Retriever, his tail wagging with fury. When Benedicta spoke, he began to bark and jump about. He then gave her some slobbery kisses on her chin.

"THIS is your Christmas present?" Benedicta laughed.

"He was left by a neighbor who moved," he said. "I thought of you. You could use a watchdog." He added, "Labs make great companions, and they have a keen sense of strangers. He could be a great partner for you."

"This dog is actually for me? Not a chance! Not a chance!" she repeated. But she knelt and petted his neck, allowing the dog to plant kisses on her mouth and chin. "He is cute," she said, relenting a little.

"He won't be much trouble," urged Jude. "He is housebroken and everything. He doesn't chew on furniture either. He's got more refined tastes, don't you, Baby?" Jude said, grinning.

"BABY! His name is Baby?" she asked, laughing.

"Really, I am serious. You need a watchdog. You need Baby," said Jude, petting the dog behind his ears.

"Ok, Ok, we'll try it for a while and see how it goes. I can just see Sister Anne, she'll think I've lost it."

That night she lay in her bed with Baby next to her. "It is only for tonight, you are not going to get used to this treatment, understand?" Baby cocked his head to one side and barked. Benedicta was secretly delighted by the gift of the dog. And with those worrisome calls, it might not hurt to have a watchdog.

Chapter Six

On Christmas Eve, Benedicta went to midnight Mass with Jude. The celebration of Christmas with the worship of the Lord seemed heavenly to her.

The church was filled with the scent of pine mixed with incense. Christmas trees, with white lights, were ablaze in the front of the church. Candles sat on every available windowsill and ledge. Red poinsettias, a whole assortment of them, were standing erect in the shape of a Christmas tree, just below the altar steps to the side of the church.

The choir, placed in the loft at the rear of the church, was in rare form. She had never heard the members sing with such reverence. The choir had a harp as well as a trumpet. And they had bells, something new for them this year. They began a half hour before Mass with Christmas carols. The sweet melody of the harp interspersed with trumpet, organ and choir were blissful to her. She sighed in contentment and joy.

The homily was about the birth of Christ and the new life that this event brings to each of us. She could see that she indeed did have a new life, and she vowed to share that new life with her sister.

The whole sense of the Eucharistic service tonight was awesome to her. Christ in His real Presence, coming to her in His

Body and Blood in the form of bread and wine, an intimate form of sharing and presence, to be sure.

If only Brie could have been here with me, Benedicta thought.

Jude left her at Pinecroft after the Mass. He mentioned he had to be up early the next morning, but she didn't know what he had planned.

On Christmas morning, she went to the nursing home to see her mother. She took Baby along with her.

Baby was an instant hit among the seniors. Even her mom seemed to enjoy the pet. She patted his ears and laughed.

"It's been so long since you've visited, forgot all about me you have," complained Lydia Malloy, as she sat in her wheelchair at the dinner table.

"Oh, Mom, it isn't that," said Benedicta, feeling defensive suddenly and trying without success to soothe her mother's feelings. *What is it about my mom that so bothers me?* She wondered. *My mom is selfish and self-preoccupied for one thing. She's never been much of a mother, certainly not a role model, and never doing motherly things,* Benedicta thought derisively.

But Benedicta refused to allow her mom to spoil her festive mood. She offered her the brightly wrapped gifts she had brought. "Merry Christmas, Mom," said Benedicta, reaching over and giving her a hug around the shoulders while handing her one of the gifts.

"Well, I wasn't expecting anything, really," her mom said awkwardly, tearing off the bow and wrapping.

The package contained a book of poetry. Lydia had once liked poetry, and Benedicta hoped this offering would go a long way toward mending the rift between mother and daughter. Or make Christmas a bit more meaningful for the two of them.

"Oh—a book," said her mom, in a deflated tone of voice. She opened the cover and glanced at the title page before quickly laying it aside.

Despite her mom's lackluster response, Benedicta persisted: "The book is written by Robert Frost, I thought perhaps you might like it. You used to like poetry," said Benedicta wistfully, adding, "These poems are some of my favorites."

"Yes, well, I don't read poetry much anymore. I gave it up when I came to this god-forsaken place," Lydia said in a complaining tone of voice, then asked, "What else do you have for me?"

"I brought you your favorite chocolates, the chocolate covered cherries in one box and the walnut truffles in another box," Benedicta said, putting the second wrapped gift in her mother's hands and retreating to a chair beside her.

The conversation between them was soon awkward once again. Benedicta wheeled her mom to the lobby to look at the brightly colored Christmas tree and the lovely decorations. There was a manger scene that Benedicta thought would please Lydia but no coaxing could get her out of her "mood."

Finally, Lydia asked to return to her room, where, with Benedicta's help, she transferred to her easy chair. She ate a few of the candies that Benedicta had brought before nodding off. Benedicta sneaked a few of her mom's choclolates and then tip-toed from the room. She found she was relieved the visit was over.

Benedicta went straight to Our Lady's on the Hill, where she visited her sister. Brie seemed surprised by the dog accompanying Benedicta. Brie gave Baby a few half-hearted pats behind its ears, and then was done with that. But they had what Benedicta thought was a peaceful time together, despite Brie's reluctance to enjoy Benedicta's pet.

Benedicta sensed that Brie was in a thoughtful, reflective mood. She was relaxed and soft spoken today, calmer than she had been on previous occasions.

"And I have presents for you, little sis. Here, open this one first." Brie pulled the wrapping paper off the box. "Do you like it?" Brie held up a soft ivory-colored robe with pink trim.

"Oh, Benie, I love it." She hugged her sister, tore open the wrapping around the second one, a leather-bound journal with a

Cross pen and pencil set. After that, there was a box of chocolates, and the last, a clip for her hair.

Benedicta almost forgot that Brie was sick, she seemed so bright and happy and alert. They dove into the chocolates and ran to the kitchen for drinks.

The day after Christmas was chilly, one below with a wind chill of −17. *Too cold to take Baby outside for a walk,* thought Benedicta. She put Baby in the basement with a bone that Jude had left for the dog, and a bowl of water. She did take him out the door for doggie breaks but then directly back into the house.

I don't know if this will work or not, she admitted to herself as she came up from the basement. Benedicta had planned to see her sister today—after what had happened with the gas turned on in her sister's apartment, she was anxious to get the full story from her. She hadn't pushed her over Christmas to talk, but now she wanted details.

The day began with weather problems. The cars wouldn't start. Benedicta called AAA. They promised to send a truck, but it would be later this afternoon. Her visit to Brie would have to wait.

Benedicta wandered about the center. There were no appointments for the day. She met Lulu in the dining room.

"You look like you could stand a neck adjustment," said Lulu, "You are really tight. I can tell without touching you, in fact. Sit here and I'll have a go."

"Oh, oh, that feels good, so good," said Benedicta, beginning to relax.

"Benedicta, I saw you the other day, getting out of a red convertible sports car, with a very handsome gentleman. Don't tell me it was your brother, either."

"No, but he is handsome, isn't he? That is Jude Forsythe, the lawyer who does some work for Pinecroft. I'm sure you have run into him here from time to time, haven't you?"

"Oh, yeah, I have. I guess it was the car that I didn't recognize." Lulu went on massaging her shoulders and neck.

"I must admit that at first I didn't even like him, I thought he was stuck on himself." Benedicta settled in the chair ready to have a real talk with her friend. "But you know," she continued, "the more I get to know him, well, he's not all bad."

"This could be interesting," Lulu said, smiling.

"It is business only," Benedicta assured her.

"Yeah, right," said Lulu, amused at her friend's insistence that there was nothing going on.

"If you don't mind my asking, are you dating anyone?" a curious Benedicta asked. She wanted to change the subject right away. No more probing questions, she found it uncomfortable.

"Well, yes, I am in fact. But it's hush-hush and all that. He's well, witty, intelligent, an outdoors man, which suits me fine, and he puts up with me, and that is saying something," she said, laughing.

"By the way," Lulu asked then, "what are you doing for New Year's Eve? We are going to a party, a pretty snazzy one."

"I think I am invited to a dance, and I am going all out for it. Would you happen to need to go shopping? I could use a companion for selecting the dressy dress."

"The dance is a fancy affair? Sure, I'd love to go. I may even get something new to wear."

Their conversation drifted to other things. Benedicta was reluctant to share about her sister, or to get too deep about anything really. True, she liked Lulu, and had reached out to her, but it was best not to divulge too much, at least not yet. *It is that trust thing again*, she thought, ruefully.

Christmas has come and gone, thought Benedicta. *I can settle down—almost. If it wasn't that I have Brie to think about, I would be free.*

Benedicta sat with her sister in the lobby of Our Lady's. Brie seemed jittery, nervous, or just kind of restless. "What's wrong,

Brie? Did Dr. Prescott change the medicine or something? You seem on edge today."

"I am. Dr. Prescott says it takes time. He added another med," she said and continued, "I am up every day and working in the craft shop. I made a belt yesterday, a wallet the day before. And I am back to my painting. I am really painting again, that means something, doesn't it?" Her face brightened as she spoke.

"Yes, it certainly does," said Benedicta.

A young man joined them in their place in the lobby and the conversation changed.

"Benedicta, this is my friend Tony Ling. He is painting too. And he is Chinese, or rather his parents are Chinese. Tony was born here, in Cincinnati." She turned to Tony and added, "I was telling my sister about my artwork."

"She's doing a great job," he said, shifting from foot to foot. "And she's a terrific ping pong player, the best. In fact, she could be a champion player. She is that good."

"I didn't know you play ping pong," said Benedicta to Brie.

"There is a lot you don't know," said Brie in a less-than gracious manner.

Tony stepped into the fray and said, "Brie and I played the other night. She beat me badly."

"What kind of work do you do, normally, I mean?" asked Benedicta.

"I am a private detective. I have my own agency. I used to work for a security company. But I don't like being bossed around. Now I am my own boss," and added, "No one can tell me what to do."

Benedicta eyed Tony. He had a tremor in his hands and a twitch above one eye. Aside from that, he seemed friendly enough. She was glad Brie was making friends.

Benedicta took I-75 toward downtown. She was dreading what was to come. Try as she might, she was drawn to visiting her mother today, and although she had just seen her on Christmas, it seemed the right time to visit.

"I don't like coming here," Benedicta said aloud as she pulled in the parking lot of Marjorie P. Lee Nursing Home on Michigan Avenue in Hyde Park.

The building was older but well kept. Her mother had a furnished room, a large one, on the first floor.

The Marjorie P. Lee Nursing Home was a two-story building. On the second floor lived the skilled-care patients, some bed-fast, some up in wheelchairs. On the first floor were the more alert and semi-ambulatory clients. They each had a private room, with activities planned for every day. There was also an exercise room available and a chapel.

Benedicta entered quietly. Her mother was napping on the couch. Lydia, dressed in a red silk dressing gown, her pudgy arms folded across her ample chest, opened her eyes drowsily, and said, "Well, it is about time. I thought you had forgotten me completely. That, or you had run off with some no-good gardener." Lydia attempted to rise from the couch. Benedicta reached out and helped her sit up. Patting her mom's chubby hand, she avoided a hug, and sat down in the sofa chair.

"No such luck, my running off with a gardener, mums," she said and continued, "and I was just here Christmas, remember?"

"I know, I know. There is bad blood between us. You blame me for Ben. But it isn't like you think." She lit a cigarette and drew hard, exhaling a cloud of smoke.

"No, I don't blame you or anyone." *I do hold you responsible for your drinking,* she wanted to say, *for your years of alcoholic haze, when you barely took care of us.* She refrained from saying something so direct. Instead, she tried to ease things a bit. "But how have you been?" She began again.

"How should I be?" her mom protested, "I am stuck in this forsaken place, no visits from my daughters, thank you so much." She puffed away on her cigarette and opened a bag of chocolates, popping one in her mouth. She didn't offer any to Benedicta.

Lydia had deep furrows in the skin on her forehead, and a sagging double chin; Benedicta watched now the bloated skin rise and fall as her mother chomped on the candy. *How has my mother ended up this way?* she asked herself. Benedicta closed her eyes for a moment thinking, *no, things haven't changed much, that is for sure.* "Forgive me for my abrupt words," she said, trying to take a conciliatory tone, but her mother would have none of it.

"Don't ask me for forgiveness, I'm not in the mood for it."

"Brie's having her problems again," she said after a pause.

"As usual, what do you expect?" said her mother.

Benedicta had had a restless night. Really, she had not been sleeping well since Brie had turned on the gas in her apartment. Something was going on and she didn't know what it was, she couldn't name it. *Generally, if things get a name they lose their power, and this is no exception,* she thought. *But I can't figure it out. And those calls, there was another one today.*

Benedicta entered Our Lady on the Hill and hurried up to Brie's floor. Brie was in her room. When she entered, Benedicta leaned down and kissed Brie's cheek, then sat down. "Well, you've been here for a month or so. It is time you were feeling better. How are you today?"

"I wish people would stop asking me how I feel. That is all that has happened today. Everyone has asked me that."

"Sorry, honey. I am just interested. And I am concerned. What did you do all day today?"

"I met with the social worker, talked to my psychiatrist, went to therapy downstairs, attended koffee klatch," she said, giving an exaggerated rolling of her eyes. "Geez, isn't it enough that I am here, do I have to be interrogated as well?"

Benedicta stopped listening and pondered the situation. Brie seemed better, easier to talk to, more relaxed despite her cranky mood of the moment. She made a mental note to call Dr. Prescott.

Brie was saying something, "And I was walking out in the yard along the walkway by the porch, and a huge flowerpot came crashing down and missed me by inches. Really, I could have been badly hurt."

"That's awful," a distracted Benedicta commented. "And have you been sleeping?"

"Do you want to hear about the accident or not?" Brie was indignant.

Benedicta was startled out of her reverie by her sister's hasty words. "Of course, I do," she said. "But let's go to the cafeteria and get a snack, I am starving. I will listen while we eat." They headed down the hall and to the first floor to the cafeteria.

"It was one of the flower pots sitting on a sill on the porch above. It must have tipped over somehow," said Brie, as they sat at a table by the window in the cafeteria. She continued, "Wooley was yards away, on the porch, and saw it fall."

"Were you hurt at all?"

"No, it missed me."

Just then, they were interrupted by two young people. One was a young man with a muscular build and dark grey eyes, the other a young woman of about eighteen who walked with a limp. They asked if Brie knew the time for group therapy, and when Brie said she did not know, they moved on.

Brie spoke of the couple when they left. "I don't know his name, but he created quite a disturbance on our floor last night. He had to be locked in a seclusion room. He became kind of argumentative and even violent. He threw a lamp at his roommate, so he was isolated from those on the floor. I didn't see it exactly. I just heard about it from that young woman this morning."

"He seems ok now, just be careful," Benedicta said.

"I think he likes me," said Brie, grinning.

Benedicta tried to bring up the subject for which she had come today. "We haven't talked much about what brought you here, the gas being on in your apartment. Have you had any further thoughts about the situation? Do you remember any more details about what actually happened?"

"Oh, for pity's sake, are we going to discuss THAT? I have been all over that with the social worker, with Dr. Prescott and with the nurses. Are you going to bug me, too?" Brie threw up her hands. "Really, that is such old news," she said.

Chapter Seven

Benedicta was in her office the next morning, Baby sat at her feet as he often was wont to do. She had been holding a difficult spiritual direction with a client who was hostile and bent on hurting herself. In the end, the woman left with a plan, but Benedicta had qualms about her ability to follow through with her plan.

What should she as an 'objective observer' do? The meeting was considered confidential, there were privacy issues at stake here, but in cases like this, she was mandated to alert the authorities if in her estimation, the individual was a danger to herself or someone else. This was a case for the authorities, Benedicta believed. It was clear what she needed to do, and she intended to call Hamilton County Social Services first thing. These kinds of situations were sticky and usually turned into headaches; the patient would probably no longer trust her as a counselor after turning her in. That was the least of her worries.

After the call, she felt a bit calmer and went to the chapel to clear her head and pray. Before she could recover from her session, a phone call came from Our Lady's on the Hill.

"Ms. Malloy, this is Helen Murdock, the nurse in charge of your sister's wing this afternoon. Please, there may be no cause for alarm, I hope not in any case. but—" and she stopped, waiting for a word from Benedicta.

"Is, is Brie all right?"

"Oh yes, she is fine."

Benedicta stood in front of her desk, thinking—waiting for the other shoe to drop. In truth, she had been expecting this very thing.

Helen went on. "This morning there was an incident that was disquieting. Brie was on her way to koffee klatch. She took the stairs, and she, well, she fell. Brie maintains someone pushed her, she insists on it. I don't know if you are aware of a previous incident, something similar. She tripped and fell down a stairwell the other day too. It is all too much to be a coincidence, I fear. Unless Brie is having balance problems or something I don't know about—" Her voice trailed off.

"You are right, Helen. Indeed, I have been expecting this very thing to happen, and I don't know yet if it is a figment of Brie's imagination, or if she is in real danger. There have been some other troubling situations. And they have been kind of threatening. Yesterday she was almost hit by a falling flower pot, and there have been calls—" Benedicta stopped, and considered what to tell Helen.

In the meantime, Helen had another question. "The doctors are still adamant that their findings do indicate she could have been suicidal when she was admitted, which is also troubling in light of the gas being on in her apartment. What is your take on that, if you don't mind my asking?"

"I think, Helen, it is all circumstantial but, at the very least, significant. Thank you for bringing these things to my attention," said Benedicta, more alarmed now than ever. She had been considering something like this but hadn't wanted to admit it.

When she got off the phone, Benedicta wished she had someone to call to talk to about her concerns. I will think about this later, she thought, as she had a spiritual direction appointment coming up shortly.

Benedicta put it out of her mind. She would regret this later.

Benedicta had another restless night. During the night, she dreamed she saw a man hitting Brie with a baseball bat. He was not facing Benedicta directly, so she couldn't see his face, but he was burly and the situation looked dangerous. She slipped from her bed, put on a robe, and tip-toed downstairs, where she raided the refrigerator. Cold chicken and a piece of apple pie. She had gulped it down, not even thinking. After she ate, she sighed. This action had not helped at all. She reminded herself it was just a dream, a nightmare really. But this dream did worry her and motivated her to visit her sister that afternoon. Brie was more composed, calmer than she had been in a while. Benedicta took heart in this, seeing it as improvement.

As they sat in the lounge on Brie's unit, an older man approached them. He was fiftyish, had a stubble-like beard on his chin, and had a kind of hillbilly accent. He stood in the doorway and beamed a big smile at Brie.

"Hullo to ya, Brie, ya going to drawin' classes today?" he asked.

"Hi, Wooley. Yes, I am, I'll be down in a little while. This is my sister, Benedicta. She is visiting me this afternoon. Benedicta, this is my friend Wooley. He is a patient here and he lives in my building downtown. Isn't that a coincidence?"

"Yes," said Benedicta. "Hello Wooley, how are you today?"

"Oh, fine, ma'am," said Wooley.

"Oh, please call me Benedicta," she said, and added, "Are you from Cincinnati? You have an accent."

"No, I'm not from Cincinnati."

"Where are you from?"

Wooley backed up as he spoke and stood again in the doorway, "I'm from away from these parts. Haven't lived here long neither. Wull, I'll see ya, Brie." And with that Wooley was gone.

As Wooley turned and walked away, Benedicta was reminded of the dream the night before. She said nothing about it to Brie.

Ach, ach, ach. I thought it would be an easy thing to do, nice and easy, he mused as he sat in his room, staring mindlessly at the television. *I figured to scare off those two by having a couple of accidents, for the one in the hospital. Right simple, mind ya. That didn't do the trick, not so easy after all, to get them outa here and runnin scared. But I'll do it, by durn.*

———————

Her visit to the hospital had been a short one and upon arriving home, she decided to take a walk around the property. The air was chilly, and she pulled her down coat about her as she took the path back through the woods. Baby was with her and kept stopping to sniff. As Benedicta walked, she became more nervous. The path wound around the lake and through some trees, where she could not be seen from the road. She wanted to clear her head. Too much was happening, things she had no control over.

She skirted the trees and took the path, which meandered along the periphery of the grounds, the path ending at the far side of the lake. She sat on a bench, the dog at her feet. It was cold, but she remained sitting there, deep in her own thoughts.

Suddenly Benedicta sensed trouble. She felt someone close by, too close, uncomfortably close. Baby was growling, which unnerved her even more. She looked around but saw no one. It was twilight. She had been sitting there for an hour or more. Her senses told her something was threatening, as if she were in danger. Quickly, Benedicta gathered her things, pulled the leash with the dog along with her and ascended the hill toward the house.

Something dark and foreboding was taking place. Benedicta did not think she had intuitive powers, but if she could have at that moment, she would have sworn that there was evil lurking in the distance. She had never been one for premonitions and she did not believe in ghosts, but this was real and uncanny. Benedicta wondered just what she could do about it. She had an idea. She would speak to Inspector Brown tomorrow.

Alerting the authorities would have been a wise choice but she delayed.

Brie stood atop the railing of the hospital porch, swaying from one side to another. "I am going to do it. It is no use, no matter what you say, I am jumping from this porch." Her jaw was firmly set, her hands clenched. She looked angry and belligerent.

Benedicta had been called this morning and informed that Brie was having some kind of "episode." She was, the nurse had reported, almost incoherent, restless, even loud and forceful in her behavior. That was not like Brie at all. By the time Benedicta arrived at Our Lady's on the Hill, things had become unmanageable. *Why was Brie not watched more closely,* she thought now, *why was she left unsupervised?* Those questions would have to be answered later, now was not the time to get into that.

Benedicta was frantic. She gauged the height of the porch, a second floor from the ground to the porch, and decided Brie was in danger. She could break a leg, get a concussion; anything was possible.

"Don't do this Brie, we'll work it out—some way—don't do this," she repeated.

Where was everyone? she mused, ready to panic. Just then, the door flew open and someone stood in the doorway. Benedicta breathed a sigh of relief.

"Whoa, Missy, what's this?" he asked, looking first at Brie then at Benedicta. It was one of the maintenance crew, accidently interrupting while making his rounds. Benedicta recognized the burley old fellow. He had always been polite and solicitous of her in the past. "Let's get you down pronto," he said. The man reached out for her.

"Don't touch me. DO NOT TOUCH ME," bellowed Brie, increasing her swaying motion in response.

"Please, get some help, quickly if you could—" asked Benedicta. "And hurry," she added.

"Sure, right on it." The maintenance man disappeared inside.

"Brie, your whole family would be lost without you. And we certainly don't want you to injure yourself," Benedicta spoke in a quiet if not entirely calm voice. "I would like to have a nice visit with you. Can't you come down now? We'll have some fun, play a game."

Brie glared at her sister, saying, "I know you are trying to cajole me. You just want to get rid of me, too."

"No, no, it's nothing like that. Please, Brie."

Suddenly the door to the hospital swung open, revealing two nurses, a male attendant, and the maintenance man.

One of the nurses promptly stepped forward and said, "What is going on here?"

"I'm not coming down, you can't make me," a defiant Brie spoke up.

"Okay, young lady, but you don't look so comfortable up there," said the nurse.

Benedicta explained the situation to those present: "She's hearing voices telling her to jump and she has chosen this place to do it."

"We will get more of a team together," said the nurse. She motioned to the male attendant who turned and left the scene. "They will bring the van. It will have an inflatable balloon on board. It could save your sister from possible injury if she does fall."

"Whatever you say," replied Benedicta, beginning to feel in capable hands. *At least Brie would be unharmed,* she thought.

"Brie, wouldn't you like a Coke? You must be thirsty. If you come down, we could get you a Coke," said the nurse.

Benedicta shifted from foot to foot. Her patience was giving out; she was fearful for her sister. This attempt to hurt herself was a new wrinkle. Perhaps the gas in the apartment had been her way of trying to respond to voices, just as now. "We always have fun when I come to visit. Don't you want to go to the canteen?" asked Benedicta.

Brie did not reply. Her anger seemed to have subsided. She looked tired and frightened. She stared from Benedicta to the female nurses and back again.

The lead nurse motioned to her companion and quietly, unnoticed, positioned herself behind Brie, kind of below her, next to the railing. She could reach up and contact Brie from where she stood.

Brie was seemingly agitated now. She took a step forward on the rail. She gazed down, took a deep breath, and looked as if she were ready to jump. The nurse saw her chance. She grabbed Brie from behind, and pulled her from the railing, setting her on her feet on the porch.

Brie seemed to wilt before their eyes. She dropped to the floor, whimpering.

"Okay, Miss Malloy, you are safe now. I just didn't want you to get hurt," said the nurse in a gentle voice. "Why don't you go inside with this nurse, she wants to keep you safe."

Brie was whisked off by the other nurse, who would medicate her and put her in an unlocked seclusion room for the next twenty-four hours. Here, she could be watched closely by the staff. And protected if need be. Benedicta thanked the team before she went up to Brie's unit. The nurse on duty upstairs informed her that she could have only ten minutes with her sister.

Brie had already been medicated when Benedicta entered the seclusion room. A big iron door with a glass viewing screen in the center was opened for her. The room was windowless and was sparsely furnished with only a mattress and a pillow. The walls attracted Benedicta's attention: they were padded. She had never seen a room like this one before.

Brie was sprawled out on the mattress, already drowsy from the medication. She looked at Benedicta and said, "Benie, why am I like this? Why do I hear scary voices? Why can I not date like other girls my age, or hold down a job, or have friends?"

Benedicta didn't know what to say. Those thoughts had crossed her mind about her sister as well. She swallowed hard, feeling a lump in her throat, and heard herself give an answer. "I know it is hard on you, honey. It is part of the mystery of God's love for us.

"We suffer sometimes, and we can offer up that suffering to the Lord, kind of to atone for our sins. And we don't always understand God's mystery. That is why it is a mystery. I know for sure that the Lord loves you very much." She hoped those words would comfort Brie. "As for the voices, it has to do with the chemicals in your brain. It is not your fault—" Her voice trailed off.

She's talking about the darkness in which she finds herself, thought Benedicta, feeling hurt for her sister. "Oh Brie, you have gifts to use like anyone else. You have your artwork, and you do a fantastic job of that." Brie didn't hear her. Brie was asleep.

"Feed the hungry, give drink to the thirsty," mused Benedicta, thinking of the Sermon on the Mount in the Gospels. She stood looking down at Brie. *This was her mission with her sister. Supporting her sister was exactly the way to live out those precepts, to feed and give drink to those in need. Brie needs to be fed, to be given drink. Not in a physical way but be given food for her soul. Brie requires help in her life, extra nurturing, to make her way on her path. For Brie, it is always an uphill climb. She requires someone to light the way, to point her toward the One.*

Benedicta turned and left the hospital, emerging out into the warm sunshine. She felt relieved that Brie was not injured, she was grateful there were nurses close by who would keep an eye on her. Nevertheless, the incident left questions in Benedicta's mind about what was happening.

How unstable is Brie? Why was she suffering so much? Is her emotional turmoil due to childhood trauma? Has Brie interacted in recent months with some strange man who didn't have her interests at heart and who is now threatening both of us? Had Brie turned on the gas in her apartment with the intent to commit suicide or was it some perpetrator, someone she didn't even know? She found no answers to her questions.

Benedicta believed more now than ever that Brie needed to come to Pinecroft for an extended stay after her discharge from the hospital. Brie would do well with some sort of routine to follow. Perhaps she would call Dr. Prescott, mention her suggestion, and see what he thought. And she would include Brie in the planning, ask her how she saw the plan.

Benedicta could not have predicted the events to follow.

Gosh, durn. It worked jist the way I figured but it still did not do the trick, he thought as he stood in line to buy chewing tobacco at the pharmacy. *I gave that sis a suggestion to jump off a ledge, a high one preferably, but I wasn't figurin on anybody being around. It would have been the way to go, too. Now I'll have to come up with somethin' more dangerous-like. I am gittin pretty tired of dreamin' up stuff to do and then it fallin' through.*

Chapter Eight

A gala affair, a New Year's celebration, and Benedicta was to be the guest of Jude Forsythe. The festive affair was something she had seen in the newspapers counting down the days until December 31st. Jude had asked her to be his date at the gala. *It is exciting*, she thought. *I can hardly wait.*

Benedicta went to the expense of purchasing a dressy dress, a formal, really, for the affair. The dress was floor length, strapless, and in off-white, with white tiny pearl beads sewn into the skirt. It had a pale blue sash at the waist. She had shopped for stilettoes and found them at Lazarus Department Store. She told herself she would make do with a pearl bag in her closet but then she and Lulu found one that she liked ever so much, and Lulu insisted on buying it for her. Lulu had gone shopping with her to get ready for the night. The finishing touch was a short dark fur coat borrowed from Lulu.

"You're all set. You will look stunning," said Lulu, holding the dress bag in her arms as Benedicta put the other bags in the car.

"Thank you, Lulu. Even though it was expensive, I haven't spent anything on wardrobe in a while, and it is a special occasion, after all. And you were so generous buying me the bag and going to the trouble of lending me your fur jacket."

"You deserve a special night out, and if that is what is needed to get you ready, then so be it."

The night was cold and clear. Jude had brought his Lincoln Town Car, and they had traveled in style to the gala.

The affair was at the Cincinnati Club on Garfield Place, downtown. They entered the grand ballroom and were awed by its spectacular furnishings. Benedicta blushed as it seemed all eyes were upon them.

The ballroom could only be described as enchanting. The room had large tall windows on two walls, and four opulent crystal chandeliers. The room was decorated in elegant green, gold, and red colors. Leather couches and stuffed chairs sat at the end of the room, just next to the bar. A buffet table lined the other end. Small tables hugged the walls with room for dancing in the center.

First, they had drinks at the bar and mingled among the other guests.

"Benedicta, I'd like you to meet Terry, Terrance Murdock. He is one of the staff at Adams, Harcourt, and Carlyle. He is Brad's assistant, and I must say I am jealous. I could use a good man like Terry on my team."

"You have a solid teammate in Hubert Ferral, you know. And then you have Connie Yeager. Who wouldn't want Connie?" said Terry, laughing. *It is an inside joke of some kind,* thought Benedicta, noticing the comment by Jude pleased Terry.

"Who is Connie?" asked Benedicta, joining in the conspiracy, as they sipped their drinks.

"Connie is a tall, willowy, and very comely brunette who is all the rage at the office. Most of the single guys want a date with her. I have to admit I was interested in her when she first arrived on the scene, but I lost interest after I got to know her better," he said quietly, and added, "to tell you the truth, Connie is something of a gold digger."

Benedicta smiled in response to that admission.

"Let's head to our table, shall we?" Jude led Benedicta by the arm to the main area of the ballroom. Here, there were tables each seating parties of four. There were about 40 tables in all, spread about the perimeter of the large dance floor. The tables were decorated with the same gold and green as the décor: a lit votive candle and a clear glass vase with red roses sat on each of the tables. Benedicta and Jude searched for their place cards and found them. They were seated with Brad and his wife, Channing.

Benedicta immediately froze upon seeing Channing. She had heard stories of this woman's reputation, mainly things she had read on the society pages of the local newspaper. Now she would see for herself. As she mentally prepared herself, she vowed to keep an open mind.

"Benedicta, you have met Brad, I think, and this is his beautiful wife, Channing," said Jude, making introductions. He held Benedicta's chair for her and seated her across from Brad.

"Flattery will get you everywhere, Jude," said Channing, a bit too loudly. "Hello, Benedicta, I have heard so much about you, I think I know you already. Now I'll have someone to gossip with. It is good to finally meet you in person. Isn't it a lovely evening?"

Channing was wearing a red chiffon strapless dress. Her gold earrings glittered as she moved. Her bleached hair had taken on a vaguely orange color. She had rings on most of her fingers.

"Yes, it is a nice evening," said Benedicta, with a little anxiety. She liked Brad, and was comfortable with him, but his wife came across as a little too brassy for her taste.

"Jude, how have you been?" Channing asked, when her husband left to get hors d'oeuvres for the foursome.

"Oh, I've been just great," said Jude, and added, "Excuse me if you would please. I'll see if I can help Brad get drinks and grab some of the nuts and pretzels or whatever."

"Channing," said Benedicta, trying desperately to think of some chatty conversation, "Jude tells me you are into supporting charity events for good causes. Is this one of your galas?"

"Yes, it is, though I was only on the planning committee for this one. I try to do two or three big events a year, in addition to this one."

Benedicta was saved from responding by the guys returning to the table. "We are in for treats. They had grilled mushrooms on crackers, chicken fingers with honey mustard sauce, and stuffed olives. I love these olives," said Brad with enthusiasm, putting the food on the table and nonchalantly popping one of the olives in his mouth.

"Careful, dear, save enough room for the main entree," warned Channing, with what seemed an edge to her voice. But she herself dug into the chicken fingers and crackers.

Jude followed with the drinks. "Here we go, a Tom Collins, for you, Benedicta, made with Beefeater's gin, as you requested, a bourbon and water for you Channing, and an old-fashioned for Brad."

"Aren't you imbibing?" asked Channing of Jude.

"Glad you asked, Channing. Here, you can see I have an extra glass, and I am going to split the Tom Collins between us. Benedicta doesn't want a whole drink, nor do I."

After a few moments of stilted silence, the group dug into the snacks. After a little while, Jude rose from the table, adjusted his tie and said, "Let's get some of that buffet while the line is not too long. What do you say, Benedicta?"

"Sounds good to me," she said. Benedicta was relieved to be moving away from the table for a few moments.

"How are you doing? You seem to be holding up despite being seated with Channing. Brad is my good friend, but I'm not a fan of Channing's. She is pretty glittery tonight, I must admit," said Jude, as he picked up a plate and scooped up some salad.

"I'm okay, really, Jude. Personally, I don't want to judge her too quickly. I am happy to be here, it is a beautiful affair, and Channing is not going to spoil it for me," said Benedicta bravely.

"That's my girl."

The buffet was fantastic, she had to admit. A prime rib, filet mignon, chicken in wine sauce, with brown rice, buttered noodles, and salad, in two different varieties, along with asparagus spears and peas, sat in silver serving dishes on the table. Tall candelabras and a red flowered and green spruce centerpiece added a touch of elegance to the table. Desserts sat on a side bar. The couple helped themselves to the salad and took some of the prime rib, rice and veggies.

"We'll come back for dessert," said Jude, and added consolingly, "We'll move around some after the meal."

When seated, Benedicta was just about to cut her prime rib when Channing waved her hand in the air, and said, "Jude, would you pass the salt?" As she waved her hand, it hit against Benedicta's wine glass, upsetting the glass. The liquid spilled onto the table dripping down on Benedicta's gown. Dark stains appeared on the delicate fabric.

Benedicta jumped from her chair exclaiming, "Oh, oh, my!"

Jude took his napkin and caught the remainder of the liquid, at the same time signaling for a waiter.

"Oh Jude, it is okay, it isn't necessary to—"

"Nonsense," interrupted Channing, "I want to have your gown dry cleaned myself. My maid will come tomorrow to get it. I am so sorry. Here, let's go to the powder room and see what we can do to remove the spots from your dress."

And Channing escorted a protesting Benedicta to the ladies' room.

"There is no need, Channing, really. These things happen," fussed Benedicta. Benedicta was sure that it had been done on purpose. She couldn't explain why Channing had chosen to knock her glass over and spill the contents on her, but she knew the act wasn't a careless move that had caused it.

They entered the quiet of the powder room. Here a brocade covered couch and two matching chairs sat in front of a mirror.

In the next area was a vanity with two sinks and three stalls. A pretty young woman dressed in a black and white uniform with a starched white apron stood stationed at the vanity, handing out hand towels.

The young woman took over when they entered the room.

"Here, let me help you. I get this all the time," she said, going to a cabinet and taking out a thick terry cloth towel and a bottle of cleaner. She began blotting the fabric of the dress. "There," she said," I don't think that will show. Unless," she added, "you want to remove the dress and I could take it to be cleaned. It would only take a few minutes. Those services are available at the hotel next door, so you see it wouldn't be any trouble."

"No, no," Benedicta said quickly, "It is fine. You are right, it doesn't show."

The maid moved on to help a client in a hurry at the sink. Channing plopped down on the couch, patting the seat next to hers, motioning Benedicta to sit down.

Cautiously, Benedicta sat on the chair next to the couch, wondering what was up. She soon found out.

"Benedicta," began Channing, "Brad has been one of the few nominated for Lawyer of the Year by the Legal Aid Society. It is a real honor. Naturally, it would be wonderful if he were to win. Has Jude mentioned anything about it?"

"N...n...no, not that I know of. Should he have?" asked Benedicta.

"It's just that I am trying to procure as many votes for Brad as possible," continued Channing, not paying attention to her question. "You understand, there will be a large monetary award attached, and a trip. We haven't traveled out of the country in a while, it would be an opportunity to—."

She stopped, looking at Benedicta, before continuing, "Would you, as a favor to me, ask Jude to vote for Brad? And see if he could line up other votes? Jude knows a lot of lawyers. And make it so it is your idea, not mine, if you would. Tell him I mentioned it and you thought it would be great if Brad won, and—something along those lines, you know? "

So that was it. That was why the trick of knocking the glass over and spilling it on her so that she could get her to the ladies' room for an extended private chat. *What a bold vixen,* thought Benedicta.

"I'll…I'll… I'll ask Jude if he knows anything about it," she said, not sure how to respond. Then she rose from the chair and headed for the door. "Let's get back to the guys, shall we?" and she led the way, Channing following.

Her head was pounding and her hands were cold. She couldn't believe the nerve of Channing.

It was with relief when they returned to the table and Jude asked her to dance.

"It was a delightful night, Jude, really," she said, her head clearing a little, as they made their way home after the dance. "Thank you, I enjoyed myself."

"You were the belle of the ball. No one compared to you, you are so beautiful tonight," he said gallantly.

They ended the night with a kiss at the front door of Pinecroft.

The next day was New Year's Day. Benedicta was preparing to spend the day with a good book, and then visit her sister in the evening. Instead, she spent it with Jude. He called about ten o'clock in the morning, after she had been to Mass.

"Would you be interested in a brunch and then watching the football games on TV? I am not a football person but it is kind of a family tradition on New Year's Day and all, and—" His voice trailed off and he was silent waiting for her to speak.

Again, she found herself confronted with mixed feelings. *Was this the beginning of something romantic?* They had had such a good time last night, aside from Channing. Or was this just a complication in her job? She found herself in a dilemma of sorts, undecided which way to go. And there was that suspicion again.

She knew this much: she was attracted to Jude. She felt they got along well, but what to do?

"I'm not much of a sports fan either, but I guess I could muster up the enthusiasm to watch a game or two. And brunch sounds wonderful. You are feeding me too much good food. I will be rotund, jolly and fat, and it will be your fault, you know," she said laughing.

"It is good to hear you laugh. Do you know that you have a musical laugh?" he asked.

"Why, thank you." She thought of her plan to read a book and decided this sounded way more fun. "By the way, who is playing today?"

"The Dallas Cowboys are playing the Oakland Raiders. The other we will catch if we can. If not, tough," he said and rang off.

After he called, she got another call.

"Hi, Benedicta, this is Channing Harcourt. I hope you are not busy tomorrow. I am inviting you to a luncheon of the Cincinnati Women's Club. It is at the Weston Hotel in the Orchid Room. It starts at 12:30 p.m. I could pick you up at 11:30 a.m.?"

"Oh, Channing, it sounds delightful, but I am a working girl. I have all kinds of appointments tomorrow. Another time, perhaps?" she was so relieved she could honestly say she was busy.

"Sure," said Channing and spoke about the gala of the prior night. "It was fun wasn't it? You and I will have to get together soon. Well, talk to you later, thanks anyway," said Channing. *Did her voice have a note of disappointment?* thought Benedicta.

Jude picked her up close to noon. She was dressed in a black wool pant suit mostly because it was warm. It didn't hurt that she thought it was sexy, too.

"Benedicta, as usual, you look stunning," he said appreciatively when he came in. "Let's go to the Quality Inn in Norwood. Theirs is the very best buffet in the city. Then we can go to my place and watch the game. The Cowboys are my favorite team and they are on at four p.m. "

"Okay, "she said, venturing a query, "Do you know who called me after you hung up the phone? You'll never guess. I'll give three tries." She laughed.

"I give up. I'm not good at guessing games," he said, smiling.

"Channing Harcourt. She was inviting me to lunch tomorrow at the Cincinnati Women's Club."

"You should go. They put on a good spread, I hear," he said, amused.

"Humph, don't you know I work for a living? Apparently, you are unaware of that fact and Channing doesn't know, either," said Benedicta as she got in the red convertible.

"And do you know anything about a Lawyer of the Year Award, sponsored by some place or other and giving a bunch of money and a trip as a bonus?" she asked as they drove to the hotel.

"Oh, yes, I have. It is sponsored by the Legal Aid Society. They do that every other year. It is kind of a big deal to some lawyers here in the city. Brad told me Channing had signed him up for it. Why would she be telling you?"

"Because she wants to enlist me to hound you about getting votes for hubby," she said. "I think she would really like a trip with her husband, and maybe she'd like the money as well."

"Well, Brad is definitely not interested in traveling. Besides, his business needs him here, and I can't imagine him spending three weeks in Europe, which is what the award entails. And it isn't like they need the money. She could go on her own if she wants to."

"Maybe she needs to go away with her husband, and this would be an excuse," said Benedicta.

They arrived at the Quality Inn and got in line at the serving table. The buffet was delicious. They had plates piled high of steaming scrambled eggs, sausage links, potato wedges, a serving of French toast, and a couple of bran muffins apiece. She carried her plate and a goblet of orange juice back to the table. Jude followed up by getting steaming cups of coffee.

"This is more than I eat in a week, a month in fact," said Benedicta as she finished her food.

"It was good, wasn't it? I'm glad I can spoil you," Jude leaned back in the chair and looked at her.

Blushing, she asked, "What are you staring at me for?"

"Can't I look at a beautiful woman?"

She turned red, and to hide her consternation, she rose and said, "I am taking a trip to the ladies' room. Excuse me. Be right back."

Jude and Benedicta were quiet as they left the restaurant and drove to Jude's. It was the first time Benedicta had been to Jude's home, and it took her aback. Situated on a hill overlooking the Ohio River, the house was stone, and had a screened-in deck running along one side. The front had tall wide windows facing down the hill. *A one-story house set on a hill, a welcoming place,* thought Benedicta.

The interior was out of a picture story book and she could see it suited Jude. The front part was all one large area, featured a cathedral ceiling, and served as a combined formal living room, more casual den area, a dinette, and kitchen. A counter divided the kitchen from the dinette. A group of tall potted palms put just in the right place made the dinette private from the remainder of the room and a huge fish tank did the same for the living room and den.

Jude saw her surveying the living area. "It is comfortable," was all he said. Then he added, "Let me show you the rest of the house."

Guiding her to the back of the home, Jude showed her the master bedroom. The room had just the right touch combined with a feminine influence as well. It made her think the room was possibly decorated by a woman. There was a brocade mauve-colored comforter and matching draperies and two lounge chairs, in blended colors. A few photographs sat on the bureau, one of two children. There were two lamps with muted lighting, as well as expensive art on the walls.

The spare bedrooms were tastefully done. The more casual room had twin beds with yellow print quilts and a rocker and chest. The other featured a queen-sized bed, a couch, a desk, and a dresser.

"Why are you smiling at me?" he asked.

"Because I like it," she said, "it is so you, somehow."

"Is that good?"

"Delightfully so," was the answer.

Chapter Nine

On Benedicta's next visit to the hospital, Brie was in a good mood and seemed more herself. While they relaxed together in the lobby, looking at the huge fish tank, Brie brought up a conversation from a previous visit: "You remember Wooley? I introduced him to you recently. He is insisting on accompanying me to koffe klatch."

"Oh? That is nice of him, isn't it? Perhaps he is trying to be your friend."

"Yeah, I suppose, but he seems a little too possessive or something," said Brie. "I don't know what it is, but it is a bit creepy, it seems to me. He lives in the apartment building where I live. I don't recall him acting this way before."

"Maybe because he knows you from where you live, he is perhaps looking for a friendly face," said Benedicta, hurrying to put Brie at ease. "Well, I think I had better head home, I have a really busy day tomorrow. Okay?"

"Sure."

When finally evening came, Benedicta couldn't wait to lock up. At last, she went to her room for the night, and threw herself on the bed, still dressed. She wanted to sleep but sleep eluded her. She found herself tossing and turning, first throwing the covers off and then getting cold again. Her thoughts were of her childhood. *We had such a controlling mom*, she mused. *It is hard to trust, for both Brie and me. Dad was never around— and when he was, he was remote. They both abandoned us, I guess.* Rising, she got out her journal and wrote:

"I am doing what I am able to do for my sister, but her acting out worries me. And she doesn't seem to be able to take care of herself. In the meantime, I have my work and need to keep body and soul together. Which is hard, because I am really struggling here myself. At times I am very depressed, anxious, and super fatigued. Sometimes I wonder if it is good for me to focus so much on my sister and leave my own wants and needs so far in the back of my mind."

She returned to bed, but still could not sleep. And so it went, all night. When dawn came, Benedicta arose, took a shower, and dressed. On tiptoe she descended to the chapel, sat before the Blessed Sacrament, the only light the candle over the tabernacle.

"It's like this, dear Lord. I know You are here for me, I know You love me— it is still hard for me to believe. Where is my faith, and how do I trust? You have said to trust in You, yet, I keep trying to do it all myself. And I believe You, Lord, want me to let go somehow. I want to abandon my old ways of being strictly independent and instead to rely on Your unfailing help and magnificent gifts, on your grace. Thank You for being here for me. I believe, help my disbelief. Thank You for Your love. Amen."

On Friday, Benedicta had a staff meeting, her first since arriving at Pinecroft. And things were heated.

It started out all wrong, she admitted later, and it got worse. Benedicta had allotted an hour and a half for the staff meeting. As she stepped into the dining room and the waiting staff, the phone rang. Sister Anne went to get it.

"It's for you, Benedicta. The caller sounds kind of funny. He said it was important."

Benedicta went to answer the phone. "Hello, Benedicta here," a breathless Benedicta said into the phone.

"Listen girlie," the voice was that of a male, it was raspy and seemed muffled. "Git you and yur s'ter out of town or there is trouble on the way. I know she's at the old psych hospital, I will be going there shortly, if ya git my drift."

"No!" shouted Benedicta, "Don't even think of it. I won't let you hurt my sister, do you understand? I am going to call the police. They'll get you." Her voice held a quaver as she spoke. He did not hear it. The line was dead. Benedicta sat for precious minutes holding the phone. What was she to do? The staff was waiting. They had no doubt heard her shout into the phone. Her staff was expecting a meeting. It was long overdue.

On the other hand, Brie might be in danger. If she took the time for a meeting, Brie might well suffer the consequences. Dialing the unit on which Brie was staying, she heard the crisp voice of Maggie Martin.

"Maggie, I am glad to reach you. It is something of an emergency. Could you find Brie and keep her in her room, and watch her, till I get there? She might be in danger."

With that out of the way for a time, she could finally focus on the meeting—and cut it short.

She returned to the dining room. Her staff eyed her curiously with what seemed big question marks on their faces. Sister Anne asked the obvious. "Is there something wrong, Benedicta?"

"I have to go shortly. Let's see how much of this we can get through quickly," she said curtly. The routine stuff was taken care of in rapid time.

When Benedicta opened the floor for new business, Beatrice, the former director, threw out the first gauntlet. "I think we should charge more for spiritual direction, much more."

"I do, too," said Father Gast.

"Actually," said Benedicta, in what she thought was a conciliatory tone, "The offering price is set by the archdiocese—" her voice broke off when Beatrice interrupted her.

"But you could make a recommendation for more, and a strong push," said Beatrice.

"Amen," said Father.

"Okay, I will approach the archbishop." Benedicta glanced at her watch, feeling apprehensive. She thought of Brie and felt her stomach knot.

"And we aren't getting sufficient Mass stipends," Father piped in again. "We need more Mass offerings. We need to change the time of Mass, it is too early for many to attend. That is why the stipends have fallen off," complained Father.

As the meeting progressed, Benedicta mentioned the matter of money for charity. "Whom do we wish to give funds to this month?"

Immediately Beatrice spoke up, "I believe it is time we thought of our center, make it petty cash for our own needs."

"Yeah," said Father.

More discussion ensued, more of a squabble.

Sixty minutes had passed, and she was further away than ever from helping Brie.

"Just why can't we use the money for petty cash?" Beatrice had returned to that subject again.

Flustered now, Benedicta managed to suck in her breath as she looked at the three staff members in front of her.

Picking up the employee hand book, fifth edition, Benedicta flipped it open, and said in a huff, "Read the rules, read the rules," and she threw the book at them. The book hit Beatrice on the forehead, before falling to the floor.

The staff sat there, stunned.

Without another word, Benedicta turned, picked up her purse, and went out the front door. They heard her car zoom out of the garage a moment later.

Benedicta dashed down the highway toward Our Lady on the Hill. *The blasted elevator would be out of order today of all days,* she thought as she stood in the lobby, momentarily delayed. Looking for the stairway, she found it and took the steps two at a time, coming huffing and puffing to the fourth floor. Entering Brie's room, she was dismayed to find no one there. No Brie.

Panic bubbled up. She choked it back. Stopping at the desk, she inquired about her sister.

"I don't know, she isn't checked out on the board," said one of the nurses.

Then she saw Maggie Martin coming toward her. "I brought her up as you directed, but when I went in to check on her, she was gone. I, I left a message on your phone," The RN looked nervous.

"Where do we look? No, I think we need to alert security first," said Benedicta to Maggie. "I had a threatening call this afternoon, and it is possible that Brie's life may be in danger."

In minutes, security arrived. A Henry Elmes, short and squat, stood in front of them, his round face seeming in a perpetual smile. Benedicta explained, giving a description of her sister, and Maggie told him what she was wearing. Henry got on his walkie-talkie and radioed the other members of the security team with the description.

"Is there someplace she might have gone? Somewhere she hangs out?" asked Benedicta, wanting to help with the search.

"She likes the swimming pool, I think," said Maggie, almost wringing her hands now.

Maggie and Benedicta rushed to a connector bridge taking them to the other side of the building, then down the steps and out the side door, where a "swim house" was standing. Its huge glass panes stood, revealing no one inside. Still, Maggie and Benedicta opened a door, and went into the cool interior. Here, a strong chlorine smell emanated from the water.

No one was in the pool, a relieved Benedicta discovered. *At least she hasn't drowned,* she thought.

"There are dressing rooms over on this side," said Maggie, moving in their direction.

Muffled sounds were heard coming from behind a closed door. Benedicta checked a restroom: they found no one. And that noise from behind the door was more insistent. Benedicta went to open the door, it was locked. "What is in this room?" asked Benedicta.

"That is a dressing room," said Maggie, her hands shaking.

Muffled sounds were heard again. "Where is the key?" A distraught Benedicta asked, trying her best to be calm. Panic was close at hand.

"Mr. Elmes could get it for us," said Maggie haltingly.

When Elmes came, Benedicta asked him, "Do you have a key to this door?"

"No," he said, his own keys jangling on a chain on his belt. "But I can get one for you pretty quickly." He spoke into the walkietalkie once more and almost at once, a man entered the area.

"Hello, I am Mr. Watts, the security supervisor, how may I help you?" Mr. Watts had a voice that was cheerful and sing-song.

"Mr. Watts," Benedicta was frantic by now. She tried to control the tone of her voice as she said, "We need the key to this dressing room, please."

"Um, well, in that case, I have a key here, somewhere." He produced a number of keys on a huge ring. It seemed forever going through the keys one by one. In the meantime, the sounds from inside grew more insistent.

"Is this the only way?" Benedicta's voice was high pitched. She felt rising terror. Her fingers tingled; her feet were numb. Her knees had a rubbery feel, and her forehead was wet with sweat.

"Oh, here it is!" Mr. Watts looked jubilant as he produced the right key.

Benedicta grabbed the key and inserted it into the lock, opening the door. Darkness and shadows were all she could make out before she heard a mumbling coming from the left.

Mr. Watts fumbled with the light switch, a glow of light emanating from a single light bulb over the mirror, helping the party to glimpse a figure lying in the corner, head covered with a bag, hands and feet taped with duct tape. They removed the bag from her head and found a rag stuffed in her mouth. Mr. Watts untied her.

Brie was angry. She was flailing about with her arms and legs. "Damn it, let me go, I can get up myself. It took you all long enough," she said as she stood up, shivering, her body covered only by her wet swim suit. Benedicta hugged her, putting her arms about Brie's cold shoulders before they were directed out to the pool area once again.

Fifteen minutes later, Brie sat on a lounge chair at the pool, still dressed in swim attire, her swim robe thrown about her shoulders, a blanket gathered about her. Benedicta had called the police and Inspector Brown had shown up. He had arrived in lightening time. He was questioning Brie, who remained frightened.

Her face was pale, her hands shaking now that it was all over. She demanded a cigarette. Someone produced one and a match. "I was swimming, I know you aren't supposed to swim alone, but you know I am a good swimmer." She adjusted the robe about her shoulders and continued, "Someone grabbed me. He covered my head with a bag so I could not see. I was fighting but he got the better of me. The guy was tying me up here in the pool area when I guess he heard a noise at the door. He threw me into the dressing room and that is the last thing that happened before I heard you all in the pool area."

"Did you get a look at him at all? Was he tall, muscular, short, did he speak?"

"I didn't really see him. He got me from behind, but I have a few impressions," she said, eagerly.

"I'd love to hear your impressions, Ms. Malloy," said the inspector, smiling at her and squinting with his bushy eyebrows, putting his hands in his pockets and taking them out before he grabbed his pen and a notebook and began taking notes.

"He was rather tall, and he had a paunch for a belly, a beer belly I would say. He had hairy arms and whiskers on his chin. A lot of whiskers, maybe a beard," she said, and let out a breath. She had been holding her breath. She was cold despite being covered. Her hair was damp and hung in ringlets. Her swim suit felt like wet skin about her. She turned to her sister.

"I didn't pay much attention to you, Benedicta. Maggie told me you called and asked me to stay in my room. I'm so sorry, really I am."

Lost in thought, Benedicta did not respond. *What is happening, who is endangering my sister and me? First the threatening calls, then the gas on in Brie's apartment, then the series of accidents at Our Lady's on the Hill. It was all too much. I am beginning to believe Brie that she had not been responsible for any of it. And he was getting bolder, it seemed.*

The questioning took time: first Brie, then Benedicta, then Maggie, and finally the security people.

"I think I have it all down now," said the inspector, closing the notebook and putting it in the pocket of his jacket.

"I am quite concerned about you both, about keeping you two safe." The inspector frowned as he spoke.

"Excuse me, sir," said Mr. Watts, "but I believe we are equipped to provide safety for Ms. Brie Malloy."

"Okay, I'll stop by your office in a bit to check on how you will provide security. Then Ms. Malloy will be taken care of during her stay here."

"Thank you, Mr. Watts," said Benedicta.

The security people left along with Brie, who was accompanied by Maggie.

"Ms. Malloy, I am quite concerned for you as well," the inspector said, looking at Benedicta pensively. "You are not to go out alone, not even to walk on your property, no, not even the grounds," the inspector added when she objected.

"We will keep a detail in the area to check on you frequently. You have my number if you need me—" He put his hands in his pockets as he spoke, "This is an ongoing investigation. I know you were worried when you got those calls, but now it is a dire situation. He is getting quite brave and making strong efforts in his pursuit of you two. It calls for your utmost caution."

"Thank you, Inspector, I know I will be quite safe at Pinecroft, especially with your men in the area. I will keep the doors locked and not go out alone, I promise." She didn't like it, but she would abide by the directions.

The following Monday morning, more to appease the troops than anything else, Benedicta called Archbishop Floersch at the Chancery. She planned to ask tentatively about raising the fee for the offering, and changing Mass time, but she couldn't get through. She was stalled by the archbishop's secretary. Edmund Wise believed his sole purpose in life was to keep others from reaching the archbishop.

"I'll put a note in with your recommendations, but I don't think the archbishop will favor any change," he added in a sharp, curt voice that allowed for no further discussion.

After the conversation, Benedicta wrote a memo to her staff, advising them of her action and the response. She also included an apology for her 'impulsive behavior.' She thought perhaps that would be the end of the commotion. She hoped so anyway.

A week passed in relative peace and quiet. Benedicta was relieved to have some "down time." She worked on the chaplain's manual and then read a novel in the evening.

They met at Ault Park, in Hyde Park, Benedicta carrying a picnic basket, and her book, Jude with a jug of wine and two glasses. She transferred from her car to his.

"What are we doing on a picnic in the second week of January?" asked Benedicta, laughing. She took off her gloves and clasped her hands.

"We're doing it in the car with the heater on so it will remain toasty warm. And don't make fun of my attempt to lure you away from the office. You are the most hardworking woman I know. And I've known a few," he added, grinning that flirtatious grin he was so good at.

"Oh, so this is just all part of a larger plan, huh? What is next? You have seats at the Bengals game perhaps?"

"You guessed it, "he said, "And I thought I was so sly."

"Well you are. You got me away from Pinecroft for part of the day today." Benedicta was not at all sure she was ready to date Jude. True, she knew she had gone to a Christmas ball as his date, and to his home on New Year's. She knew too, she was attracted to him. That was part of the problem, as she saw it. *Wasn't it best not to mix business with pleasure? Was it already too late for considering that?* she wondered.

Jude unpacked her picnic basket. "Oh, I see we have fried chicken, potato salad, and choclate cake. Wise choices for sure." They laughed.

He turned on the sweet sounds of classical music and began to switch the station.

Benedicta grabbed his hand from the dial, "No, you don't, I am not listening to jazz again. Classical music, okay, but not jazz." She adjusted the dial. Rock music blared from the speakers, mainly drums and a steel guitar.

Jude raised his arms in the air. "I give up," he said, laughing.

They finished eating and then they took a walk, each wearing a heavy coat. When they finally returned to the car, they were silent for a while, both thinking their own thoughts.

"A penny for what is on your mind," he said at last.

"I was thinking how much fun this has been and it is mostly spontaneous fun today. I like that."

"We'll have to do it again, m'lady."

He leaned over and kissed her, full on the mouth. He lingered for a moment and then drew back. She didn't object.

"Was that part of the spontaneity?" she asked.

"It seemed just the thing to do. I hope you didn't mind," he said.

"Well, I am not at all sure we should be doing this. But it does show where we've come from. A few short months ago, I would have been offended."

He kissed her again, softly, longer this time.

They said nothing more, but gathered their belongings and departed, each in their own car.

Benedicta was gearing up in her work. More clients were coming to the center, more groups were scheduling long weekends or several days during the week, even week-long affairs. She was glad they were prospering but with Brie in the hospital, it was all a lot to keep track of, even for her, and she credited herself with being very organized.

Benedicta was sensitive to the tension between her and the other staff members. Each day brought new and fresh complaints from Beatrice, orders from Sister Anne, and requests for further privileges from Father Joe. *I will handle it,* she thought, as she took a break in her office. How, she wasn't sure yet, but she must take charge.

It occurred to her she hadn't seen Mother Margaret Mary for a while and she, Benedicta, might like to talk things over with Mother. She would make an appointment. It would be comforting to see her again and bring her up to date on happenings.

As she rounded the corner of the hall to go into the office, she collided with someone with a large bundle. "Oops," she said, "I didn't see you."

Lulu peeked out from behind the hooded barricade. She was pushing her portable massage equipment. "So sorry. I was in a hurry, I am having someone for a massage in an hour or so and I thought I would get this set up in the basement."

"Lulu, it is great to see you. How about a Coke? What do you say? I could use some company."

"Sure. Just let me get this downstairs first. Could we make it after I finish my work? I'd love to have a chat."

They met after her massage appointment and spent the evening together. They had supper, then hung out. Benedicta was glad for the company. She didn't mention much of what was transpiring but she found herself unwinding a bit.

"What has been going on in your life?" asked Lulu.

"Not much. You know Brie is in the hospital. It is crazy-making, trying to fit in seeing her, keeping organized here—" She let her voice trail off.

"And what about your life, Lulu?" asked Benedicta.

"Same story here. Hectic, chaotic at times. I don't know where the time goes anymore. I rather think it is busier at Pinecroft now than even a few months ago. I know I get more business." Lulu drained her Coke glass and put her fork and knife on the plate. "We'll have to do this more often, it has been fun."

"I am glad we could get together even for a short time; it helps to have some girl-talk now and again, don't you think?" Benedicta put the dishes in the sink and ran soapy water. "Lulu, let me ask you something. Do you think Sister Anne is bossy?"

"Well, I don't know. I don't think I ever thought much about it one way or another. Where is that coming from?"

"Oh, never mind. I just thought perhaps I could get an objective opinion from you."

"Are you having conflicts with your staff? I have always thought they were an imperious lot."

"Well, not to say exactly that, but yes, conflict would be the right word. I'll work it out."

"I'm sure you will. And if you want, I'll keep my eyes and ears open."

"Fine, thank you."

———

"I'm so glad to see you looking so well, Brie. And taking my advice and coming to stay at Pinecroft is a step in the right direction," said Benedicta. It was the third week of January, bleak and cold. Benedicta had a mountain of paperwork, a tentative plan to oversee a group coming in for a three-day conference, and a date to give a speech at a women's club the next day. She felt a bit harried.

All in due course, she thought. *First, let's get Brie squared away.*

"You can stay in the room next to mine," said Benedicta. "And Sister Anne wants to teach you the fine art of cooking.

Not that you can't cook now, but she knows all these secrets. I thought it would take your mind off things and help you relax." She stopped and took a deep breath.

Brie threw her a dark look and said, "Benedicta, I do NOT want to learn to cook. If you want me to stay, you'll have to forget all the plans for me." She continued, "I do not want a bedroom next to yours. I'll take one on the first floor."

Despite her testy attitude, Benedicta was heartened by her presence here, and she did seem, all told, in a better mood these days, more cooperative, and there was no talk of carousing at night. Benedicta didn't want to even mention it.

"I expect I'll have to get up earlier than I am used to. Life here is different and runs on a different schedule than my apartment," Brie said.

"Good thinking," said Benedicta. "And if you want a downstairs room, well, you may certainly have one. It will be more private, probably. What about trying just a few sessions with Sister Anne? You never know, you might love cooking."

"I don't think so."

That evening Sister Anne hosted a party in honor of their new guest. Sister Annie made pizza and had beer and Cokes. Lulu stayed over. Jude was invited, along with two of Brie's girlfriends. And Sister Anne privately put in her two cents worth about what Brie would be doing.

"You can't be telling a grown woman what to do or not do, Benedicta. Please don't worry. I'll ease her into activities. I think I have a way with Brie."

There is that bossiness again, thought Benedicta. *I must put a stop to these kinds of orders, but at the same time, if she takes over with Brie, I am very thankful.*

For the next week, life was complicated. Things got off to a rocky start. Brie refused to get up in time for breakfast, and usually missed Mass at 9 a.m. What's more, she was untidy. Her room looked trashed. Benedicta was trailing behind Brie, picking up after her. Benedicta found herself eating to her frustration over Brie and how she was settling in. Benedicta was just about to admit this arrangement was not working. She was going to have a "talk" with Brie, when life suddenly began to settle down.

While Brie continued to get up late and go to bed even later, in exchange for a late breakfast and a snack at bedtime, she agreed to "practice" cooking in the kitchen with Sister Anne a couple of days a week. Sister Anne had challenged Brie to doing an afghan with her in the evenings, all under Sister Anne's supervision, of course.

Benedicta was surprised when Brie agreed to and was excited about taking swim lessons at the YMCA. It meant two mornings a week someone would have to drive her to and fro. Sister Anne volunteered for the job. And Lulu had Brie "assisting" in her massage work. Then a sewing class was begun at the Y, and so the two days Brie went swimming, she stayed over for her sewing.

One day, Benedicta was doing the small payroll, when she heard a commotion in the hall. She opened her door to hear Sister Anne screaming. And the fire alarm was going off.

"Fire! Fire!" Sister Anne was frozen in place in the hall shouting. Knowing the fire department would be arriving shortly, Benedicta followed Sister Anne out the back of the mansion. A tool shed they had erected some time back was ablaze. Smoke was belching from the window and the door. Benedicta ran for the garden hose, fearful that the fire would spread to the house. As she succeeded in dragging over the hose, she could hear sirens in the distance.

The flames shot up into the air and rapidly destroyed the sturdy shed. Suddenly, there was a crackling, a popping, a varoom, boom, varoom, and the roof began to disintegrate. Parts of the roof were being propelled about the vicinity. Flames erupted, spewing sparks about the yard. Bits of roofing plus chunks of wood were hurled into the air, confirming Benedicta's worry about the safety of the house.

A final explosion of fire, an intense rupture of sparks, and the roof caved, sending what was left of it sinking into the destroyed mess below. The last of the flames and a lot of smoke could be seen and a strong smell of burnt wood emanated from the vicinity of what was once a shed.

Benedicta was thankful the firemen were now on the scene. They were dragging their hoses and spraying water onto the charred remains and parts of the garage still ablaze. Soon the fire was contained, then out. Equipment stored in the garage was tossed from the ruins, but there was little hope for any of it.

Suddenly, Benedicta had a terrible sensation of falling as she recalled that Baby, the dog, had been playing in the shed only this morning. Where was Baby? Was he burned in the fire as her brother had been burned so many years ago? A tearful Benedicta began calling his name. It couldn't be, it just couldn't. Saying a silent prayer, Benedicta watched the men wrapping up their work as she called and looked around the area.

Sister Anne came up beside her and asked, "Are you looking for Baby? I put him in the basement with a bone. Don't worry, he is safe."

Relief mixed with gratitude flooded Benedicta's senses.

"We'll be inspecting for arson. It is standard procedure," said the fire chief who came up to the house as they completed their work.

"And I rather think that is what you will find is the cause of the fire. We've been having some very mysterious things happening," said Benedicta.

It occurred to her that she needed to alert Inspector Brown about the situation. She could do that. She intended to keep her sister safe. *I'll make a note of that*, she thought.

Chapter Ten

The storm raged outside, rain beating relentlessly against the window panes, thunder crackling, and the lightning rising fiercely. Inside, the fire raged too. She was trying to see in the flames, find Ben. The room was hot, the smoke thick. She was suffocating from the black smoke. There was a figure in the room across the hall. Benedicta saw him. She could call him, reach out to him, but she did not. Later she would think about that action, the hesitancy to reach out to someone, and wonder if it was an issue with trust. She had a weakness here, she knew. Her trust level was never high.

Benedicta awoke with a start. She was drenched in sweat and was shivering. The storm was fierce and blowing rain outside her window. She was momentarily disoriented by the dream in which she saw an image of herself peering into the darkness, looking for a way through the smoke. Suddenly she realized where she was, in her bed, and the fire she had just experienced was a dream.

The window was open a little, and rain water was seeping onto the sill, dripping on the carpet. She heard it rather than seeing it. She got up and closed the window.

Unnerved by her dream, Benedicta tried unsuccessfully to piece it together in her mind. The fire, a picture of a man, the danger to Ben, all served to upset her. She silently screamed into a pillow. No one heard her.

It had all been just a dream, she told herself. *Why does it feel monumental?*

The power it wielded in her made her know beyond doubt that there was something deep within that wanted to be voiced.

And she knew what she would do: she would see a counselor.

Agatha Forest, Psychologist, PhD, read the sign outside her office.

Benedicta put her hand firmly on the door knob then backed off as if she had touched a hot potato.

Pacing a few yards, her mind racing, she tried to get a grip. *I can always leave, I'm not sure about this, we'll see,* she thought, and straightening up, she entered the office. Five minutes later she was met by Agatha Forest.

Dr. Forest had a graceful figure, soft features and kind, blue eyes. Benedicta liked her immediately. She was well dressed in a well-made tailored suit; her hair had an expensive cut, Benedicta surmised, and she walked with an air of confidence.

"Ms. Malloy, I'm Agatha Forest. Glad to meet you. Come this way." She ushered her up a flight of stairs and into the office on the right. It was a warm, inviting room. The first thing Benedicta noticed was the light, lots of it, coming from a wall of windows. Two massive black leather chairs and a desk, a book case and a potted plant were the only furniture. It felt spacious.

"Please sit down," she said and indicated a leather chair. They both sat.

"Would you like some tea? I have peppermint, raspberry and chamomile. The peppermint is the best." Pouring the tea before Benedicta had responded, she handed Benedicta a mug and poured one for herself.

"Thank you for the tea," said Benedicta. It was warm in her hands and the aroma was comforting. She inhaled the steam and took a sip.

The tension built within her, it seemed palpable. *What am I doing?*

When she had had the dream, Benedicta had known this action was the way to go. She would see a counselor, to try to put her trust in another. *Therapy would not be easy* she had surmised *but it could be fruitful. Anyway, the dream is disturbing. And I don't know anything else to do.*

"This is more difficult than I thought it would be," said Benedicta, tentatively. Looking out the windows, she watched a bank of clouds suddenly hide the sun. The clouds looked almost mystical, sent by God it seemed. The room fell into shadows.

"I had a severe depression when I was in the convent. I think I am getting over that now. I still have some symptoms though, difficulty sleeping, crying jags, difficult moments---" her voice trailed off.

Benedicta glanced back out the window. The sun was now shining brightly.

She turned her attention back to the matter at hand. "I had a terrible dream the other night. It seemed real. There was a fire."

"Had you had any dreams like that before?"

"I, I'm not sure."

Benedicta shifted in her chair and began again. "My life is a mess. No, just parts of it. I have a hard time trusting."

"Why don't you tell me about it?"

"It doesn't affect my work but it does make relationships difficult and intimacy is impossible."

"And what do you do about these relationships?"

Pausing, her mind wandered, and she looked out the window once again. *Agatha is a regal priestess, bestowing her healing powers on those who come here. And I do want healing.* Suddenly she had a premonition that this experience could be a momentous one for her, and for a second, she felt better.

"My, my sister is emotionally ill, I think, to answer your question. Brie's been very unpredictable lately, depressed some, impulsive, it seems to me. She's seeing a psychiatrist, or just beginning to. There was a run to the hospital just a few weeks ago.

She was hospitalized for a few weeks, in a psych hospital," she said, taking another sip of the tea from the cup in her hand. "I've had all I can do to be there for her, I've always tried to look after her, ever since—" she stopped, chewed on her lip, and shifted her position again in the chair. The chair felt hard beneath her.

"How does that feel to have your sister to care for?" asked Agatha.

"Exhausting at times," said Benedicta, and again she was distracted by the clouds—a vision of heaven. *A priestess is here in this room with her own cloud formation.*

"I enjoy working because it distracts me from the time spent with Brie. My work gives me something to concentrate on other than my sis. My job is stressful, though."

Benedicta paused. She took a handkerchief from her bag. She laced the cloth through her fingers, studying her hands, and fidgeting with the hankie. Suddenly the room was spinning, she felt a chill. *Why don't I just say it, say it out loud?* "My baby brother died in a fire when he was four. Brie was supposed to be watching him. We don't know how the fire started," the words were tumbling out now. "The fire was in the kitchen. His body was burned beyond recognition before help could arrive."

Agatha nodded, "That must be terrible for you to think about."

"Yes, yes, that memory is blurred but devastating. When I think of it, it is all I can do to avoid panic. Brie thinks someone was in the house. Mom was passed out upstairs drunk. By the time mom got down there and the fire department was called, well, they discovered Ben was —" she caught her breath. "It was too late."

"Let's slow down now. This is important," said Agatha. "How did you feel about losing your little brother?" Agatha's tone of voice was gentle, almost a whisper.

"He was burned alive. I was very upset. We don't know how it happened. I thought it was my fault—Brie thought it was her fault. And Mom was nowhere in sight." The last words were spit out, and she felt an anger she had never experienced before.

Knotting the hankie again, she looked directly into the eyes of the woman facing her. "He died in that fire. He died in that fire," she repeated, rocking herself in the chair. "How did that happen? How did the fire begin? There are so many unanswered questions, really,"

Benedicta felt a fire akin to that in her belly. The anxiety was coming in waves, the oh- so-familiar thought of that night, even though she had thought of it so seldom these past years.

"You are angry at your mom?"

"Yes," suddenly banging her fist against the leather arm rest.

"Is she still living?" asked Agatha.

"Yes, she is alive. Our relationship is strained, disrupted by that day, broken by our whole childhood, really. My parents weren't bad people, they tried, well, they hardly tried—." She put away the hankie. "I don't much want to see her, visit with her, but my feeling of guilt gets me there. It is overwhelming. It has affected my faith, my trust."

"Sure, certainly," said Agatha. "So, you think the dream you mentioned may relate to the fire in childhood?" continued Agatha going back to the reference of her brother and the fire.

"I do think so." There is more, that intuition came to her, persisting, but she pushed it away.

Agatha spoke again, glancing at her clock. "Benedicta, our time is almost up, we've covered a lot today. You've taken a risk and begun a process, a journey really. There will be more feelings. We can talk about them. If you journal, keep it up, otherwise you might try beginning one. Here is my private number. If you need to speak to me, please call. I mean that."

Outside, she took big gulps of air and struggled to get control of her breathing. Stumbling to the car, she managed to unlock the door. Once inside she leaned against the seat and closed her eyes. *What am I doing?* she thought. Benedicta knew she had stirred up feelings that had been kept at bay for so long. *And why did I not tell the whole story?*

"January is a time for football, things are exciting, and this is the time of the playoffs. The weather is cold, the stands are filled with fans, and Boomer Esiason is playing great football," said the man sitting next to Jude.

Jude and Benedicta were attending a Bengals vs. Browns game. "The Bengals have done well this season," said Jude to the stranger, giving a sly smile to Benedicta.

Just then a thirty-yard touchdown was scored by the Bengals'running back, Ickey Woods, who then did a version of the "Ickey Shuffle," and had them on their feet, laughing and clapping.

"Would you like a hot dog and a beer?" asked Jude, "Or do you want to stop on the way home for a snack?"

"Let's have that famed hot dog and beer," said Benedicta, grinning.

They sat in the stands, huddled under a blanket, eating their snacks and watching the game.

The Bengals won, much to the amusement of Benedicta as the fans were ecstatic.

On the way home, Jude commented, "Well, for two people who are not much interested in sports, we did good today, rooting for our team, don't you think?"

"Yeah, I do," said Benedicta, touching his arm affectionately.

She was seated at her desk as she did every other morning after Mass. The gospel had been the attempted stoning of the adulterous woman and Jesus saving her from the Pharisees. Somehow, in the listening, a memory had been jogged loose; she felt uneasy, distressed, and thoughts were beginning to come to consciousness, or wanted to. *What was it?*

Benedicta closed her eyes and saw in her mind's eye, her bedroom in her childhood home. It was dark, nighttime. She saw only shadows. She was in her twin bed, covered with a wool blanket, holding a stuffed bear, clutching it tightly to her chest. She was sobbing into the bear's soft furry coat. She was not alone.

Instead, there was recollection of someone, someone with her on the bed, someone with a knife to her throat.

Alarmed by what she recalled, she felt waves of terror strike at her as the memory played out. Benedicta dropped the cup she was holding and sent it clattering onto the tabletop, spilling tea on a sheaf of papers. The cup was left unnoticed. The images were strong, forceful and came now unbidden in rapid succession. A man's face was close to hers, she could remember his breath on her neck, could feel his hand pressing on her shoulder.

At this present moment, her heart pounded against her chest wall, her breathing was uneven and difficult. She believed herself to be having a panic attack. She had no power to stop it. There was a sense of something as being a menace, a threat, something encroaching upon her that she was helpless to avoid.

In her imagination, she saw something, and she was taken back to that time long ago. A hand reached out and grabbed her throat, caught it tight. She jerked away but was unsuccessful in righting herself. She choked. She tried again to get away. She was afraid even to speak, to say a resounding "NO!"

A sense of foreboding and agitation pierced her now, leaving her chilled and disquieted as she went back, time and again, to that place in her mind. She shivered at the thought of it and pulled her sweater about her. The next moment, overcome with a feeling of shame, the shame of the image so overpowering her, she sat quietly in her office staring into space.

"It was my fault." A voice from out of nowhere seemed to grab her attention. "I did it. I didn't mean to, I swear I didn't, don't tell." The voice was more persistent now, the thoughts coming fast and furious. "Get away from me," she heard herself say, pushing the tea cup on the desk onto the carpet. "I've got to get away. Don't let it happen." She remembered now, she had seen blood on her hands, spilling onto the bed, blood dripping down onto the sheet.

Coming back to the present, Benedicta sat in her chair. Her hands shook. Her body rocked in an uncontrollable manner, back and forth in a swaying motion. That body felt traitorous as she sat there rocking. Captivated by the images coming to her, her mind raced.

Benedicta wasn't at all sure how long she sat there, she wasn't sure of what had just happened though she had a good idea of its intensity. When the shaking subsided and her thoughts became calmer, she managed to stop rocking. She retrieved a card from the drawer. On the card, printed in italics was: "*Agatha Forest, Psychology.*"

"Agatha, this is Benedicta Malloy" She could hardly speak, her mouth was so dry. "Something has just happened. I would really like to see you, today, if possible." With the appointment made, she relaxed momentarily at the desk. Then she abandoned herself into a flood of tears and cried aloud, wanting to shriek, as she considered her experience.

Two hours later, Benedicta sat in Agatha's office. *More tea, more talk*, she thought, but today was different; she was committed to getting through this, of getting this part of her story out in the open. The thought came to her, "*The truth will set you free.*" Wow, how she hoped for that.

Agatha did not offer tea. Instead she wasted no time on small talk and sat calmly looking at Benedicta in silence, waiting for Benedicta to speak.

Agatha was dressed in a black and white plaid jumper with a black turtle neck top. Pearls adorned her neck. Her hair was swept up and away from her face, fastened in a clip that let her hair cascade around her shoulders. She looked angelic.

"When I was in your office the last time," began Benedicta tentatively, "I had thoughts about the past come to mind, thoughts I had no recollection of until that moment. It seems unreal but I recall the incident vividly now. There was something that happened around the time of Ben's death, after Ben's death." She stopped, struggling to take a deep breath but failing, adding in short, jerky sentences, "Someone. Came. To. My. room. One night. He was scary. He told me. To. To be. Be quiet. He said he would hurt me. He. He had a knife. He. He. He hurt me."

"This is important, Benedicta. Did he hurt you with the knife?" asked Agatha.

"He—he touched me." Benedicta closed her eyes and allowed the words to come tumbling out. "He touched me—in private places—he held the knife to my throat and told me to be quiet—. I asked him to quit but he didn't—not for a long time." The words flowed in fits and starts, and as if in a dream. As the words were said, a refreshing mist seemed to manifest itself, to wash away the disgrace that had been under those words. Decades of thinking she was to blame, that she was not good enough, came to the surface and were washed away by this mist.

"I, I feel cleansed," remarked Benedicta, "I didn't know how powerful it would be to get this said." Now she took a deep breath and felt the renewed energy course though her body.

"It was not your fault," said Agatha, seeming to know what was going through Benedicta's mind just then.

"It seemed like it was. I did some stuff about that time, some boy/girl stuff. I was about fourteen at the time. It was all new to me."

Benedicta became quiet. Her mind went back to that time. It was all so hazy. She recalled her feelings experienced just that morning. The feelings had been strong and intense.

Now she realized she had felt all her life as if the attack had been her fault. She had put the blame on herself. Now Agatha was telling her to let go of that. She wondered if she could, even when she knew she had already begun to let go.

Agatha interrupted her reverie and said to her, "You must have felt bad about yourself?"

"Yeah, I did. Now that I look at the situation in a new light, I realize the memory has kept me hostage. I think it affected my ability to trust. I tend to be kind of suspicious. And I have what I call an eating addiction, sometimes I turn to food in a frenzied way. This began about the same time as the attack. I guess I realize now that the eating was a way of pushing the feelings away. Do you think the food frenzy will go away now?"

"It could be healed by this talk," Agatha said, reassuring her.

"I also know the feelings have kind of colored my perceptions. My life in the convent was affected. I could not make a go of it; something, this story, always stood in the way, somehow."

"Benedicta," Agatha said, glancing at her watch, "this revelation took a lot of courage for you to share with me today." And Agatha was quick to add, "We'll talk more about this attack soon. How do you feel now?"

"I feel freer. I feel something has been washed away."

"Good, we'll talk more next week." And the session ended.

———————

Jude invited Benedicta and Brie to a play at the Playhouse in the Park. A business associate had given him the tickets.

On the way to Eden Park, Jude was heading down Fifth Street towards the park, when all at once, a jolt, a loud bang, was followed by the sound of crunching as metal hits metal and, when the dust settled, they realized the Lincoln Town Car had been ploughed into by a car coming down Sycamore.

No one was hurt, thankfully, but the police had to be called and waited for, and by the time everything was resolved, the play was not an option for the evening.

"Come to my place. We will relax and watch a movie and eat cheesecake," offered Jude.

After the tow truck came for the car, they took a cab to Jude's.

They settled in the cozy den and watched "North by Northwest." Brie got scared by the movie, and Jude teased her about her fear of scary movies. Then they enjoyed cheesecake. Jude made a fire in the fireplace. They roasted marshmallows and had them with melted chocolate.

"Now this is a party," said Benedicta, "I like this way better than a play."

Jude got out his BMW and drove Benedicta and Brie home.

Brie had been quiet throughout the evening, so Benedicta said to her when they were in the house, "Did you enjoy the evening?"

"Yes, I did. It was fun seeing you and Jude together. I am sorry you couldn't see the play, but it was a good evening, even so."

The next week at her appointment with Agatha, Benedicta felt again that sense of refreshment. She took a seat in the soft leather stuffed chair, putting her feet up on the ottoman she shared with Agatha.

Agatha was dressed in a mint green suede zip-up sweater and green plaid wool slacks. Benedicta considered her something of a fashion guru.

"Would you care for some hot chocolate in place of tea today? I brought it in as a treat for us." Agatha looked at Benedicta. "You've had thoughts about our last talk?" Agatha poured hot water into the chocolate mixture in the cups and handed the steaming concoction to Benedicta. It was a welcome change from the tea, *just right,* thought Benedicta.

"Yes, I've considered the discussion. Those things were distressing, you know, the touching and all. And yet it was freeing to get those feelings out and look at what was bothering me. I do feel better about myself. I even look better, don't you think?" She stood up and gave a little bow.

She was dressed in a navy-blue jogging suit, with a crisp white top. She wore a cross and chain about her neck.

Agatha smiled and nodded. "You look quite bright and fetching! And you will continue to feel better about yourself, I expect. We may need to discuss those feelings again, however."

"I know." Benedicta sipped the hot chocolate and made eye contact with Agatha. "That experience makes me kind of vulnerable, it seems to me, but that may not be a bad thing," she added, putting the cup on the table to her side. Benedicta looked out the window and mused. It hadn't been long ago that she was thinking of Agatha as a priestess with her own cloud formation. *What do I think of her now? I respect her,* thought Benedicta, *and more than that, I am beginning to trust her.*

"I went to see my mom over Christmas. And I went again a week later. I don't know why I managed two trips when I normally can't bear one. I don't want to go, but if I am to be charitable, and honor my parent, well—" Benedicta stopped in mid-sentence. She stared at her hands in her lap, and then gazed out the window. It was a long moment before she spoke. Finally, she said, "I, I, I feel distress talking about my mom."

"Is it because of your thought that you must be charitable and honor her?"

"What do you mean? I don't understand."

"Well, Benedicta, from what you have indicated, your mom has never been there for you, even in childhood. It might be difficult to face that, to realize that she didn't protect you from the intruder, and it might be more productive to look at how you feel about her role in your life, especially when you were a child."

"I see." Benedicta was quiet for a long moment. "Well, I remember when in school, I wanted my mom to be like the other moms, to bake cookies, to help with homework, to listen." She stopped, then began again, "That was a problem as she was never there for me or for Brie either. And when the intruder incident happened, I knew I could not go to my mom with it."

"Are you saying you never had a connection with your mom, and that you wanted that?"

"Yeah, something like that."

"Benedicta, what are you feeling when you think of those days?" Agatha refilled Benedicta's chocolate and her own.

Benedicta reached for the cup, her hand was shaking.

"I was afraid so often. I'm still afraid—" her voice trailed off. She took a sip of the rich thick liquid and put the cup on the table. She was quiet for some time, reflecting on the past, her thoughts were focused on her mom and how she saw her then and now. *It is news to me, I'm afraid all the time,* thought Benedicta. Then she spoke, "I am always focusing on Brie and seeing her afraid, I hadn't realized I am afraid as well,"

"Do you want a relationship with your mom?" asked Agatha.

"I used to, really bad. Now I would just like to get along with her, and not mind so much visiting her."

"And what about fear, would you like to feel that and let it go as well?"

"Yes, I would."

"Then, let's see what we can do here. Okay?"

"Like what?" Benedicta put down the cup and looked directly at Agatha.

"Stop a minute, close your eyes and see if you can get in touch with that fear. Really feel it if you can."

Benedicta closed her eyes and did as directed. A long time, she sat, nothing happened. All at once her gut spoke to her, and she said, "Yes, I, I do, feel it, sort of."

"Good. Now just be with it. Take your time on this, try feeling it, staying with it, and then letting it go." Agatha sat and watched Benedicta intently, before she finally said, "See a balloon in your hand, and kind of let it go, up, up into the sky, if that would help."

When they were finished, Benedicta collected her belongings to go. She looked at Agatha and said, "I really got into that, the meditation was good, I think." And then she added, "And it is news to me that I'm afraid a lot, but I see that I am."

"Let's discuss this some more, it is important," said Agatha as Benedicta headed for the door.

———

On Sunday, Benedicta and Jude went to an ice skating rink on the west side of town.

As they skated across the ice, trying to balance and avoid a fall, Jude said to Benedicta, "Remember our first ice skating expedition?"

"Remember it? How could I ever forget it? I thought we were going to be drowned in that pond with the broken ice."

"You were very brave," said Jude now, attempting to twirl her around.

"No, I was foolish, and afraid, and I wanted like everything just to go home. But no, you persisted in getting me out on that ice," said Benedicta, dodging a teenage skater in her way.

They skated in circles about the rink, enjoying the music and the easy moves they were making. Afterward, they got hamburgers and fries and listened to music on the car radio.

Benedicta sat in Agatha's office, now more enthusiastic about talking over her problems. The last two sessions had dealt with her sexual abuse at the hands of a stranger at knife point and her relationship with her mom in those growing-up years. Today, they reviewed those talks and the consequences coming from the ordeal of sexual abuse.

Agatha, as ever, was well dressed. Brown suede pants and beige pullover sweater, a cross and chain about her neck, and a new hair style. The blonde hair remained long but she had side bangs and wore her hair a bit shorter in the front and on the sides. *She looks the picture of the goddess today*, thought Benedicta.

"Agatha," said Benedicta, at a mid-way point in the session, "this fact may not be earth-shattering, but the behavior, the habit, has affected me almost my whole life." She sat gazing at the cloud formation outside the window and mused once more about Agatha being a goddess. Th*is will put that notion to the test*, she thought, and she began once more, this time in a reflective mood.

"It began the night of the abuse, the incessant binging, a kind of out of control eating pattern. I am like a person addicted. I don't do it all the time, it comes in fits and starts. When I am sad, or mad, or worried, especially in those times I eat, but also when happy or excited. Any excuse at all. Occasionally, I binge, more often, I overeat or simply graze."

"But you are not overweight," commented Agatha.

"Well, thank you, but I am a bit pudgy, and I could be heavier, I realize. The fact that I am not as overweight as I could be, that is fortunate for me, but it does not change the facts or keep me from eating. All these years," she continued, moving about in the soft leather chair, "I have wondered what is wrong with me. I have considered why I have no better control."

"It is how you cope?"

"It must be. If I get stressed, or angry, or even happy, it begins. Often, I eat for comfort. I can see why now, it makes some sense. And I have no control at all." Benedicta kind of threw up her hands in seeming bewilderment.

Agatha eyed her intently, and said, "Oh, I think you have more control than you realize. What happens if you admit your powerlessness?"

"What, what do you mean?" Benedicta reached for her tea, this time a hazelnut variety, and sipped the hot, steaming liquid.

"Admit you are unable to stop this, that you have no power over it or that it could make you fat and that you do not have the say-so over its effect on you."

"I don't know, I've never tried to do anything like that," she said, considering Agatha's words.

She had heard of the twelve steps, she knew that admitting powerlessness was the first step.

"I will try that," she said at last.

Agatha refilled the hot water in the tea pot and added the bubbling liquid to her cup, tipping it to ask Benedicta if she wanted a refill. When she had refilled both cups, she put down the teapot and said, "You admit you feel much freer now that you have dealt in some ways with the abuse. Does that translate into a relief with your eating patterns?" asked Agatha.

Benedicta thought hard while absentmindedly looking out the window at the treetops in the distance. They were the winter colors, grey and black. The day was a cloudy one, a common occurrence in the Ohio valley. She sighed and brought her mind back to the question.

"Well, yes, I suppose I have experienced a lot of relief. In fact, I can't say I have had a binge attack, or even a temptation to overeat since we began talking about the abuse," she said, realizing this change all at once and nodding her head in agreement. She felt a sense of relief and thankfulness.

"Have you thought any more about the man who accosted you in your room? Who he was? Did you recognize him? "

"I don't believe I'd ever seen him before. He was very young, maybe about twenty or so. He pinned me down. I wanted to scream but was afraid. Do you think he had something to do with Ben's death, that he was the man Brie saw the night of the fire?"

Brie may have been right, Benedicta realized instantly, *there may have been a man in the house the night Ben died. Her sister had always believed that, Benedicta had not given it much merit until now.*

"Have you had any more dreams?"

"Yes, but they are unclear," she answered.

The session ended then. On the way home, Benedicta realized that Agatha was right, that she did have some control over her eating.

Chapter Eleven

"I am powerless and my life has become unmanageable," she wrote the sentence in her journal. Well, it was certainly true. *My life is sometimes chaotic,* she thought as she sat at her desk the next morning.

"Come to believe that a power greater than myself can restore me to sanity." Benedicta recited the second step aloud as well as writing it down. *Well, it is true* she thought, *I do agree with that.*

"Put myself and my care under God, praying only for His will for me and the power to carry that out."

Now that one is harder, she observed. *I know generally that God's way is best, but I seem to want some input myself.*

"What is God's will for me?" she wrote in her journal. "God wants me to pray daily, to worship Him, to be a part of a Christian community of the faithful, to keep the commandments. What else? He wants me to practice my faith, to live a virtuous life and avoid sin. And He wants me to pray with the Bible, and to help others, to think of others and treat them as I wish to be treated."

Reflecting, she wrote the word "temperance." "It is a little-used word today," she wrote. "In our society, so many are concerned with satisfying their cravings, why gluttony is not even mentioned." *It seems,* she thought, *a matter of balance, and a matter of conscience too.*

"Oh, yes," she wrote, "the Lord may want me to meditate and journal some as well," and she wrote, "to lead a healthy life, to eat a healthy diet."

I think I have just done the first three steps. Not perfectly, but it is a start, she thought. *Wow, I am working a program, as they say in OA.* She resolved to look for literature online about addiction and to find some info on the Overeaters Anonymous group.

Benedicta threw herself on the bed. It was well past midnight, but sleep eluded her. When she had been suffering from depression, she often had difficuly sleeping. This was improved now but still cropped up from time to time. Tossing and turning about, she pondered her situation. She was having memories come back of her childhood, and anger too, at her mom.

Mom was an alcoholic, she left much of Ben's care to Brie and me. And I left it to Brie. I am as much to blame as my mom.

Today she sits in that nursing home, sits in front of the TV. I know she still drinks, I don't know where she gets it—it is so hard for me to visit her. Brie doesn't even make the effort.

And so it went all night. The voices of accusation and blame were nothing new to Benedicta but they seemed more offensive tonight.

She considered that this temptation to negative thinking may have come because she had been feeling so free, her mood so brightened, her resolve so awakened. When dawn came, Benedicta gave up trying to sleep and got up, dressed, and went down to the chapel. She sat before the Blessed Sacrament, the only light, the candle above the tabernacle.

"If you hear me, Lord, please know that I am here. I want to believe, I want to trust, to have faith in You and Your Word. On my better days, I know You are a God of Love. Where is my faith? Where is my trust? I thought that faith and trust were returning when I related to Agatha and trusted her. I still do trust her. Yesterday, I put myself in Your hands in the third step, now I am unsure once more. Am I taking it back?"

She fingered the rosary in her hand. "Would You help me get my life together? Would You help me get my life together for my sister's sake, and for my own growth? Thank you for being here, thank you for Your Love." And making the sign of the cross, Benedicta genuflected and left the chapel.

Benedicta had invited Jude to go on a day trip to Red River Gorge just past Lexington, Kentucky. It was a bright sunny day but the wind was fiercely cold even for February. The red convertible BMW that Benedicta had once thought so gaudy now seemed a treasure as she settled back on the black suede cushion of the car seat.

The radio was playing jazz.

"I have never been much for jazz," she said to Jude, "but once a few years back, when I was in the convent, if you can believe it, we took a trip to New Orleans, a couple of nuns and I. I was intrigued by the French Quarter and loved the infectious music. Wasn't Al Hurt or someone from New Orleans?"

Jude chucked and said, "It was Al Hurt, and he actually lived in the French Quarter. I visited there. I am surprised we didn't run into each other." They both laughed then.

Jude held her hand as he drove I-75 through Lexington to Red River Gorge.

"I have heard there are some plain people in this area we are approaching," she said to make conversation.

"You mean Amish?" he asked.

"Yes, I've always held a curious fascination for these folks," she said and continued, "Their holding onto tradition as they do, reminds me of our way of holding onto Catholic traditions. We have so many ancient ones, in the case of us Catholics, dating back centuries," she said, marveling.

She continued, "How daunting, if you consider our rituals have endured for many eons, our church started by Christ, and passed on by apostolic succession, passed down through the ages." She thoughtfully put her hand on his leg, "Even in Old

Testament times, there was a foreshadowing of what would be. It is awesome really, if you think about it, truly awesome."

"Yeah, I guess it is," he agreed.

They stopped for lunch at a country store, getting slabs of cold cuts and cheese, and putting them on fresh buns, eating at a picnic table along the way. Benedicta zippered her jacket and moved closer to Jude. He put his arm around her shoulder and held her tight.

"It is so good to be relaxing with you, Jude," she said, squeezing mustard from a tube onto her sandwich. "It lets me know that I have come a long way; I used to be so depressed all of the time, I never enjoyed any fun things, like a picnic."

After lunch, they toured Red River Gorge and stopped at a few shops along the way. One was a furniture store with hand-crafted furniture made by the Amish. There were chests and desks, dressers and beds, all made by hand. "They certainly put a lot of pride in their work, don't they?" remarked Jude, caressing a hand-crafted desk.

It was after dark when they returned to Pinecroft. Benedicta and Jude stood in the doorway. Jude had his arm around her. She was painfully aware of his other hand firmly placed on her behind. She turned red.

"I don't want this day to end," he said, dreamily, stroking her hair, that other hand still placed on her derriere.

"It has been so much fun," she said, trying to breathe normally.

"We'll have to take an overnight trip, maybe a couple days, and go somewhere, maybe the dunes in Michigan, or even a trip into Canada." He traced an imaginary line across her back, she couldn't help holding her breath.

Benedicta felt her face grow warm as it deepened in color. From the porch light, Jude looked at her. They both laughed.

"Good night, sweetheart," he said at last, then as an afterthought, he continued, "Benedicta, there is something I want to talk to you about, and it is important. Something you don't know about me. Let's discuss it, not tonight, of course, but soon."

"Okay, goodnight," she said

"Be careful," he added, turning to go.

"I am Abby, a compulsive overeater," said the woman in jeans and a blue tank top.

"Hi, Abby," said the group in unison.

The next woman, a tall redhead, repeated the introduction, "I am Kate, a recovering overeater."

"Hi, Kate," chimed the group.

There were about fifteen men and women sitting in a circle, some drinking coffee, one fidgeting with her keys, another fussing with her clothing. Benedicta joined the circle hesitantly.

"Welcome," said Kate, smiling at her. Benedicta nodded and waved a hand in the air but said nothing. The meeting progressed. There was a general discussion of the first step tonight. Benedicta learned some new information. She learned that just like with smoking, you can have psychological addictions—with possible withdrawal symptoms. And she learned a craving may come, but never lasts and just like with cigarette smoking, the craving subsides.

Benedicta was offered literature and accepted the pamphlets. When the meeting came to an end, the group huddled together, saying the "Our Father." Benedicta slipped out unnoticed.

On her next visit to Agatha, Benedicta was determined to face rather familiar feelings about her relationship with Jude.

Agatha, inspecting her array of teas, said, "Let's see, we have chamomile and Earl Gray. Why not cranberry? This is a cranberry day, is it not?" Benedicta watched as she poured the hot water into the cups. It had become a ritual for them, a beginning, a way of easing into the session together.

"What shall we focus on today?" asked Agatha, smoothing the smartly tailored navy pants she wore. Her hair was awash with soft curls piled high on her head. She had on long dangling earrings, and a matching gold necklace. Her blouse was navy and white print and went well with the pants. It was always of interest to Benedicta, "the fashion of the day" she called it. Coming into the office and seeing Agatha's apparel, she got more ideas for her own wardrobe just from observing Agatha's.

"Well," began Benedicta, slowly, as if reflecting on what she wished to discuss. "I would like to talk about Jude Forsythe. Things seem to have taken a turn of late."

Agatha nodded.

"When I first met him," she continued, crossing her legs and getting comfortable in the leather chair, "I kind of came across as rebellious, I think, calling him on everything. I thought him showy, arrogant even." She pondered this insight for a moment before she continued, remarking, "Now I really, really like him." Benedicta's color changed as she talked, her face became ruddy and more animated.

"Go on, please," said Agatha.

"I see him as a good man, considerate, kind. He likes fine things and doesn't mind being showy, but that is not the biggest part of him." Benedicta drummed her fingers on the arm of the chair, her foot was swinging back and forth.

"What is it, Benedicta?" asked Agatha.

"At first," said Benedicta, ignoring the question, "I was uncomfortable with him, now I like the affection he gives me. I find I am, sort of, attracted. Well, very attracted."

"And?" asked Agatha, refilling her teacup.

"Well, it scares me for one thing." She accepted a second cup of tea and put the steaming liquid to her lips. Then blotting her wet lips with a napkin, she continued, "I don't really know how far to let it go. It hasn't so far gone—" she said, her words trailed off. "I meant to say nothing has really happened, but it could, you know?"

"How about going with what you are comfortable with?"

"Well, on the one hand, that sounds very sensible, but, as you know, I am Catholic, and there are certain proprieties, you could call them, certain rules to live by. I am not saying this very well. The church does not allow pre-marital sex, or much in the way of petting for that matter." She blushed and squirmed in the chair.

Reaching down, Benedicta picked up her purse, and retrieved something from within, a photo of Jude. She showed the likeness to Agatha, smiling, beaming really.

After a moment, Benedicta said, "It is difficult to discuss this. I find, it is, after all, private, and—" again her words trailed off.

"You don't like putting your thoughts into words because it makes it more real?"

"Yeah, that sort of sums it up." She thought for a moment and looked out the window at the skyline in the distance. It was marked by the presence of high rises, and the rooftops of buildings among a horizon of treetops. "The more I see of him, the more I like what I see," she began again.

"Do you return his affection?" asked Agatha, pushing a little.

"Yeah, I do, I do." She nodded emphatically and continued, "I like his kisses, they are sweet, and I am hungry for them. And yet, so far, I have considered my faith, and its requirements for abstinence, you know?"

Rising from the chair, she went to the window and stood, glancing down on the park below. There were a few skaters on an ice rink in the park. She watched their graceful motions. *I am doing a dance with Jude*, she thought, *just like those skaters, and I am trying to do it with grace and aplomb.*

When she turned back, her face was serious, and when she spoke, there was an odd tone to her voice. "If I were to look at this, I would say that when I met Jude, I was emotionally repressed. It has helped getting to know Jude. It has helped me grow up a little."

"Do you see yourself as marrying him?" Agatha spoke softly.

"That is the question, is it not? I don't believe I am ready for marriage, but there is more. There is something he is not telling me. I don't have any idea what it is. He has referred to it on several occasions but thus far, he has not explained. I am waiting."

Benedicta returned to the window, and stared into the distance, unseeing. As she returned to her chair, she said, "There are questions. He has something important to share with me, he says. I don't know what it is."

"Have you thought perhaps he is married?"

"No, but he could have skeletons in his closet, you know? He could have a dead wife, maybe? Ghosts like that are hard to compete with. Don't you think so?"

"It depends," said Agatha, glancing at her watch.

Then as quick as the session had begun, it was over.

On her drive home, Benedicta went over in her mind the meeting with Agatha. It occurred to Benedicta that her feelings were becoming deeper when it came to Jude—she was more at ease with him. *In fact,* she thought, *I kind of feel that "zing" with him.* She saw this as a good sign, but a feeling of fear was there, too. *What would the future hold with this man?* She did not know.

Chapter Twelve

Lulu lay on the lavender flowered sheets, her head resting in the crook of Jake's arm. It was not quite 10 p.m. in the evening. Her mind wandered and she thought about this apartment whose charm had weaved a spell of magic for her.

Lulu lived in a row house in Mt. Adams, a suburb of Cincinnati, perched high above downtown and the Ohio River. The area was commonly referred to as "The Hill." Lulu had only a passing acquaintance with its history; she knew the land had originally been owned by Nicholas Longworth and that he had used a few acres as a grape arbor where he produced the then-famous "Golden Wedding Champagne."

She had heard part of the land then became the Monastery of the Holy Cross Fathers. Lulu had participated in a tradition, dating back to the time of the Monastery, in which pilgrims, like herself, on Good Friday, climbed the steep hill from Columbia Parkway to the church of the Immaculata, there to ascend the steps of the church, praying on each step. The monastery had long since been sold but that particular tradition had remained and had been part of her Easter celebration for several years.

Part of the magic of Mt. Adams was its art decor. It had at one time, she recalled, been an area favored by artists and hippies. It still retained some of this flavor in the shops and restaurants.

Lulu had rented the apartment to be a part of the art scene. Her apartment was small, meant for one person. The living room was the most spacious room, a combined living room/dinette, and this room wasted no space. Outside a double door was a patio, from which light streamed in and gave a glow to the entire living room area. From here was a view of the city, especially the downtown area.

The floors were hardwood and shone from polish. Sitting in front of the patio door was a set of white wicker furniture, a couch and a chair with pink floral cushions. The apartment wasn't big enough for any large pieces of furniture, and besides, the wicker was purchased on sale. She liked to think they added a bit of ambiance to the apartment. A small dinette set was in the corner nearest the kitchenette, the set a remnant of the last owner's left-behind-belongings. A potted palm stood before the window. That potted palm stretched her ever-loving patience during the winter months, as she worried over it, repeatedly carting the plant to the bathroom to let the shower run steam on its leaves, thinking this helped keep it alive.

The kitchenette and bathroom had been concessions to her budget as they were outfitted with old fixtures and sat in tight spacing.

The only other room on the first floor was a very tiny room she used for her massage appointments. Here were her table and the oils needed for massage and a stereo for playing soothing music.

In the living room was a circular stairway to a loft, which housed a queen-sized bed. This was the part of the apartment that had sold it for Lulu. The look was unique, and she liked the out-of- the-way feel of the loft.

Lulu stretched and turned to look into Jake's brown eyes. He was taller than she. In fact, her bed was too short for his frame. He had rippling muscles, which he kept by working out regularly. She wove her fingers through his shiny brown, wavy hair and whispered, "I miss you when you're not here. Can't you sleep over tonight?" Then she added, "Puleasse, Puleasse,"

Easing out of her embrace, he sat up looking at her.

"Nope, I've got a late business meeting—a couple of old friends wanting financial advice," his eyes refused to meet hers.

Lulu wondered about that. The avoiding her eyes as he was so prone to do. She dismissed it once again.

"You can't expect me to stay over and miss out on wining and dining prospective clients, now can you?" He was an investment counselor with a prestigious firm in the city. The markets, he had told her, had been good and were getting better. He had suggested they were beginning to prosper and she guessed he would have more meetings in the future.

"Will I see you tomorrow?" They had only recently been sleeping together. Lulu knew this arrangement probably was ill-advised. She knew too, that it was not in line with the practice of her faith. And Lulu realized she was being clingy, possibly even obnoxious, but she couldn't help herself.

"I sense something altogether different is going on inside you tonight," she ventured to say to him.

All he responded was, "I'll call you." He finished dressing, descended the loft steps and went out the door.

Suddenly Lulu saw a dark cloud surrounding the area where he had just stood. Scurrying from the bed, she ran down to the door, opened it and in nightgown and bare feet, went out into the hallway. She saw Jake just walking down the side walk.."Wait," she appealed. Jake looked up, surprised. Leaping toward him, Lulu bounded into his arms, her arms tight about his neck.

"Don't leave, not yet. We need to talk," she said, and persisted, "It's important."

"Uh-uh," he said, grimacing. He loosened her grip on his neck, disengaged her, and left her standing on the walk, merely saying, "I've got this meeting, I'll call you first thing tomorrow." And he was gone.

Tears in her eyes, Lulu retraced her steps and entered her apartment. Something was just not quite right. She had felt it before, now she was sure of it. But what was it?

Lulu went to bed but had a restless night. She dreamed of Jake being chased by a man in a dark cape.

The next morning Lulu showered, dressed, and looked at her appointment book. Nothing until 2 p. m, Glancing at her wristwatch, she realized she had time on her hands. She could go shopping or go out to eat. She didn't much want to do either, to tell the truth.

Lulu decided she would visit her dad. Driving over, she had those "feelings" about Jake again. She saw him in her mind's eye surrounded by that dark cloud. Lulu tried to shake off the mood that engulfed her. The disturbance seemed to rumble around within her, wrecking her confidence. In the past, such feelings had proven true, she reminded herself.

Putting the key in the lock, Lulu opened the door of the two-story frame house in Norwood. She could hear her dad. He was in the basement working on his much-loved carpentry work. Coming down the steps, she saw him brighten and throw down his hammer. Lulu reached her arms about him, "Dad, how the heck are you?" Then she added, "I've missed you these past weeks."

"Yeah, that beau of yours keeps you busy, I imagine. Too busy for old dad." But he pressed her cheek and gave her a peck.

"Dad, I have my work too. No," she amended. "You are right, I have been spending a lot of time with Jake. I've been steadily dating him for months. He is attentive, he takes me out to dinner, treats me to seats at the orchestra, which you know I love. We go to the movies on weekends and sometimes we get a video to watch at my apartment. I've never been to his place or met his family, though." She sighed, looking down at her pink sweater, fussed with a button, and continued, "He has hinted that his family has money. They live in Indian Hill. I must admit, I've wondered why he hasn't introduced me yet, but then again, he is a private person."

Smoothing the sweater, she added, "And frankly, it's getting kind of serious, at least my feelings for him are serious. I believe

I love him, and I haven't been able to say that about anyone in a long while." She looked beseechingly at her father.

"Is it reciprocated, honey?" he asked, leading her to an old couch along one wall. Lulu recognized the couch. That same piece of furniture had been in the living room upstairs, along with a matching stuffed chair, when her mother had been alive.

"Well, possibly. I believe it is." She pondered the situation for a moment, then said, "But there is a mystery of sorts. The more I get to know Jake, the more I see things are not quite right. You know? I get this idea that there are walls up, words we are not saying. He avoids my questions at times, won't make eye contact, and disappears for days at a time. It's just not all wine and roses." She stopped and gazed at her dad. He had been the one person who had always been there for her. Her mom had died when she was ten in a disastrous accident involving a shooting incident. Her dad had never remarried.

"You sure he's not married?" he asked, his frown across his forehead deepening.

"No, I don't think so," she assured him. "But I suspect he is preoccupied by a problem, you know how I sense things at times?"

"Well, I know you've always had a 'sixth sense,'" he said, taking her hand and adding, "Whatever it is, it'll come out, you just got to be prepared for it."

Yeah, that is what I am afraid of, she thought.

Lulu kept her thoughts to herself regarding Jake and the mysterious aura he seemed to have around him. One mid-February morning while on assignment at Pinecroft, she had lunch with Benedicta. Sister Anne had gone to visit her sister, who was ill.

"What's in this casserole, Benedicta? It's delicious," asked Lulu.

"I put it together with a mix of noodles, tomato sauce, a filling of cottage cheese and spinach and parmesan cheese, topped off with melted provolone. Careful, it's hot," said Benedicta. "I can give you the recipe if you're interested. "

"Yes, I'd like that. It's good," said Lulu. "Thanks for inviting me. I don't often get to have lunch here. I appreciate the invite, and time to spend with you."

"And I, too," said Benedicta.

"How are things coming between you and Jude? The last I heard, you had gone to a ball game together," she served herself a second helping, and added salt. "I'm trying not to use so much salt," she said shaking the salt onto the casserole, "but I like the taste much better."

"Help yourself. It does need salt, and to answer your question, we have been having fun together. Going out with Jude seems to take my depression away for a time. We drove to Red River Gorge a couple of weeks ago, and we are going away for a long weekend somewhere, maybe. I am quite content, at least about the time I spend with Jude. Thanks for asking. Sometimes I am concerned as to whether it is a wise idea to be spending time with Jude, but I am doing it, nevertheless. And you, Lulu?"

"Well, I've had some serious misgivings about Jake, but I am beginning to think it is far-fetched. In the last month, he has taken up painting with pastels. In fact, he has taken over a portion of my massage room for that purpose. Not that there is much room in there," she hastened to add. "It seems to relax him, I have noticed."

Then pausing, and seeming to choose her words carefully, she looked at Benedicta, and said, "We are actually thinking of moving in together. Or more to the point, he is moving some stuff in with me, provided I can find room. You know how cramped my apartment is."

"You had mentioned something about his going off for days at a time, unexplained," said Benedicta, buttering a piece of bread.

"Well, I've had some mis-givings but I am trying to think positive about this," said Lulu taking a bite of the casserole and washing it down with wine. "We are going ahead with the move-in. My nerves are finally calmed."

"I'm happy for you both," said Benedicta. "Here, let me wrap up a bowl of this concoction for you to take home," she said as they finished their meal. "You can surprise Jake with the treat. Tell him it is from my kitchen."

He did not want to awaken her, the sleeping Benedicta, lying next to him in the massive four poster bed in his master bedroom. The time on the digital clock said four in the morning. He heard the bong, bong, bong, bong, of the grandfather clock downstairs chiming the hour.

Reaching out, he gently put his hand on her arm. It felt soft—she liked to cuddle he had discovered, to his delight. Benedicta opened her eyes, turned to look at him, her gaze catching his, her eyes saying, I trust you.

Rolling over aside her, he kissed her mouth, ran circles around her lips with his tongue and kissed her once again. She stretched with a sigh and drew closer. He would have her. He would have her now.

Then he awakened. For a brief instant he was downcast. It had not happened. It was a dream, a nice dream, but nevertheless a dream.

"Wow, where did that come from?" he asked aloud, as he cleared his head and he saw that he was alone in the bed. It had crossed his mind before, almost every day of late, but he wasn't free—he wouldn't impose that on Benedicta. *Maybe later,* he thought, *when things are settled.*

"I had a dream about you last night," he said that evening as he held her hand and rubbed her back with his other hand.

"Oh? What was the dream?" she asked.

"Not telling," he said, "It could incriminate me."

"Now I am interested. Was it good sex?" Benedicta could be teasing when she wanted.

"It was outstanding sex. Blow your mind out of the water sex," he said grinning.

"Wonderful!!" she retorted and giggled, "Are you thinking it is practice for the future?"

"It could be, could it not?"

"Possibly," she said and kissed him.

The day was a warm mid-March day. The sun was shining, but there remained a chill in the air, a reprieve from the very cold weather of the previous month.

Benedicta drove, her sister in tow, from Dr. Prescott's office. They had stopped at St. Peter in Chains Cathedral for noon Mass before going on to his office. Now, they were driving north on I-75. There was, as always, a good bit of traffic.

"The doctor thinks I am doing well. And I feel like the meds are working. I am happy for the first time I can remember, Benie," Brie said, as she changed channels on the car radio.

"That is so good. It is really great news, honey." Benedicta felt perhaps that she could relax a little.

Since the fire, there had been nothing eventful going on at Pinecroft. Benedicta was glad for the break. Brie had adjusted to life with her and Sister Anne, and was learning to bake bread, something she took pleasure in. Benedicta could not remember a time when her sister enjoyed something so much.

Benedicta noticed a car, an old Honda, in the next lane; he approached, coming close to her car, practically touching the fender. Tapping the horn, Benedicta moved into the next lane, only to see the Honda move in unison.

"That's weird," she said, and thought, *I don't like this.*

Speeding up, the Honda followed suit. Locking the doors and gripping the wheel, Benedicta knew there was trouble ahead.

The Honda got behind her car and hit her bumper with a resounding thud. Her Nissan lurched forward, then the car seemed to steady itself. A concrete wall was on her left, and the Honda, pulling alongside now, was on her right. There was a scraping of the side of the car, an apparent effort by the driver of the Honda to push her car into the concrete dividing wall.

Tires screeching, Brie screaming, the Nissan scraped the dividing wall, wobbling on the road. A curve in the road appeared, and even as she applied force to the brakes, the Nissan crashed into the concrete wall, careening across two lanes, and, hit by a vehicle in the far lane, her car belched smoke as it dove down into the ditch.

Glass was everywhere. The horn was stuck and was blowing, keeping up a constant noise. Several cars came to a halt and a few individuals left their cars and came running toward the ditch.

Benedicta felt the impact as the car hit the wall. She heard Brie's screams and felt her own trepidation as she lost control of the car. It seemed as if things were happening in slow motion now.

When her car was hit by the car in the far lane, her seat belt suddenly became unfastened. As the car landed in the ditch, she was thrown forward, and her head hit the dashboard.

Benedicta felt her body descend into a hole of darkness and nothingness.

On that same day, in Hyde Park, Lulu entwined her arm in Jake's as they toured the Spring Arts Festival. The festival was being held in March so the weather was passable. It had been her idea to come browse. Every year, the suburb hosted an art fair, where artists displayed pots and jewelry and paintings. Lulu had encouraged Jake to submit some pastels and much to her delight, he had done just that.

"You think of yourself as kind of an art connoisseur, don't you, Lulu? Confess it!" he exclaimed and added, "What do you think of this painting?"

It was a picturesque scene of a flower-strewn meadow, a babbling brook meandered through the lush brush. A young girl with blonde hair was picking flowers in the distance. Lulu examined the painting with a critical eye. She knew what she liked, and she loved this painting. It spoke to her of hope. "Yes," Lulu said. "I like it. The sky is so blue, and the painting radiates light. I like it a lot."

"Would you want to have it?" he asked.

Nodding, she looked at him wistfully and said, "Well, that would be lovely." She squeezed his hand, beaming.

"Wait," he took his wallet out of his pocket before saying nonchalantly, "Oh, I forgot, I left my credit card in my other jacket. Could you lend me yours to buy this for you? I'll pay you back promptly."

"Sure," she said and dipped into her purse for her wallet.

The painting was purchased and wrapped. They took the painting and moved on down the square. Jake pocketed the credit card in his own wallet and said nothing.

After a while they left the art fair and headed home.

Benedicta moaned and tried to move her arm. Pain shot through her body at the slight movement. Moments later, she felt herself being yanked and pulled through the mangled car door and onto the ground. A siren whined in the distance. Voices she couldn't make out were shouting something.

Where am I? What has happened? Suddenly memory returned, Benedicta sucked in her breath—and vomited a grey greenish liquid mixing with the red blood dripping from her forehead. It made a purple stain on her white blouse.

She felt her face wiped clean.

"Ma'am, can you hear me?" a calm voice spoke.

Benedicta nodded her head and felt a return to life, to reality. Her head hurt terribly, she was nauseous, and she couldn't seem to move her left arm properly. With effort, she gingerly moved to sit up, a hand on her shoulder gently pushed her back down.

"Miss, steady there, work with us. We'll have that arm in a splint in a minute. Can you hear me?" he said again.

"Yes, I hear you," she mumbled.

"Can you wiggle your toes? Good, there you go, good girl."

"You're alone?" the voice asked again.

"No," Benedicta opened her eyes, and shot a look at the man crouched over her. He was dressed in navy shirt and trousers, a patch on his chest identified him as Nathan, EMT. Making an effort to speak, she said, "My, my sister is with me. Where is she, please?"

"Fellas!" shouted the EMT, "look for a second one. She's got someone with her."

"Over here in the bushes," yelled one of the firemen, and a second EMT with a stretcher tore across the ground headed for the bushes.

"Steady, Miss," said Nathan, "we'll have you to the hospital shortly."

Benedicta returned to the darkness and nothingness.

Whew, I don't think they saw me clearly. They were pretty shaken up by the antics I was pullin. Now, maybe they'll listen and high tail it outa here. I hope so. I am gitten pretty durn tired of messin with them, he thought, pulling his car into the parking place in front of the apartment building. The dents in the car he had gotten in the crash added just a few more dents to an already beat-up car.

Lulu was enjoying having Jake share her small apartment. He had all but taken over the massage room with his watercolors. He had an array of brushes and art books lining her one and only shelf. Lulu had made a drawer for him in the chest in the loft and a space in the tiny closet as well, but now the massage room was pretty much for his use.

Still, that nagging voice within reminded her that things were just not quite right. When Lulu considered the situation, she tended to become disturbed and she preferred to leave well enough alone.

For now, life went on. Lulu missed talking to Benedicta and was concerned as well for her friend. She could not make herself go to visit: there was too much distress in that for her. She promised herself she would visit when Benedicta was out of trouble. Instead, she preferred to send her a get-well card.

Chapter Thirteen

"Ms. Malloy," a voice she didn't recognize spoke to her, "Can you feel this pin prick? Good. Grip my hand, great, good girl."

Benedicta opened her eyes—she saw herself lying in bed in a blue pastel-colored room. The sign across from her bed said, "Good Samaritan Hospital, March 15, 1986. Nurse/Ruthie.

What am I doing in the hospital? she wondered. And she drifted back to the darkness, only to feel herself being pulled back to consciousness once again.

"Ms. Malloy, it is Inspector Brown. Are you able to talk?"

"Yes," she said in a whisper, wincing at the pain as she attempted to move her arm. The arm was in a sling of some sort. Feeling the front of her head, she realized it was covered with a dressing.

Blinking, she tried to focus on the inspector but found she had double vision.

"Someone smacked the hell out of your car and led you on a merry chase. Your sister told us what happened. Now, I know there have been a series of mishaps, to your sister at Our Lady's and at Pinecroft. And of course, you have gotten those calls."

"Yes," was all she said.

"These incidents have all been unexplained, it seems. Are you able to talk about it?" The inspector took out a pen and note pad.

"Yes, let me sit up first," she said, but found herself dizzy as she stirred, her head fell back on the pillow.

"It was a Honda, a black one. He forced me into the wall. Then things happened so fast. I couldn't control the car, I think we hit another car or something, I don't remember much." She wanted a drink of water. Her mouth was very dry.

She glanced over at the bedside table. A jug and glass sat there. "Inspector, could you possibly give me a drink, my mouth, it is so dry," said Benedicta.

"Sure, just a minute," said Inspector Brown. He fumbled momentarily with the glass and straw, before putting it to her lips. She sipped a cold drink of water, feeling refreshed for a brief second.

Putting the glass back on the table, the inspector asked, "Did you recognize the driver? "

"I didn't get a good look at him. I'm sorry, but I can't identify him."

"So, you wouldn't recognize the perpetrator?" asked the inspector, and then continued, "Did you get the license number?"

"No, I don't know the license number."

And again, she fell back into the nothingness. —

A week and a half passed after the accident and Benedicta became more alert. One of her concerns was what had happened to Brie. No one had told her anything. *Are they keeping something from me, trying to protect me?* she wondered.

Finally, awakening as a doctor unwrapped her head dressing, Benedicta asked, "Could, could you possibly tell me how my sister is? She was in the accident with me, wasn't she?"

Dr. Donard-Smith smiled at Benedicta and said, "Now, there is a question I am able to answer and give you good news. Brie was shaken up a bit, but she had no injuries and is feeling better. She was seen in the emergency room that afternoon and released. I'm surprised no one informed you, but then, you have been kind of—" he let his words trail off.

Relieved, Benedicta sighed softly. Brie was safe at Pinecroft, and she, Benedicta, was going to get well.

"Jake, is that you?" Lulu put down the book she was reading. Jake and she had been living together a short time. He was gone a lot and Lulu found she was often alone. *That aloneness is too much,* she thought.

"Yeah, it's me," he said, coming into the room. "How is Benedicta? Did you talk to anyone today? I know you have been very concerned. I am very sorry," he said solicitously now.

"No, I haven't had an opportunity to see anyone. I talked briefly with Sister Anne, who said she is still listed in critical condition." Lulu tugged at the belt on her robe and looked at Jake. "Where have you been? It's after eleven."

"Checking up on me already?"

"No, of course not, silly. I miss you when you aren't here."

Suddenly Lulu thought of her premonition over a month ago as she saw a dark aura surround Jake now. A nagging intuition assailed her once more, and the thoughts came unbidden. Those thoughts had been coming and had intensified at moments like this one. Lulu could not shake this feeling no matter how hard she tried. *What is the matter, what do I not know?*

"Lu," began Jake, stretching his arms out, and then plopping down beside her. "I miss you, too. I am trying to make time to be with you." He continued, after hesitating a long moment, "I have some things going on, not business really, some—things,"

"You make it sound so mysterious. Will you tell me about it?"

"Eventually, maybe," he got up and poured a drink. "Let's go to bed. It's getting late."

Two days later, Lulu was at home in her apartment. She was planning a visit to the hospital today to see Benedicta. *I must do this,* she thought. The phone rang. Lulu, washing dishes, dried her hands, and answered. "Hello?"

"Ms. Ennis, Lulu Ennis?" a muffled voice asked.

"Yes, this is Lulu Ennis, how may I help you?"

"Ms. Ennis, you don't know me. I have some information—information you might like to hear. This may be of interest to you. It is about Jake Bannon," the voice was silent.

Lulu sucked in a deep breath. *Here it is. Here is where I find the messy part,* she thought.

"Yes, I know him well." *How well?* That question was her next thought. She found a fear ratcheting up in the pit of her stomach.

"Well, Ms. Ennis, I am calling you for your own protection. Are you aware that Jake Bannon is involved in gambling? He has racked up a sizeable debt and continues to gamble," the voice sounded gritty and hoarse. She could barely make out the words. "I just thought you should know. And he runs around with a pretty tough crowd as well. Be careful."

"Who are you?" Lulu demanded, "Who are you?" Lulu insisted, but the line was dead.

Lulu stood holding the phone for some minutes. She seemed reluctant to move, feeling the call required some response.

Who was making these accusations? And what did it mean?

Suddenly, Lulu gasped. Recognition hit her like a ton of bricks. *The day of the art show, I gave my credit card to Jake. He has not returned it.*

Caught off guard, Lulu considered what to do.

She went to her lock box. The lock was loose, the keyhole bent and the box easy to open. Lulu sat down quickly. She suddenly felt panicky. Hands clammy and trembling, she fumbled with the lid. *What did Jake do?* Opening the box, she found that her three other credit cards were gone.

Lulu dialed the number for her major card, only to discover that the card was maxed out. Numb now, she checked online, the other cards had high balances as well.

When she could stand it no longer, Lulu dialed the number of the bank. Jake had put her name on his account and credit charges. She had to know more.

"I'm sorry Ms. Ennis, but that account is in arrears. You want to know about the credit cards? Let me see, they are maxed out." The news hit her again, like a slap in the face. She added up the figures on paper. The total would be about $40,000.

Lulu stared at the paper with the figures for a long, long, time.

Lulu pulled the car up in front of the brokerage firm Wygal, McDowell, and Frost.

"Could I please see Doug McDowell?" asked Lulu upon entering, her voice faltering. "I just phoned and he said he would see me."

Lulu sat in the lobby, waiting to see McDowell. She knew she felt frazzled, but she had to do this, to get further information, to find a way to know what steps to take.

"Come this way. Mr. McDowell will see you now," said the receptionist.

Upon entering the office of one of the principal brokers, Lulu looked around. She had been here only once before, for a benefit to help AIDS victims. She looked about. Expensive artwork lined the walls, very modern, very contemporary furniture sat in the highly decorated office. *No doubt a decorator's delight*, she thought vaguely.

Approaching the massive desk, Lulu held out her hand, trying to put a smile on her face. Doug McDowell took her hand and came around the desk and hugged her warmly. "Lulu, what a surprise. It's been too long," he said, motioning her to sit in the chair opposite the desk. "May I get you coffee, or tea?"

Lulu sank down into the cushions of the plush arm chair. Any other time, it would have pleased her to be so graciously welcomed, to come here to Jake's former colleague. She reminded herself of her intent.

"No, thank you. And yes, it has been a long while," commented Lulu. "Jake and I live together now in my apartment in Mt. Adams We can see your offices from our patio."

Small talk made, Lulu attempted to clear her throat and begin. She found her throat dry and parched, and she realized she was thirsty. She licked her lips and began again. "Doug, you know Jake as well as anyone. He used to work with you and you two were close. I can't help thinking something is wrong, what is it?"

Doug McDowell frowned, picked up a gold-leafed letter opener off his desk, fingering the sharp perforated edge of the knife. "Lulu, leave well enough alone," was his input.

"But Doug, if there is something going on—?" Her words trailed off. What could she say, then summoning her strength, she spoke more firmly, "I received an anonymous call this morning—warning me —and the credit cards are maxed out—I checked—mine too," the words spilled out now, she couldn't help herself, "And he has been acting so strangely, he is gone for days and nights at a time without explanation."

Doug McDowell traced the edge of the knife in his hand, seeming caught in thought. Finally he said, "Do you know about Jake's gambling debts?"

Taken aback and caught off guard, Lulu stammered, "Well, well, I didn't until the call came, and now you are confirming that." Regaining her composure, she asked, "What do you know about this?"

"I know he has a sizeable debt, and he's trying to cover it any way he can. His house just went up for sale. You didn't know that, did you?" he said, when he saw her gasp. "I don't know that he has done anything illegal, yet, or that he would, mind you, but he had better be careful."

McDowell flipped the letter opener onto the desk and stood up. "I hate to rush you, honestly I do, but I have a meeting. Anyway, it was good to see you. And tell Jake to watch himself."

"Thank you, Doug," Lulu said and left.

Lulu sat in the shadows of the gathering dusk. It had been a long day. Disappointment weighed on her like a heavy too-tight garment. Waiting for Jake to come home, Lulu had been sitting here for hours. She had not gotten to the visit with Benedicta. She would do it tomorrow. This was important, too.

She had had some further thoughts since talking to McDowell. *How much did McDowell know? Was Jake in debt to him and his* company as well? *Were they putting pressure on Jake to pay up? Was Jake in danger, real danger? And who was the person who called me? How did that man know to call me on my home phone?'*

Lulu didn't like any of the questions and she had no answers.

There was a click of the lock of the door and Jake stepped inside.

"Hello, honey," he said, "Is that you sitting here in the dark?"

Lulu thought about the time since this morning and the difference a few hours could make in a relationship. "Jake, I want to talk with you, "she finally said.

"Okay," he said, plopping down beside her and taking her hand in his.

Lulu pulled away.

The air seemed to fill with tension. She felt it collide with her spirit and bounce against the walls.

When she spoke, it was with difficulty. "Jake, I know about the debt. And the credit cards, all of the credit cards, and mine as well. What possessed you, what did you think, that you could keep it from me? And how did you get into this mess? And, and—" she finally stopped. Her chest was tight, her heart beat was pounding away, and her hands were clammy and cold.

There was a silence. Lulu could feel him steeling himself.

"This is something I have to work out," he said finally.

Flicking on the lamp of the side table, he put his arm around her, squeezed her shoulders. As he did, he noticed the luggage at the door.

"Are, are you going somewhere?" he asked.

"Jake, I'm leaving until you can work this out. You need more support than I can give. And more advice than any I have. I suggest you find help, quickly, before it is too late, before you are in trouble you cannot escape. "

He seemed to crouch in a corner of the couch. His shoulders sagged, he lowered his eyes, he was quiet and continued to seem to listen.

"This isn't something that is okay. It is not, you understand. And it seems to put me in some danger as well as you. There was a man who called here today. How did he know me or my name?" Her hands moved in an expansive gesture and she would have continued, but she found she could not.

I just have to make it past the door, she thought. *How am I going to do that? Just to the door.* When she was able to speak again, she said with effort, "I am not locking the door on us yet, but I am closing it, for the time being. I will be out of the apartment until you make arrangements for a place for yourself. I know it would be appropriate for you to leave now in place of me but I am giving you that courtesy. And I will expect you to take me off your account and your credit cards tomorrow. I will certainly check. And when you can return the money to my cards, that would be appropriate as well."

Finally, she stood wearily, and said, "We get second chances all the time, Jake, but sometimes we use up all our second chances. You are worth saving, you are a good person, but only you can put in the effort to save yourself. If you do, you will find all the support you need. I am sure of it."

Rising, and before she could change her mind, Lulu threw on her coat, picked up her luggage, and disappeared out into the night.

Lulu sat in a rocking chair in the basement of the house in Norwood. Her dad had been winding up upholstering a chair, when she had burst in, tears streaming down her face.

Now, her crying over, the facts revisited, and hot cocoa in hand, Lulu sat with her dad.

Like a baby bird with a broken wing, Lulu glanced at her dad, almost hoping he could fix this for her.

"I'll be glad to pay off your credit cards if that would help. You know I'd do anything I could," he sat on the couch next to the rocker and patted her hand.

"No, no, Dad, this is my responsibility. I know you are there for me. That is enough. I'll clean up my own mess," she said, in a tremulous voice. *I wish I could,* she thought, *but I am unsure just how to do that.*

"Oh, I know you girl, you can be as tough as nails when it's called for. Just like your mom, bless her soul."

"I'll be okay, Dad," she said, and meant it, even if she had moments when she doubted it.

"Benedicta, it is Jude, are you awake?"

"Yes, I am, though I seem to be asleep all the time or so they tell me."

He took her hand and squeezed it tightly. "This is the first time they would let me see you. The nurses say you are coming around. I've been so worried about you. If anything happened to you—well—" his voice broke and he stopped talking. He recovered and said to her, "You gave me a terrible scare."

"So sorry, Jude, "she said with a wan smile.

"Benedicta, I want to say, I love you." Their eyes met and held.

"I love you too, Jude," was all she said.

"Get better, Benedicta, I need you."

She closed her eyes, when she opened them, he was gone.

"Hi, Benie, it's me, Brie," her sister said, patting the hand so still on the sheets of the bed.

Benedicta opened her eyes. "Hi honey, I'm awake. That's all I'm doing is sleeping. But I am feeling much better. The doctors say I was incredibly lucky, that I'll be good as new when this is over. "

"Wow, that is great, cool," said Brie, then turned and indicated the person next to her. "Here is someone else to see you. "

"Hello, Benedicta," said Sister Anne, affectionately giving her a soft hug. "I hope you are getting the rest you need. Brie is doing okay at Pinecroft. She is learning to bake pies and cakes. We are keeping her safe. Inspector Brown has a detail of men checking on us several times a day."

Benedicta sighed. "Good," she said at last. "I am so glad you escaped injury in the accident. And I know you are as safe as possible at Pinecroft." In a whisper, Benedicta said as if an afterthought, "Keep up the good work, Brie"—and she drifted off once again.

The days stretched out before her. Her dad working in the basement on the upholstery business, and she upstairs rambling around. At first it had been a suffocating nightmare, thinking of the situation she had just left and what Jake was facing.

Now, Lulu had begun to have a regular schedule. She could sleep better, and her work habits, though not focused on massage, put her in good stead. She kept house for her dad and cleaned the place as if it hadn't been cleaned in a decade.

She had begun to eat a bite for lunch and dinner, even if she picked at her food. Of course, her face was haggard, as her father pointed out to her, and her clothes were loose on her thinning frame. The afternoons seemed interminable. And she wanted to make plans. *What do I do?* She waited.

It had been over a month since she knocked on her dad's door at midnight. Lulu had stayed at her father's house and put her massage business on hold.

Today, she was preparing a cherry pie, her dad's favorite. Lulu put the pie in the oven and set the timer. Glancing at the pile of dishes to be washed, she heard the phone. A funny feeling filtered into her gut. *What is it?*

Lulu had been on alert wondering if she would receive any more distressing calls. *Who had had her number? Could they call her here?* She had considered changing her dad's phone number but wanted to keep it open for important calls.

Lulu took a deep breath.

"Hello?" she said, bracing herself.

"Lulu, this is Jake, how are you? I have thought about you so much—"

"Oh, you know, all right, I guess," she said, though that didn't begin to describe it.

Jake began again, "I only want you to listen," he said. His voice seemed unusually quiet and thoughtful. "I didn't sleep at all for weeks after you left. Your words were a wakeup call. And I needed that desperately." He hesitated, then said, "You were right. My behavior lacked good sense. I wasn't using my brains. I could have gotten help for my addiction when I saw it heating up. I thought I could stay ahead of it. And then I got in over my head.

"I have been getting help. I am progressing, slowly, carefully—" His voice broke, and she felt a tug at her heart strings. He continued, "I am seeking out those who have good judgment. Hopefully I have acted before it is too late."

"Jake—" she said wishing to support him in some way.

"No, let me finish, please. My father has paid off the debt. I will pay him back eventually. I have joined a twelve-step group called Gamblers Anonymous, and I have the support of my sponsor and the group." He went on, his voice more even now, taking on an animated tone, "I have a counselor I trust who is holding me accountable." There was a pause.

She waited, not exactly knowing what to say. Her heart gladdened, but in some disbelief.

"I want you back, Lulu. I realize you mean so much to me. Maybe not now, it may be too soon to resume our relationship at this stage, my counselor thinks I need more time to get stable, but in the future—" His voice trailed off.

Then he spoke in that same animated tone again. "I have joined a Catholic men's group at my parish, iron sharpening iron, as they put it. Anyway, it seems the best thing I have ever done—" She thought he was finished with the conversation, but he continued. "Will, will you consider resuming our relationship if I can get it together?"

Lulu reflected upon his words. *Everything was all out on the table now. And he had a plan. And the plan seemed a pretty good one. It is more than I can say for myself.*

"Yes, I will consider you being in my life once again, if your words hold true. But, one thing though, I won't be sleeping with anyone ever again, getting so involved before marriage. I have had to own that mistake. And I've had to repent. You must know that. You must decide if you are able to handle such an arrangement."

"I respect your decision, Lulu, I really do," said Jake. "It sounds like you are going through some changes yourself, and that is good, I think. I am glad we talked. I will be in touch later.",

They talked about the Reds then, of all things. And she had asked when baseball season had begun. Neither of them were sports fans. They just needed a buffer it seemed to her. He didn't ask her what she was doing and this was a relief to her.

"Thank you for calling," she said at last. Then the phone conversation ended.

Now, after hanging up the phone, she considered their conversation. She, too, needed a plan. And she had some ideas that weren't apparent to her just a few minutes ago. Those ideas had been gelling for weeks. Now it was time to act, she had been set free.

It was high time she resumed her massage business. And, although she knew her dad was happy to have her, the time had come to get past her father's house. She would move to Pinecroft and stay there for a time before returning to her much-loved Mt. Adams' condo. And she would get a spiritual companion.

Someone she could talk to about her personal life. Benedicta would be able to recommend someone, she felt sure.

These thoughts and ideas came to mind as Lulu realized she felt hungry. Heading for the refrigerator, she stopped and remembered the pie. Peeking in the oven, Lulu found it ready to be removed.

Lulu saw that the time had come to move forward. Tentatively, Lulu felt her hopes come alive once again. *Whatever happens, I will be ready now,* she thought.

March had come in like a lion and left, as the saying goes, like a lamb. And April brought showers and those May flowers. Benedicta had chronicled some of the time from her hospital bed as she wrote in her journal. She had been moved to the rehabilitative unit at the hospital. It was a real joy, writing about the days, as was reading, and visiting with her friends. It was expected she'd require speech therapy but that was not the case. She had physical therapy to regain the movement in her arm and to strengthen her legs. Benedicta would continue these activities with the physical therapist for some time after returning home.

Benedicta found she had no trouble curbing her appetitue while in the hospital. She was eating a regular diet and didn't think about snacks or overeating. *An improvement,* she thought.

On a beautiful June morning, with a blue sky overhead, Benedicta was released from the hospital. Arriving with Jude at Pinecroft, she was carefully escorted in. Upon entering she said, "It is so good to be home."

"Sister Anne tells me Lulu is staying at Pinecroft for a spell," said Jude.

"Oh, that is news to me, and good news," said Benedicta.

Entering the front door, Benedicta was met by a banner posted above the mantel in the living room. "Welcome home," it said. Looking around, she saw Sister Anne, Brie, and Lulu. Benedicta hugged each one.

"We're so glad you are back. Look, here is Baby, he is glad too," said Brie as Baby jumped on Benedicta's lap.

"Thank you everyone," she said, overcome with joy.

"That is not all. We have a cake baked by Brie, and ice cream, and tea," said Sister Anne.

The day went by in a blur. Everyone huddled around, not wanting her out of their sight. Jude stayed long into the evening. Finally, he carried her up to her room and Brie helped her undress for bed.

"You all are spoiling me," she said, "but thank you so much."

And it was good to know that the police had a lookout on the place.

———————

Benedicta stretched at her desk. She had been busy for days catching up. She had been ordered to rest part of each day, so her mornings were taken up by getting up later than usual, going to Mass at 9 a.m. with a late breakfast, and afterward time in her office until 2 p.m., when she took a nap. In the afternoon, she visited with Brie, sometimes with Lulu, and helped Sister Anne a little in the kitchen.

She was surprised at how much time recovery was taking. However, the naps were helping her energy level and she was sleeping better again.

Today she had met with Inspector Brown at 4 p.m.

"There have been no further incidents since coming home. Not even those worrisome telephone calls I was getting," she informed the inspector.

"Good to know, but I don't think this is over," he said. "Be careful and don't go out alone, even to walk on the property. Let others know of your whereabouts. "

"Will do, Inspector," said Benedicta.

———————

Chapter Fourteen

Benedicta thought she had this down pat. She could easily get through her counseling sessions. She was even good at it, she surmised.

Then it happened. She had a call from Edmund Wise, the archbishop's secretary. The earth moved.

"Archbishop Floersch wishes a meeting with you in the near future. I have scheduled it on Thursday, day after tomorrow. Plan to be at the Chancery at 1 p.m. sharp." And he was gone. This meeting was highly unusual. Granted she reported to the archbishop, but that usually meant a paper report or a few words with Edmund Wise. Or possibly she heard word through Jude.

She spoke with Sister Anne. "I am a little uptight about this meeting. What could the archbishop possibly want with me? Have I done something wrong? Is he going to fire me? "

"Oh, Benedicta, you've done a grand job. Maybe he wants to tell you what a superb director you are." *Welcome words*, she thought, but I *cannot own them.*

Benedicta even mentioned to Jude the archbishop's summons, but he was no help, either.

On Thursday, Benedicta did her hair up in a bun, carefully applied makeup, and put on her best go-to-the-office dress and headed downtown to see the ever-unflappable Archbishop

Floersch. She showed up at 12:50 p.m and was greeted by Edmund Wise.

"What does Archbishop Floersch want with me, Edmund? Have I, have I done something wrong? Has someone reported me? Am I in trouble?"

Wise was non-committal as usual. His face was a mask of non-communication, and she could not discern what she was called for. Here she was, seated in the lobby of the chancery, waiting to see the archbishop. Benedicta fiddled with her clutch bag, put her keys in, took out a handkerchief and wiped her brow, immediately replacing the handkerchief in her purse.

"The archbishop will see you now," said Edmund Wise, coming out in the crowded lobby. She was escorted down a hall to a double door. Wise knocked and immediately opened the door, ushering her in.

The room was modestly but expensively furnished. The floor was carpeted in a thick plush pile. A massive grandfather clock stood between two windows. Soft easy chairs sat in front of a huge desk; a few straight chairs sat against one wall. A bookcase filled the space on another wall. A portrait of Cardinal Bernadine hung above the straight chairs.

Some expensive-looking church memorabilia, like an old chalice, a beretta, that is a kind of hat worn by the priest before the council, a mitre, which was a staff used by the bishop or archbishop for official functions, and a cape worn at one time by the bishop or archbishop sat on the bookshelves along with shelves of treasured ancient books.

The bright light from the windows momentarily blinded her as she stood just inside the door, facing the desk.

The archbishop sat signing papers. He looked up, and without smiling, directed her by a wave of his hand, to one of the soft chairs in front of his desk.

"Ms. Malloy," he said at last, putting down his pen, and shuffling the papers. "Please come in, have a seat." He waved again toward a chair, and then said as if an afterthought, "Would you like a cup of coffee or a glass of water?" Without waiting for a reply, he said to Edmund Wise, "Please, bring us each a glass of water."

"There has," he began without any further small talk, "been a discrepancy occurring between funds I used to receive from Pinecroft—and what I now receive, even though attendance is up. And I want to know the reason for the discrepancy."

Benedicta was startled. She felt the tension rise within her. *This is not good*, she thought.

Edmund Wise entered with two glasses of water, and Benedicta absentmindedly took one of them, and downed a large gulp of the cold liquid.

The archbishop was a big man, muscular, a slight paunch for a belly, nothing unusual for a 60-year-old man. His hair was thinning, his face was full and round. He had a slight goatee. He wore a clerical suit with a cross and chain about his neck. Another gold chain was attached to a pocket watch.

He seemed to be waiting for her to say something. "What, what do you mean?" she said, almost gasping as she did so.

"I believe funds are being 'lost' or God forbid, stolen. There is a diminution in funds this year from last, and according to your reports, the numbers are even up. I want to get to the bottom of it. Now." he said emphatically, and repeated, "Now."

The archbishop fingered the gold cross about his neck. Then he took out the gold pocket watch and glanced at it, rising as he did so.

"Come, Ms. Malloy, I am a busy man. I have many things to do. My schedule is full. I expect you to solve this mystery and get back to me. Promptly," he added the last word seemingly for emphasis. "Is that understood?"

The archbishop scooted back his desk chair, came around the desk, and took Benedicta's hand in his, saying "Forgive me for my being curt. It is just that I don't know where to go with this discrepancy. It is something of a mystery." She felt momentarily relieved.

The archbishop retrieved his glass of water from the desk, took a sip and sat down in the other easy chair. Seeming to reflect, he was silent for a long moment.

Benedicta sat quietly as the archbishop remained thoughtful. A long pause ensued. Then the archbishop said, "Ms. Malloy, I must be honest with you. I do not like conflict or even mystery. And this situation seems to present me with both."

He fingered the cross and chain about his neck, and said, "If I knew a way to solve this dilemma over funds missing, I would perhaps not have to ask you here, or put the burden of this situation on you." He rose from the chair and went to the window, looking out on the street below. "As it is, I do not know the answer to the question that plagues me. Would you, Ms. Malloy, help me with this? I would be most grateful."

With a wave of his hand, the archbishop returned to the far side of his desk and, pressing a button on his answering machine, said, "Edmund, would you show Ms. Malloy out, and give her the papers we have for her?"

"Thank you for coming in to see me. Work on discovering what you can about the missing money and keep me informed."

Edmind Wise immediately opened the door, stood at attention, and Benedicta saw that her time here was over. Benedicta was mystified by the interview with the archbishop. On the one hand, he was businesslike and brusque, curt even. Yet somewhere in the middle of the twenty minutes with the archbishop, he had softened his tone, he had become more human. *He seems genuinely stumped,* she thought.

Benedicta hoped she would be able to answer the question for the archbishop but she had her doubts. At present, she knew nothing about the "missing funds" or who might be to blame.

Out on the street headed to her car, she looked at the papers handed to her by Edmund Wise. They were a summary of the funds from this year and from the previous several years. And at a cursory glance, the papers did show a sizeable reduction in money collected for this fiscal year.

Benedicta considered the meeting she had just attended. The archbishop was evidently putting this matter in her hands, with the warning to figure out where the funds had gone without delay. He clearly wanted results.

Benedicta went home with the unwieldy task of finding who had absconded with the funds from Pinecroft. And the archbishop had made no mention of the possible consequences if she did not solve this problem.

For several weeks, Benedicta mulled over the appointment she had had with the archbishop. She prayed about how to discover who was behind the disappearance of funds, if indeed, they were missing.

Benedicta went through the paperwork to see if she could find where the funds might have gone. Nothing seemed obvious. On Monday she talked with Jude when he visited to take care of another legal matter.

"I just don't know what to tell you, Benedicta. The fact is no one here seems a likely candidate or suspect for taking the money. But the figures don't lie. The money is missing. How much do you see as gone?"

"I don't know for sure, but it looks like about $12,000 to $15,000 might be missing. I have decided I can no longer store money in the safe in my office. I'll have to get it to the bank as soon as possible, which may cut down on any pilfering. If such a thing is happening, I want to know about it."

Jude invited her, Lulu, and Brie to dinner at his home that night. Benedicta was surprised by the invitation. She was glad Lulu and Brie were included. Their joining her and Jude was a nice touch.

Jude served chicken cordon bleu, rice, gingered carrots, a salad and a freshly baked chocolate cake for dessert. Brie had been delighted with the cake and had eaten a second helping.

As they lingered over the desert, Benedicta remarked, "Jude, you didn't tell me what a good cook you are, this dinner was delicious."

"Thank you, madam. I once took a gourmet cooking class. I surprisingly learned a lot and I use those recipes every chance I get. This dish was one of those recipes. The cake as well came from that particular chef."

"Well, that was a good investment. This dinner was so good."

As they sat over coffee, Jude asked, "Lulu, how long do you plan on staying at Pinecroft?" The question seemed more a part of the conversation than any kind of confrontation, and Lulu appeared unruffled.

"I don't quite know. I am having my apartment in Mt. Adams painted soon, and I will decide sometime after the paint is dry. I had also hoped to use a couple decorating ideas. Why do you ask?"

"No real reason. Just curious, that's all."

"Lulu is good company for us all," said Benedicta. "She is cheerful, funny and plays a mean game of checkers."

With that, the evening ended.

On Wednesday, Benedicta and Lulu made a trip into town for a beauty salon appointment. The two planned to make the day of it, having lunch and doing some shopping. She had signed out at Pinecroft until 8 p.m. Benedicta knew Sister Anne was away today. Brie was visiting a girlfriend, and there was no one at the center.

Benedicta had second thoughts about whether to leave the place unattended. At the last moment, she cancelled her lunch date, leaving Lulu in town, and returning to Pinecroft. She was home by 12:30 p.m.

There was a car in the drive behind the garage when she got home. She didn't immediately recognize the car, and she knew none of her staff was there. So where was the person with the car?

Entering through the back door, Benedicta made her way to her office. The door was closed. Benedicta heard noises like the rustling of papers coming from behind the closed door. Benedicta stood in the hall, stopping short of opening the door.

What do I do? Benedicta thought. *If it is an intruder, and he is dangerous*—she let her thoughts trail off. Now, Benedicta was just plain curious. *Who is occupying my private room?* She cautiously put her hand on the doorknob, and quietly opened the door to her office.

Benedicta gasped. Her first instinct was to be relieved. And she was surprised. "What, what are you doing here?" she stammered.

Beatrice Hartung, the part-time chaplain, froze in the chair as she sat at the secretary. The finance book lay in her lap. The safe in the corner stood open. The pen she was using dropped to the floor with the sound of metal hitting wood. Beatrice looked shocked. It was evident she had not been expecting Benedicta's return.

Neither spoke for a moment. Another moment of silence ensued. And a third moment went by.

Beatrice spoke first. "I, I can explain, it, it really isn't as it looks."

"I certainly hope you can explain," said Benedicta sharply, more sharply than she had intended.

"I, I had a contribution I was including in the paperwork."

"There is a protocol for that, and it is not what you are now doing," said Benedicta tersely.

"I, I," began Beatrice, "I have a reason. It is not what you think, really."

At first, Benedicta thought perhaps the archbishop had enlisted Beatrice's aid in finding the missing funds. After all, she had been director in recent years.

Just what was the meaning of this situation? Had someone been siphoning money from cash and cooking the books as the archbishop seemed to surmise? And was this someone Beatrice?

"I, I know it is not the usual way of putting in contributions," said Beatrice, as Benedicta stood, startled, in the doorway, "but, but that is what I was doing."

Benedicta came into the room as she composed herself after the shock of finding Beatrice at her desk with the safe open. Benedicta said, "There is already a procedure in place for such things," and, she said, leaning over the safe and peering in, "You are well aware of that fact."

"I, I know," was all Beatrice stammered in response.

"Really, Beatrice, this looks bad. Do you have anything to say for yourself?"

"It isn't what it looks like," was her only response.

"Please, give me that book," said Benedicta, holding out her hand for it.

An awkward pause ensued.

"I, I wasn't finished, not just yet," said Beatrice.

"Please leave my office, we will discuss this later."

"Benedicta," said Beatrice as she slowly handed the financial book to her, "I know this looks bad, but—" her voice trailed off.

When Beatrice had left, Benedicta shut the door and inspected the safe. There was a deposit made only yesterday of $2,500.00. She counted it now, 50, 100, 200, 300: there was a total of $600.00 remaining in the safe. Benedicta opened the book and looked intently at the latest set of figures.

Sure enough, the $2,500 deposit had been altered in the book to read $500.00. The books indicated that the total funds in the safe were $600.00.

"Ouch," she moaned now. *I do not like where this seems to be leading*, she thought.

Benedicta called Jude then, asking him to meet her at Pinecroft at 4 p.m.

I do not like thinking Beatrice is responsible for the change in these numbers, but what else am I to think?

"You see," she said to Jude at their meeting, and after telling him the whole story, "it looks like Beatrice has been cooking the books and taking money."

She rose from her seat before her secretary, financial book in hand, and handed it to Jude, saying, "But is there sufficient evidence to accuse Beatrice? And what is to be done?"

Jude shook his head, before saying, "I think you need to have a heart-to-heart with Beatrice. There must be something we are not seeing." He looked intently at the page as if the answer could be found there. He handed the book back to Benedicta and said, "I can't rightly think Beatrice would do this. She was, as you are aware, director before you came on the scene. She would know there would be trouble if she were caught. She just wouldn't do this without a good reason."

He handed the book back to Benedicta and turned to leave, then changed his mind and came back, saying, as he sat down, "But, speaking as the archdiocese's lawyer, we must get to the bottom of this matter. If Beatrice is guilty, and it looks quite likely that she is, Beatrice will be prosecuted." He sat in the pink wing chair, tapping his fingers on the armrest, thought for a moment, and said, "If you need me to talk with her, I will. It is your call."

Benedicta locked the front door before setting the timer. She glanced at the clock, which read 10:35 p.m.. She was late getting the place settled for the night. Switching off the lamps in the living room, she headed for the kitchen. That pie left from supper was too good to pass up. She wanted a second piece.

As she opened the fridge, the doorbell rang. She wondered, who would visit at this hour of the night. Should I open the door? Looking out, she saw Jude standing, hat in hand, on the far side of the glass screen door.

"Hello, Benedicta," he said as she opened the door, ignoring that he had come unannounced.

"Why Jude, this is a surprise. Come in," she said, unlocking the screen door.

"Is it too late? I mean, I wanted to talk with you. It's kind of important."

"Okay, I guess. Let's go in the kitchen. I have cherry pie and milk."

The pie was served and the milk poured. Benedicta took a seat at the table. Jude seemed nervous and sat fidgeting with the salt and pepper shakers.

"What's up? Shoot," she said.

"There is. There is," he repeated, twirling the shakers in circles, "something, I, I have to tell you. Something I should have made known months ago. I haven't really lied to you. I haven't been totally honest, either." Jude took a handkerchief from his pocket and wiped his glasses, then folded them and laid them on the table.

He took her hand in his, kissed it, and said, "You are my world to me. I don't want to lose you or lose our friendship."

"Okay, what is it? You're scaring me." Benedicta couldn't imagine what he would say. Benedicta sat back in her chair. She recalled the time at the restaurant, his wanting to tell her something. Putting aside her misgivings, she was ready to hear what he had to say.

"I'm, I'm married. Technically, I'm legally separated. Six years now, separated." Jude looked at her and saw her flinch.

Benedicta swallowed hard. There was a lump in her throat, her eyes were smarting. She automatically pushed the pie away. *What?* She wanted to shout. *What do you mean, married?* She said only, "I see."

"No, I'm afraid you do not, Benedicta. We've been married thirteen years, Charlotte, my wife, has been unfaithful since our honeymoon, with a series of lovers." His eyes were downcast, he wasn't looking at her. He couldn't, he found. "I haven't exactly been perfect," he went on, "but I never played around. I was never even interested in anyone, until—you—came along—." his words trailed off as he saw the color of Benedicta's face change to red.

"Are, are there children?"

"Yes. There are two. Charlie is nine and into basketball. A real boy, he is. Hannah is thirteen, plays the piano and is on the honor roll. I am very proud of them both."

Benedicta's color remained ruddy. She examined her fingernails. *I should polish them. I will paint them plum, a new color. I'll get some polish at CVS,* she decided.

She had heard of married men going with single women. And there were, she knew, married men who seduced single women. She had always thought these behaviors a lose-lose proposition. It came as a shock, no doubt about it. She had trusted Jude, kind of. *I never considered for even a moment that he was married. Or did I? Am I naïve?* she wondered.

A knot formed in the middle of her stomach. She pushed aside the cherry pie. She found it difficult to breathe. Her mouth was dry.

"Say something, Benedicta," an unnerved Jude exclaimed.

"It is hard to wrap my head around this news. I wasn't expecting it. You waited this long to tell me?" she asked, incredulous. Her voice rose, her hands shook. Her face turned a scarlet hue.

He put his hand over hers, but she drew hers away. "You have every right to be angry. If it is any defense, I have thought of myself as unattached—" His voice broke.

Benedicta desperately tried to put a spin on this conversation that would explain it. She could not.

"I am very sorry. It just didn't seem like the time was right to tell you—" again his voice broke.

"The time was right?" Her words were flung at him.

"As I say, I am sorry. I have no excuse."

"No, you don't!" she exclaimed.

"The truth is," he began again, picking up the shakers once more and twirling them, "the truth is, we never had a marriage. We were both selfish, and into our own stuff. My work, Charlotte's social life—and her men friends, that is all we ever had. Our so-called marriage never happened, it seemed to me, and that's the truth.

"I just assumed you were single," she said, more subdued.

Jude went on. He wanted this out. All of it, on the table for good. "The children have been our connection. There will always be the children. I'm telling you this, even as late as it is, because I want to be upfront with you. You and I have struck up a pretty close friendship. I want to keep it that way. I thought maybe—well, I thought, I don't know what I thought," he stopped. It was all out now.

There was a silence. The clock in the dining room struck midnight.

"What more can I say?" he said at last.

"This is pretty astounding," Benedicta said. She didn't want to have to deal with this new event.

"Tell me about the children," Benedicta's good sense was kicking in. She needed all the facts.

"They live with Charlotte, their mother. I pay alimony and child support. They live in a brownstone in Westwood. They are in grade school. I think Hannah is in middle school," he amended. "I have them a week-end a month, some holidays, and a month in the summer. They're great kids." He finished the milk and tapped the glass on the table top reflectively.

Benedicta sat silent. The clocked ticked in the dining room. Twelve fifteen. Jude waited. He felt the jury was out.

"This is all such a concern," said Benedicta. Her hands trembled. "I don't really know how to handle this situation." Her color was returning to normal except for a round red splotch in the middle of each cheek. She touched his arm in an affectionate gesture, and said, "I'll have to think about what you told me. It is all so new."

Grateful for the sign of friendship, he looked at her intently. "Sure—sure—take your time." And picking up his coat, he left the house, leaving her sitting at the kitchen table.

~~~~~~

Chapter Fifteen

Despite feelings of shock and grief, life must go on, thought Benedicta. The next morning as she sat in her office beginning work, work she was reluctant to do, she refused to think of what had just transpired. Instead, Benedicta phoned Beatrice for a formal appointment. Beatrice entered her office saying nothing, her face masklike.

"Beatrice, I have spoken to Jude about the books and the missing money. Yes," she waved Beatrice's objections away, "There is money missing and the books look intentionally doctored."

There was a silence. "Beatrice," Benedicta began in a gentler tone of voice, "what is it?"

Beatrice looked as if she wanted to be anywhere but here. She seemed to want to speak, but stopped, preferring instead to reflect on the situation. Finally, she spoke, "My, my husband has been very ill. He must undergo a serious surgery, a heart surgery, the doctors say. The medical bills and cost of the pending surgery is taking a lot of money. Believe me, a lot.

"I didn't exactly plan on taking the money. I thought I could have replaced the funds before you noticed. You see, I am getting a second job, I am going to moonlight as a night chaplain at Mercy Anderson Hospital."

Beatrice stopped and looked at Benedicta. Guilt and shame clouded Beatrice's face.

Benedicta pondered what she was hearing. Beatrice had admitted to the theft, and the irregularity of the books. Okay, she had pressure on her for money.

"That will be all, Beatrice. I will be in touch with you soon. I will do everything I am able to avoid a legal matter or a charge, but I cannot guarantee this. You understand?"

"Yes, yes, I do," said Beatrice, and with tears in her eyes, she left the office.

Benedicta returned to her position in front of her secretary with the financial book in hand. She felt real compassion for Beatrice. True, Beatrice had been part of the staff with whom Benedicta had been conflicted. Nevertheless, she felt for her. Would she have done any differently under such circumstances?

Taking out stationery, she began writing a letter:

"Dear Archbishop Floersch:

"In reference to my visit to you and the search for the missing funds, I have found where the money has been going. There was a misunderstanding about the money. The funds are being appropriated and will be reflected in deposits in the coming months. Adjustments have been made to deal with the problem. Rest assured, there will be no further discrepancies in the financial statements. The situation that led to this impropriety has been cleared up. It will present no issues in future statements.

Thank you,

Best regards,

Benedicta Malloy

Benedicta had a plan in mind. She would not inform the archbishop where the money had gone. She would make a sizeable contribution of her own money. When Beatrice could make deposits, the remainder and her own contribution would be replaced. Beatrice could pay her back when able. No real crime was intended, she felt sure.

The next day, Beatrice was in the house and seated at a table where she worked in the basement. Benedicta came down the steps and greeted her.

Beatrice was pale, her hands were shaking. She smiled wanly.

Good morning, Bea, I am here to let you know I did not report the details of the loss of funds to the Chancery. I will cover a sizeable amount personally now, and as soon as you get going on your job, you can make up the difference. And pay me back over time. Over a matter of months, of course, you should be able to replace the stolen funds. We will leave it at that. Okay?"

Tears filled Beatrice's eyes. Benedicta felt near tears herself. She stood before Beatrice, leaned over and hugged her. "You would do the same for me, I am sure. Now, dry your eyes. It is all going to work out. How is your husband doing? When is he to have surgery?"

Beatrice wiped her glasses, and said, "In a matter of weeks. I will probably need some time off."

Benedicta patted her shoulder and said, "You have time coming to you. You'll be paid for any missed work. Take all the month off or more. Whatever you need is fine."

"Benedicta, I don't know what to say. You've made this bearable."

"Think nothing of it."

———

In the coming weeks, Benedicta came to a revelation. Suddenly, all of Benedicta's perceptions of Beatrice trying to show her up on the job, of making others think Beatrice knew more about the job than she did, all of that disappeared. Beatrice in fact, stopped irritating Benedicta.

Benedicta saw in a flash of insight, that all her efforts to have "discipline," to "let them know who is boss," all of this was changed overnight.

Benedicta was aware she had made a friend in Beatrice. And Beatrice, it seemed, influenced Father Joe Gast as well. He stopped all his requests for special privileges. The staff was, in a word, coming around.

And Sister Anne and Benedicta attempted to mend their relationship. At supper one evening, Sister Anne spoke up: "Benedicta, do you think I am bossy?"

Benedicta looked Sister Anne directly in the eye and said slowly, "Sometimes I do, Sister Anne, but I have come to realize you mean nothing by it."

"Well," said Sister Anne, "You would not be the first to think that. I have always been a bit bossy. When growing up, I drove my two brothers crazy. I was always telling them what to do." Sister Anne smiled and continued, "Fortunately, I have out-grown most of that, but it sneaks back in at odd times, you know?"

"Sister Anne, you are just fine," said Benedicta with exuberance. Benedicta patted Sister Anne's hand, and Benedicta's eyes filled with tears. She rose from her chair and went around to the other side of the table, putting her arms about Sister Anne's shoulders, saying in a whisper, "You are indeed a friend. You have taken Brie in hand. You have more than welcomed me here. We are okay, as far as I am concerned."

"Now you have me bawling," said Sister Anne, wiping her cheeks with a napkin. She seemed pleased as she composed herself.

"We make a good team," said Benedicta as she returned to her place at the table. *The tension I have always felt with this woman is gone,* thought Benedicta, taking a deep breath. *I am relieved to have a real friendship with Sister Anne.*

Benedicta related all of this in a meeting with Mother Margaret Mary after church on Sunday morning at St. Xavier's.

They sat in a pew in the rear of the church. People were still milling around just after the noon Mass. There was to be a baptism at 2 p.m. The proud parents and godparents were part of the remaining crowd.

Benedicta shared with Mother Margaret Mary a report of her deepening friendship with Sister Anne, and how her efforts to save Beatrice from criminal prosecution ended with more of a sense of harmony with her staff.

"I can't get over it, Mother. All the while, I have been struggling to be in charge and now the situation has become balanced without anything from me. There is a natural give and take, a professional relationship with all three, I haven't had since coming here."

"All things work together for those who love the Lord," Mother intoned, repeating the Bible passage she so often used when talking with Benedicta.

"Well, it truly has come together. I am grateful, really."

Brad dribbled the ball down the court, set it up and passed to Jude for the shot. Jude lobbed one in. Tied: 10-10.

The other team, the "Lucky Louts," as they called themselves, a men's group composed of businessmen from CG&E, as well as a few other firms in town, marched down the court and dunked one in, the score: 10-12.

The ball came back to the lawyer's group, nicknamed the "Brave Warriors," and the ball was then stolen by the Lucky Louts, who slammed another one in. Score: 10-14

Brad made a shot, then the other team lost the ball. Jude tried and missed, but the ball was saved. A basket was made by another team member. Score: 14-14.

The buzzer sounded in overtime. The Brave Warriors made two in a row and won the game, Score: 18-14,

Jude mopped the perspiration from his forehead with a towel. He approached Brad as they were coming into the locker room.

"Do you have time for a drink?"

"Sure, always, great," said his friend and partner.

The bar was quiet, dark and smoky even though early afternoon. A patron or two sat on stools at the massive oak bar in the front. A few tables, a row of booths lined the sides of the room, a piano stood in the back. Brad and Jude chose a booth near the rear. The two came here after their pick-up basketball games. It gave them a private place to talk freely.

O'Grady's was just down the street from Adams, Harcourt, and Carlyle, Attorneys at Law. The three lawyers had a two-story renovated house for their practice, situated downtown near the Hamilton County Court House.

Brad Harcourt was not only his partner but his best friend. They had a long association, having been in the Navy together and then having attended the same school, Harvard Law. A few years after graduation, the two men and Leo Adams set up shop in the offices they now occupied.

It was a good arrangement. The three were about the same age, each had their own specialty. Jude's was criminal law. The three got along well.

"I'll take a beer, Miller Lite," said Brad, sitting down in the booth.

"Make that two, if you would please, and could you rustle me up a salad, with blue cheese dressing on the side? Thanks," Jude said as the waiter noted their orders.

"How's Channing?" Jude asked politely. He had been best man for Brad and Channing's wedding four years ago.

"She's bustin her chops on her charity shindigs," said Brad, "always into her charity balls and benefits."

"Well, it keeps her happy, doesn't it?"

"Yeah, I suppose it does," said Brad, then added, "That was a bang-up game you played, Jude. You're getting good, too good. Have you been out practicing?"

"No, no, nothing like that, just nervous energy, a way to take charge at something besides work in the court room," said Jude, shoveling a handful of peanuts from a bowl on the table into a napkin in front of him and nibbling at the treat.

"What's on your mind?" asked Brad, accepting the beer, and giving the waiter his credit card.

"Here you go, keep the change," said Jude, then he dug into his salad. Chomping on the greens, he put a napkin to his lips, wiped his mouth, then said, "Damn it to hell, Brad, I just got a call from Charlotte. She wants to see me. This can't be good. I find myself distressed at the thought of a face to face," he said and added salt and pepper to the salad before pouring more of the dressing into the mixture.

Leaning his elbows on the table top, he said, "Brad, you know Benedicta. I like her a lot. I envision a future with her. You understand?" He looked at his partner, catching his gaze and holding it.

"Yeah, I get the picture," said Brad, calmly taking a sip of beer, smiling as he did so.

"No, no, it's nothing like that. This is different, not some casual affair." And he went on. "I just had a heart-to-heart conversation with her at her place night before last. I laid it all out. She was a bit shocked, surprised you could say, but she listened, accepted it, I think."

"What happens now?"

"We are kind of taking a break from each other until she knows what she wants to do; I guess you could call it a sabbatical, a time off."

"It is a good plan, I would say," said Brad.

"And it just so happens I have a case that is taking me to London. I plan to be over there for a few weeks, if not longer. It will give her a chance to have her own space and to think."

Jude leaned into the table as he scooped up the last of the salad and said, "You are aware just how punk things have been between Charlotte and me. She was unfaithful right from the get-go. And it just continued thereafter—it was a pattern. She never kept the commitment to marriage. I don't think she knows the meaning of the word. Heck with her anyway, for all the effort she made."

He pushed the salad dish away from him, and said, "I was not without blame. I horsed around and put my work ahead of her. I never tried to reach out to her once I discovered how she behaved. It seems there was never any love between us. If there ever was, it was gone by the time the honeymoon was over."

He took a long pull on his beer and wiped his mouth with the napkin.

"Whoa, hold up now! That's not exactly the whole story, is it?" said Brad. "You offered marriage counseling, bugged her to see your pastor together, kept up pretenses, for what, seven years?"

"Mainly that was for the sake of the kids, they were just babies. I have always thought a family is important for children," he said, as he fished a quarter from his pants pocket. "I never tried to get custody of the children after we separated. Despite her flaws, she is their mother and kids need their mom." Jude left his seat and went to the jukebox, pressing the button for the song, "You don't love me anymore."

Returning to the booth, he fiddled with his tie, loosening the knot, and said, "What do I do now?"

"Perhaps it is important to see what Charlotte wants, hear her out. My advice for you is to have a little space for thinking for yourself, too."

"Yeah, I will go with that for now. I have a lunch date with Charlotte tomorrow. Hell, I'll see what she has to say. Maybe it's nothing. Come on, let's get out of here," Jude said, rising from the booth.

"These things have a way of working themselves out," said Brad, putting on his suit jacket.

———————

The lunch couldn't have been more awkward. Charlotte had already had two drinks and was on her third when he arrived. *She is 'plastered,'* he thought, and he considered leaving immediately. Jude could tell she was three sheets to the wind because she was slurring her words, and was, frankly, almost incoherent.

Tongue tied and embarrassed himself, because he had an interest in a woman, he sat there morosely.

Charlotte ordered a club sandwich and onion rings. He put in a request for a dressed hamburger. He asked for a scotch and water while he waited for the meal.

He glanced for the first time at the woman opposite him at the table. She had put on weight. Charlotte had always been a bit heavyset, now she looked forty or fifty pounds past her ideal. Her hair was tightly permed and bleached. Dark roots showed at the part. She was dressed in a red dress with a lot of jewelry, and her makeup looked as if it had been applied with a putty knife.

The years have not been good to her, he thought. Her face had lines on her brow, crows' feet around her eyes, and deep wrinkles at the corners of her mouth. Her arms also had loose flab, from lack of exercise, he supposed.

As Jude considered Charlotte, his own embarrassment fell away. He felt pity for this maladjusted woman. *And she deserves kindness*, he thought. *After all, she is the mother of my children.*

"How are the kids?" he asked, trying to start a conversation.

"T'riffic, just t'riffic," was her only comment about the children.

The drinks came. He wanted to tell her to go easy on this one. It was her fourth.

Before he could say anything, she blurted out, "I wanna d'vorce." The startling exclamation came out slurred and a little too loudly. "I'm gittin' married, I wanna d'vorce," she repeated, then said, "As soon as poss a ble." She drummed her fingers on the tabletop, then lit a cigarette, and blew the smoke directly at him.

Through the haze of smoke, he looked at her again. She had led a life of dissipation. It came as a surprise, a shock, really, that she wanted a divorce. He had always given her a large spousal support. He didn't think she'd want to jeopardize that. *I underestimated her*, he thought now.

Not knowing what to say, Jude leaned over the table to take her hand, and in a strained voice said, "Congratulations." *I am going for conciliatory*, he thought. She pulled away.

"I, I think that, that's great," he said at last, wondering just how big a lie this statement was. "I'll agree to a divorce, I'll have Brad act as my lawyer. You may want to get one of your own, but you wouldn't have to. I'll meet any reasonable financial demands, and of course, care for the children."

"That's bullish of you!"[1] Charlotte said crossly. "I already have a l'yer. I'll have him contact Harcourt mediatley. And I'll take you to the cleaners. I will. I swear I will."

"Would it be possible to get you to co-operate for an annulment?" he said quickly, ignoring her threat to fleece him.

"What?" she looked aghast.

"Just think about it if you would."

The meal was served, and Jude did his best to carry on a semblance of a conversation during the remainder of their time together. Charlotte seemed to have lost any interest in talking. She plowed into her sandwich and ordered a fifth drink. Jude was relieved when he put her in a cab and sent her home.

The days seemed to creep by in a long-lasting parade. The routine was virtually the same. Up at six, breakfast at seven with Lulu and sometimes Brie, a sit-down in her office, Mass at nine, and spiritual direction appointments following. And, of course, the calls coming in to fill the schedule, and a list of other duties, all were what filled her days. When supper came at six, she couldn't wait to lock herself away in her room for some quiet and peace.

At supper, Brie and Lulu usually chatted nonstop. Benedicta made an effort to join in, but more and more, she craved quiet.

No Jude around. She ached to see him, to hear some word of him. He had taken a trip, she heard from the Chancery, from Edmund Wise. "A trip out of the country," said Edmund Wise vaguely.

She wanted to see him, to hear his voice, to be held in his arms.

She found herself becoming irritable at the least infraction of her rules. Brie was her main target: "Brie you are late." "Brie, you are not doing that right." "Brie, when will you learn?" It went on and on. At the same time, she breathed a sigh of relief that her sister was safe. She was pleased with her sister's steady progress. Her sewing classes were going well. Brie was taking a class in conversational French at the Y now. She hadn't ever done that before.

"Are you aware of how much better you are?" Benedicta asked Brie one day.

"Oh, I don't know. I still have bad moods, I hear voices some. Nothing like earlier but they are still a part of my life. Much as I hate to admit it," she rolled some of the yarn she was using to make an afghan, and continued, "it has been a life saver for me to come to Pinecroft. I have you to thank for that."

Benedicta was grateful to hear Brie's thoughts about coming to Pinecroft. It confirmed her belief in the power to heal.

The situation was improved by everyone in the household assisting Brie. The group remained diplomatic about Jude's absence. They said very little.

Brie had an unexpected visitor one day, Wooley, from the hospital. He didn't stay all that long. When Benedicta asked about the visit, Brie was noncommittal. "He seemed to be checking up on me," was all she would say on the subject.

Benedicta was glad that Brie was fitting in at the center, and she was happy she had friends. There was something about Wooley however, she couldn't quite put her finger on. Something, she didn't know what, was wrong. It was about his demeanor. Mostly though, she gave it very little thought.

In the meantime, Benedicta was lonely and missed Jude. One day, Benedicta tried to talk with Lulu about Jude. They commiserated with each other.

"I'm wishing you would just call him," said Lulu. "I know you want to, he would be relieved to hear from you."

"Where do I call? He's out of the country, remember?"

"Well, write him a letter. You two have just got to connect back up. It is a different situation with me entirely. No comparison. I know how much you miss him. I can see it."

Benedicta went to her office, sat and typed, "I miss you ever so much. Where are you now? When you get back, let's get together. Love, Benedicta." She sealed the envelope, affixed the stamp, then changed her mind, and disposed of the letter. She would wait; he was in her prayers. Something would bring them together again, she just knew it.

One early July evening, Lulu and Benedicta were walking the back edge of the property, on the trail leading around the lake. As they emerged from the thicket into the soft dusk, Benedicta saw a man standing in the front yard of Pinecroft. She stopped and put her hand out to Lulu who had been speaking.

"What's wrong, Benedicta?"

"Look! There in the yard, someone. I don't recognize him. I can't see him clearly."

When the man saw that they spied him, he turned and started running toward the roadway.

Benedicta called Inspector Brown. "This is why you must go out in pairs," warned the inspector. "I will notify the detail in the area to keep checking on your place."

The next day a call came.

"Listen girlie, ya and ya sister are gonna make me mad. And ya don wanna do that. When I'm mad, I am dangerous. Do ya understand?"

"You are a coward and a liar. Why should I believe anything you tell me?" Benedicta tersely replied.

The time was coming when she would regret these words.

She called Inspector Brown immediately. *By now this has become a habit,* she thought, then she gave thanks that the inspector took her seriously.

When she had Inspector Brown on the line, she gave him all the details. "He is threatening you two, so don't venture out at night and know each other's whereabouts at all times. Remember, be cautious."

She missed Jude as things on the home front escalated.

Her answer was to stay busy, and to wipe out her thinking at night with sleep. Except, Jude invaded her dreams. His hugs, his kisses, his comforting words, never left her for long.

One morning things came to a head. She was in her office, Brie came to the door.

"What are you up to, Benie?" asked Brie.

"I'm working. What does it look like?" Benedicta said sharply, then she caught herself as she saw the look of hurt on Brie's face.

"Oh, honey, I'm so sorry. Really, I am. Too much going on, I think."

"It is okay, Benie," said Brie, and she added philosophically, "everyone has a hard day now and again."

She had had a string of bad days, Benedicta realized with chagrin.

Chapter Sixteen

Benedicta had no idea what the evening held in store for her and for those at Pinecroft as she worked in her office late one night. Things had been going well. A routine was established and Brie was thriving. No incidents had come up, at least for a while. And her desire for Jude was still there but seemed less urgent.

It was well after 10 p.m. Benedicta had already locked up the house and was sequestered in her tiny office working on a schedule on the typewriter. Baby slumbered at her feet. From time to time, the dog would jump up and growl, growing restless. Benedicta turned on the lights outside and peered into the darkness. She saw nothing amiss. She returned to her typing and ignored Baby when he sniffed and pawed.

Suddenly the lights flickered, the window unit air conditioner sputtered, went off, and the lights dimmed again as darkness fell in the room.

"Goodness, what a time for the electric to go off," exclaimed Benedicta, "I'll have to go see about the circuit breaker in the basement." Heading for the hall, she stopped momentarily to rummage in her desk drawer for a flashlight and started for the basement. Lulu met her in the hall, candle in hand.

"Be careful on those steps," warned Lulu, holding onto Baby and standing at the head of the steps just in case Benedicta needed her. Baby was growling and growing restless.

Benedicta warily descended the steep basement steps. Suddenly she stopped mid-flight. Intuition told her that there was trouble below, something was amiss. She heard Baby growl once again. Treading carefully now, flashlight in hand, Benedicta took one deliberate step after another. Her alarm rising, she made her way down the staircase. The steps creaked a warning.

Reaching the bottom of the steps and the entryway to the basement, her anxiety increased as she flashed her light into the dimness and shadowy darkness of the room. Suddenly, a big, heavy arm was about her neck, pinning her in a choke hold, and pressing her down against his torso. She gurgled. "No, don't," she tried to say but it came out as a mumble. The arm squeezed tightly against her throat all but cutting off her breathing.

She and her assailant scuffled. She thought desperately, *I'm going to pass out.* He tightened his grip. She choked and sputtered. He now thrust his foot between her legs to throw her off balance and topple her, she fought to stay aright, as she smelled his sour breath and gagged.

At the same time, Lulu showed up in the entranceway. Baby charged down the steps with Lulu, barking and growling in a menacing manner as he reached the landing. A look of horror passed over Lulu's face at what she was seeing. Without wavering, she pulled a pair of scissors from her pocket, and brandished the scissors like a weapon. Lulu struck the assailant on the shoulder time and again, the sharp point of the scissors digging into the soft flesh.

While Lulu was stabbing the assailant, Baby was biting at the attacker's legs, thighs, and butt.

Blood spurted from the torn tissue on the man's shoulder. The intruder yelped, loosening his hold on Benedicta, and holding his hand over his wounded shoulder, he retreated toward the outside door. "Damn lady, you almost killed me. And you sic that monster dog on me one more time and it is all over for him." Limping and bleeding, he moved toward the door. "I'll be back you damn bitch, you can count on it." And the door closed behind him.

Baby suddenly stopped barking, sensing that the danger was over. An air of stillness descended on the basement. "Benedicta, are you all right? Who was that? What has just happened?" A confused Lulu sputtered into the darkness.

Benedicta picked up the flashlight from where it had landed on the floor and peered into the darkness before her. The scene looked chaotic. Chairs were toppled, a lamp was shattered, stuffing was pulled from the couch as if it had been grasped in a powerful battle, but worse, there was blood, a lot of blood.

The stuffing from the couch was wet, the cushions, and the adjacent carpet suggested violence had occurred here. Stains of blood were apparent everywhere. A dim trail of reddish brown tracks led across the floor to the side door.

There had been a fight here and it had been messy. Benedicta immediately thought of Brie. There was no one else in the house, she could think of no other explanation. "Where's Brie?" A panicked Benedicta asked the question they were both thinking. A search of the interior of the house ensued, but no Brie. If she had been the target of this fight, she had not gone willingly.

Why hadn't someone heard the commotion? Baby had given her clues. She hadn't followed up on any idea of an intruder as she could have. Scratch marks on the door gave another indication that Brie had not gone peacefully.

Twenty minutes later, Inspector Brown with a huge police-issued flashlight in one hand and crime scene tape in the other, was beginning to cordon off the area. Lulu and Benedicta stood on the lower steps, both perplexed and tortured.

Brie was gone. A second search of the house had confirmed the suspicion. No one had seen or heard anything. But Sister Anne, who had come in just after the scuffle, had something to report. "I, I came in and the house was dark, I surmised everyone was in bed, but I thought it odd that the porch light was not on. And, when I drove in, there was a truck parked a few yards away on the roadway, just short of the drive into Pinecroft. Do you think? Do you think—?"

She was interrupted by the inspector who remarked, "No doubt about it, that truck was his. Did you happen to see anyone, anything else unusual?"

"No," said Sister Anne, "Nothing at all, I am afraid."

Benedicta was grief stricken that her sister was gone. Between sobs, she said, "It looks like she may have been hurt. We don't know the extent of her injuries. Let's pray the injuries were minor, that it was nothing serious, but oh, this is worrisome. We have to find them quickly. She will be without her medicine. And she won't be in good shape without it."

"We'll do everything we can. We'll check the hospitals, we'll check the airport and train station and bus terminal. And we'll put out a missing person's alert."

Benedicta spoke up, "I just tried to reset the circuit breaker but nothing works. He must have damaged it. What was that about do you think?"

"He or they were probably going to take you as well as your sister. It was a ruse to get you down here, maybe."

Benedicta shuddered. "If it had not been for Lulu and her quick thinking, I don't know what would have happened," said a trembling Benedicta.

"The perp sure underestimated the two of you," said Inspector Brown patting her shoulder.

"I'll call the electric company. Is there anything I can do for you, Inspector?"

The inspector was making notes in his notebook, and now flipped it closed, putting it in his pocket, saying, "Ladies, I will have a detail at your doorstep for the night. Lock your doors and check the locks on the windows. And remember to leave in pairs and know where everyone is."

Perplexed, bewildered and heartbroken that Brie had been taken, Benedicta locked up as the inspector left the premises.

Brie lay in the bed of an old black Ford pickup truck, her hands tied behind her back. She was lying under a tarp, struggling to get free, as she tried to comprehend what was transpiring. Since being forced into the truck at gunpoint last night, blindfolded, and her hands tied, she had faced this danger with all the courage she could muster.

The ride was rough, jolting her stiff body, that body hot and sweaty under the tarp. The August heat was stifling and no less so for Brie. She was thirsty and hungry, her mouth parched. *Is he going to starve me?* Brie thought desperately. She hadn't been given any food or water since they had begun driving last evening.

I wonder where we're headed, she thought. *We didn't stay long at that flea trap of a motel. What is going to happen? Will he kill me as he threatened? I DON'T WANT TO DIE.* She wanted to scream those words out loud to anyone who would hear. *Anything,* she thought. "Help me now," she muttered.

And I don't have my meds. What am I going to do without them?

The truck jerked to a stop. A scruffy man in fatigues, with a beard and a bandanna over his face, roughly pulled her, half dragging her, from the truck.

"Ya can go to that bathroom in thar, if you want. I'll fill up on gas and get us some snacks," he growled, and pushed her ahead to the bathroom. "And don't try any funny stuff," he warned her.

He is attending to my needs, she thought ruefully. When she returned from the bathroom, he said, "Ya can sit up here in the cab of the truck, it is cooler, and ya can eat some of this stash of snacks. Here is a cold drink." He shoved a Coke into her hand and threw her a bag of chips and a candy bar. She accepted the snacks readily. *At least he isn't going to make me starve.*

"And you get to be free and sit up here as long as you behave," he opened the door of the cab of the truck, pushed her inside, and locked her in.

––––––––––––––––

Well, finally, something is takin place. I got one of em. I'll have to be careful though, no mess-ups. Those women are stronger then I woulda given em credit fer. I wasn't planning on gittin caught. No more mistakes.

"I want to find my sister." Benedicta sat in Agatha's office on Tuesday, her third visit in a week. "I don't like this, don't like it at all. This is a crime, isn't it? Kidnapping someone is a crime, a Federal crime?"

The weather was hot and humid. Agatha went to the window air conditioner and adjusted the controls, turning it to full force. A blast of cold air was emitted from the unit in the window.

Benedicta sat kneading a handkerchief in her hands, almost unaware of her surroundings, it seemed. Her hair was matted and in need of combing, as if it had not been brushed today. Worry lines were etched on her forehead. She had on no make-up and was wearing dark clothes, despite the summer heat.

Unconsciously, Benedicta opened the top buttons of her blouse, and looked at Agatha, speaking once more. "It is so warm, I am afraid Brie is suffering because of the weather. Does heat make her condition worse?" She looked with a haggard expression at Agatha, her eyes reflecting her state of mind; they were dark, blood-shot, unfocused.

"Benedicta, at the moment it is you who concerns me most. For Brie's sake and your own, you've got to take charge here. Stress can do a number on us, and I can look at you and tell how you are feeling. I can bet you are not sleeping, not getting any exercise, not eating meals—" She was interrupted by Benedicta.

"How do you know all of that about me? It is true, but how am I to go on when I know Brie is in danger?" She pushed her hair back from her face and rubbed her eyes.

"Well, Missy, you go on because you must go on. And you take care of yourself because you will be no good for her, or anyone else, including yourself, unless you make an effort here." Agatha watched Benedicta closely, continuing, "At the moment, you have no control over what is happening to your sister, Benedicta. Sorry, but you do not. You can, however, make a conscious choice to care for yourself. Then, when Brie is back in your life, you will be ready for what comes."

A silence ensued. Agatha made no effort to pick up the slack. Finally, Benedicta took a deep breath and said, "What can I do?"

"You can eat three meals a day and if it is too much, eat smaller meals more frequently. Go for a walk every day, walk farther each time. Get a partner to go with you. See if you can enjoy the walk. Yes, I said enjoy yourself. Just a few hours at a time. Do something good for yourself that you will enjoy."

"And," as if an afterthought, she jotted something down on her notepad, and said, "Get some sleep. I will call your medical doctor and ask him to order you a sleeping medication. Here is the name of it. And Benedicta, as my grandmother used to say, 'This too shall pass.' This is not the end, though it may seem so. You've got to see you have a life. No matter what comes, have a life, then you will be ready."

Benedicta went to the window and looked down at the park. Strollers were there, moms pushing baby carts, a couple holding hands, some, leisurely sitting on benches, the world went on. She was being asked to do the same.

"I know your words to be wise ones. They are the truth. I will try."

"No, trying doesn't cut it. I want a commitment." Agatha was no nonsense in this situation.

"Okay, I will do it. I will take care of myself.

Benedicta left Agatha's office full of resolve. When she reached Pinecroft, she went to the kitchen and took the makings of a fruit salad out of the fridge. She made a fruit plate and dished up some yogurt. Taking a tray with the food, she went to her office and sat in one of the wing chairs and tried to enjoy eating. She was surprised at how good it felt and how tasty the dish really was

Benedicta then went upstairs and took a shower and shampooed her hair. She wondered what to wear; she went to her closet and selected a pink top and navy shorts. After dressing, she applied some make-up. Benedicta looked at herself in the mirror.

Her face glowed from the hot shower and the use of a moisturizer. Soft curls fell about the nape of her neck. She needed a haircut, she realized, but she looked immeasurably better. Yes, Agatha was right, she needed to care for herself or she would be no good for Brie or herself.

After taking a nap, Benedicta went looking for Lulu. She felt a special bond with her these days. Lulu was without Jake, she without Jude.

"Lulu, I just realized, after a firm talking to by Agatha, that I am doing myself and everyone else no good by moping about the house. It won't do at all. It isn't going to help Brie if I am depressed."

"Oh, that is music to my ears," said a delighted Lulu. "I've been so concerned about you," she added.

She and Lulu made a plan to exercise together each day, either with a walk, or a trip to the Y.

"I just wish I knew she was alive, that she is okay," said Benedicta mournfully.

"Benedicta, do you have any idea of anything that might help Brie now?"

"Yes, I do," said Benedicta. "I know, and this might sound terrible, but Brie has had experience with street people, with those down and out. She knows how to befriend them. I can't help but think this trait may help her stay alive."

For days afterward, Benedicta made a special effort with her appearance, with getting extra sleep, with her diet, with exercise. And she had to admit she felt better; her worry was more manageable.

~~~~~

Chapter Seventeen

Yet, Benedicta remained terrified. She had an intuition that her sister would be found alive, but despite that sense of certainty, it wasn't happening soon enough. Ten days since the kidnapping, and they had heard nothing from Brie or the perpetrator. Inspector Brown stood in the office facing Benedicta, who sat before her desk. Today his hands remained in his pockets. He still had a frown on his forehead.

"We're doing everything we can. We just haven't found any leads, but we'll find her," said the inspector, and continued, "I promise. Now could I have a second article of clothing for another fresh scent? We may be using dogs this afternoon, and we want to be ready, standard procedure really."

"I just wish I knew for certain she is alive," said Benedicta, handing him a blouse of Brie's.

"We'll be in touch," said the inspector and left.

———————————————

They know, he thought pensively, stabbing the knife in his hand vehemently into the wood in front of him. *They must be shut up, for good. It's the only way.*

I have captured the younger one. I will hide out till I know jist how to do this....to take the next step. Yeah, that is what I will do. I don't really wanna hurt em but they must be silenced. They know too much. I can't have them spillin the beans.

Brie was having a hard time of it. She had barely eaten all day, those snacks she had early this morning had helped but now she was famished and needed a meal. They had been traveling west, if the signs on the road indicated anything. She was hot and sweaty and tired. But she couldn't let on about her growing fatigue, she needed to have all of her senses ready for anything that happened.

The perp is wasting no time staying in any one place. We have just stopped for the night at a flea bag motel somewhere in Kansas, she thought. Thinking about her situation, she figured her only hope was to befriend her kidnapper. Toward that end, she began carrying on a running conversation with the perp.

"Where are we headed?" she asked now.

"None of your damn business," he snapped at her.

"I was wondering," she continued, undaunted, "if I could be a help with the map. You know, ride shotgun, so to speak, and give directions."

"That is right kindly of ya, but naw, I can manage," he said now, but softened his tone of voice.

"You know they are searching for us. They could find us before nightfall," she said now, unable to keep the fear at bay.

"They are not going to know that we tore out across country. I figure we have a head start on em. Well, I think we need to eat some lunch or somethin, before I fall into a faint." He turned off the main highway and into a truck stop down the road. "Look, if you keep yer mouth shut, and don't give off any signals, ya kin go in and eat, but if ya make one peep, yer done fer, understan?"

"Yes, yes, I get it. You don't need to worry about me," she said at once, again attempting to befriend the kidnapper.

"Good, then le's go, git out of the truck."

Brie scrambled down from the truck and headed toward the Sunny Side Up Restaurant, where the lunch specials were posted on the window. Her mouth watered, she was ready for just about anything to eat.

"I goin int that thar bathroom, I want t see ya sittin right thar when I git back, understand?"

"Sure, I will be here," she said quickly, and headed toward a booth close to the men's restroom.

When he returned, Brie was looking at the menu. The waitress had brought water and was coming back for their orders.

"The waitress said she'd be right back," Brie offered now to the perp.

"Okay dokie. Now what's fer lunch?"

Benedicta had settled down some since her last visit to Agatha. That visit was on Tuesday, today was the following Monday, the third week since the disappearance.

She sat now in Agatha's office. Agatha was dressed in a silky-looking blouse and pants. The blouse was white with lace around the collar; the pants were lavender. She had on flats and had a ribbon tying back her hair. She looked, as always, beautiful.

A cool front had come through last evening. The temperature was more bearable, upper 80's.

Benedicta had walked daily, she told Agatha now. And she had eaten a good meal every evening since her last visit. She informed Agatha that she had even tried to meditate and found her prayers more peaceful. She was getting a better night's sleep. Somehow, they would find Brie; she was beginning to believe that again.

Once home, Benedicta went to her office to make out a schedule for the coming week. The phone rang and she answered it, distracted, "Pinecroft House of Peace, Benedicta here."

The voice on the other end was familiar. Benedicta jerked to attention, gasping. "Brie, Brie, is that you? Are, are you all right? Are you hurt? "

"Yes, I am okay, and no, I am not hurt," she whispered, then continued, "I am in a bathroom in a restaurant. There is a phone in here. I only have a minute before he begins missing me." For a brief moment, there was silence on the phone. Benedicta fought her feelings, trying to keep calm. Then Brie spoke again, "Take this down quickly, the license for a black Ford pickup truck, Ohio license XL 5840."

Benedicta jotted down the number, then interrupted her, "Is it really you, I can't believe it, Oh Brie, I am so glad he has not hurt you!" Her heart did a flip flop. *It is Brie. She is alive, thank God, she is alive,* thought Benedicta.

"Did you take down the number? Do you think," Brie said now, "I mean, can they find me with that information? We just came into Kansas. He has roughed me up but he hasn't hurt me. He frightens me. It is hard, you know?"

"Brie, where are you exactly?"

"Oh, Benie, I have to go. I hear someone coming," and the phone was dead.

Benedicta went immediately to call Inspector Brown. He was not in his office. The inspector had given her his private number. Now where was it? She rooted through her desk drawer and finally found the card with the number scribbled on it.

"Inspector Brown, I have just talked with my sister. She is okay but is having a hard time of it." She relayed the license number of the black Ford.

"Great work. Did she say any more about where she was?"

"No, she suddenly ended the conversation. If she calls back I will get the information."

"This may help us. Good work," the inspector said and rang off.

Benedicta followed up with a few moments in the chapel in thanksgiving for Brie being alive.

Sitting in a restaurant in a roadside truck stop, Brie was left alone at the table, and saw her chance to act. Taking a napkin, she wrote in lipstick from her pocket: "Help, I have been kidnapped, call the police." Brie put the napkin with the message on top of the dirty dishes, and sat back, as her captor returned to the table with two roast beef dinners.

"Well, let's eat while it is hot," said the perp, setting Brie's food in front of her.

The waitress came to remove the dirty dishes. "Hot, ain't it i?" remarked the waitress. Brie held her breath. The waitress put the napkin in the bin, never once glancing at the writing, and with that, she left. The waitress had not seen the message.

Brie sighed. It was just a shot after all.

"Inspector," her voice was shrill, the words coming out in rapid fire, "We've got to find her, she will be off her medicine now for four weeks. She needs this medicine."

Benedicta felt a sense of panic clawing at her. Her pulse was bounding, her thoughts racing. She, Benedicta, had been so confident on Monday when in Agatha's office, now she was unsure and befuddled once again. She had only one thing on her mind, to find Brie, and find her alive.

She continued her conversation with the inspector. "For her mental health, she needs the medicine. I spoke with my psychologist. She says how Brie would fare without medication is strictly individual. She may be unable to function or she may slowly become depressed. One thing is sure, the sooner we find her the better."

Benedicta sat in her office. The inspector sat facing her. He listened empathetically. Benedicta went on, "It endangers her health being off of her drugs. We must find her now."

Taking a deep breath, and choking back panic, she lowered the tone of her voice, slowed down, and continued, more subdued, "I figure things are getting bad by now. And the longer she is with him, the greater the danger."

"I understand Ms. Malloy, honestly I do, and we will find her. It takes time, and patience. We are doing everything we can."

"Is there any word on finding the truck?"

The inspector ran his fingers through his hair, nodded, saying, "Yes, yes, there has been. I just did not want to tell you this news. We found the truck, in Kansas. It was stolen here in Ohio. The truck had been left, there must have been a fire in the truck, and, and," he added slowly, "there was a body in the bed of the vehicle. We have forensics working on it now. The body was too badly burned; we couldn't make any sort of identification. We may want to compare dental records. Could, could you give me the name of Brie's dentist?"

The sense of panic intensified. Benedicta felt a pain in her gut, and a knot in her throat. "Do, do you think it is Brie?" She was reminded of her brother and his death. Her mind traveled back to that time. *I was panicked then as well.* Benedicta gripped the arms of her chair now. She felt herself sinking into a black hole. She fought back the feeling, trying to fathom this new turn of events, trying to understand.

Coming back to the present, Benedicta eyed the inspector. The inspector shook his head and said, "I doubt it, really I do. More likely it is a drifter they gave a ride to, but we will know shortly."

"I thought we had him, I thought we would find them."

"He must have heard her tell you the license number and ditched the truck. That is a possibility and the only thing I can think of." The inspector rose now to leave, "We will be in touch," he said and was gone.

They drove straight through the next day and into the evening, in their new stolen vehicle, a newer model Dodge truck. It had a bigger cab and more leg room.

"Just where are we headed?" asked Brie, as they made their way across country.

"Ya ask too many damn questions," the perp said, frowning and taking a chew on his tobacco.

"I am just trying to make conversation. I am a little homesick for my sister and my friends. Do you have family or friends that you miss?"

"Naw. Good riddance to them, I say," he said now, passing another truck and veering back into the curb side lane.

"Would it be possible for me to call my sister, let her know I am all right? You could monitor the call, I wouldn't give anything away," asked Brie, opening a wrapper of a candy bar and taking a bite.

"That ain't gonna happen, sis. I can imagine ya being a bit homesick as ya say, but there is nuttin to be done bout it. Now git all those thoughts outta yur head." The perp honked at a slow-moving vehicle, and did another swerve to go around the car, yelling at the driver as he made the swerve.

Brie went on asking questions, trying to get to know her captor. *I am making some headway*, she thought, *he is not shutting me down.*

She was going to do it now. Benedicta had been planning to do this for weeks. *Heaven knows it needs doing,* she thought. There just had been so much going on, no time was a good time. Benedicta directed her car along Michigan Ave. A few minutes later, she entered her mother's room at Marjorie P. Lee Nursing Home.

Lydia Malloy sat in her Lazy Boy recliner, watching TV and eating from a bag of chocolates in her lap. The TV was blaring. Benedicta made an effort to talk above the noise.

"Why are you interrupting my soaps? Couldn't you have picked a better time?"

"Don't worry, Mom," she almost shouted, "I can't stay very long." She was almost glad to have an excuse to leave early.

"Mom," she cleared her throat and plunged in, "I have something to tell you. Please try not to be too upset." Confiscating the remote, she lowered the volume. "Brie is missing," she said, "She's been kidnapped."

"Don't turn down that volume!" thundered her mother, seeming to ignore her announcement.

"Mom, stop!" Her hands shook as she spoke, and tears welled in her eyes. "Did you not hear what I said? Brie is missing. She could well be in danger."

"Yes, I heard you. What am I supposed to do about it?" her mother said, reaching for the remote and turning back up the volume on 'General Hospital.'

"I, I thought you'd want to know," Benedicta said, wiping tears from her eyes. It was at this moment that Benedicta realized just how bad off her mom was. She guessed that she had dementia.

"Well, I don't," her mom was saying. "Let the police worry about her. That is their job."

Benedicta shook her head. She was disappointed. Benedicta noticed the pile of newspapers stacked on a table. She asked her mom, "Do you want me to take these newspapers and throw them out?"

"You could," remarked her mom, not paying her much attention.

Benedicta went to pick up the stack to put them in her car. An old dog-eared notebook fell out of the pile.

"Mom," Benedicta asked, "do you want this notebook? It was in with the papers." She picked it up and opened it. It was filled with her mom's handwriting. Her mom seemed to ignore the question.

"Mom, what is this?" Benedicta leafed through the aged notebook.

"What's what? Oh that. It is an old diary. I was reading about the time of the fire. You can have it if you want."

Benedicta gasped. What she read in the notebook was of vital interest to her.

"Could I borrow this, Mom?"

"Sure, sure, now let me watch this program in peace."

Benedicta put the book in her bag and left. When she reached home, Benedicta changed clothes. She put on shorts and a halter top and went outside to sit on a bench under the trees. It was humid and hot, unseasonably warm for late September, but a little breeze was blowing. And she felt the need to be close to nature.

Opening the book, she again saw her mom's slanted, even script filling the pages. Glancing more closely, she read from the diary: "Their father is not attentive—he is never even around. But I have found a way to get even. With perks, you might say."

And another entry dated a week before the fire: "He has been here every evening this week. We are doing it on the sly. No one is the wiser. And all of this is harmless for sure." And another entry with a blurred date, "His name is Wooley, he is my kind of guy. A little young, but heck, I like them young."

Benedicta blinked. Could it really be that simple? Was the Wooley who was mentioned in her mom's diary the same Wooley who had been a patient at the hospital with Brie, who lived in her apartment building? Her mind was racing, her thoughts were wild as she read the remainder of the entry.

She re-entered the house and called Inspector Brown. She would make an appointment for this afternoon if possible, for this kind of information couldn't wait. And she would make an appointment with Agatha.

The following morning, having talked with the inspector the evening before, Benedicta entered the office of Agatha Forest.

Agatha was dressed in a lavender jumpsuit and a matching print jacket. She looked the picture of the professional she was. Today, Benedicta was ready for her. Her hair was stylishly cut, makeup in place, her nails painted with a pink frosting, and wearing a pale blue pantsuit, she sailed into the office and offered Agatha her hand.

Agatha looked at Benedicta as she poured the tea. "Is this the new you? You look—different, calmer, prettier, even."

Benedicta smiled.

"I take that as a compliment. I must say thanks for your kind words. I realize something I haven't realized before. I haven't trusted my own instincts. The key was right here in front of me all this time." Benedicta rose from the leather chair and went to the window, glancing down at the skating rink and the intersection beyond. Cars were buzzing past, people were hurrying about. They were safe. She wanted her sister safe, too.

"I realize now I have been reacting to the kidnapping rather than responding," said Benedicta, still looking down on the city below. "And I haven't been trusting. Oh, I have put my trust in the Lord because I have had to, and I have made progress there, but I have felt so suspicious and afraid.

"I know who the man in the dream was. And I know who is responsible for Brie's disappearance. It is one and the same man."

She returned to her seat and made herself comfortable.

"Well, this is news, indeed," Agatha said, excitement in her voice.

"The man who kidnapped Brie was visiting my mom the week of the fire, years ago. I am certain of this information. And all this time he was right under our noses. The man who kidnapped Brie is Wooley Catrell, alias Wooley Castle, also known as Wilson Catrell."

She let the words she was speaking sink in before continuing, "You see, he was in the hospital with Brie, and he lived in her building. I knew he looked familiar when I was introduced to him at the hospital, but I didn't put it together until I got ahold of my mom's diary."

"Wow," was all Agatha said.

Benedicta couldn't hold back the news any longer, she wanted it all out. "He has a rap sheet. He is wanted right now for aggravated assault and robbery in Indiana, and car theft in Kentucky, plus the Ford he stole here in Ohio." She paused, smiling, "I know, because I went down to the police station late yesterday afternoon and worked with a photographer. From the

185

picture I was able to give, the police identified him in their mug books."

Benedicta briefly described her mom's diary and what was in it.

"Oh, Benedicta, you are so close to finding your sister, ever so close," said Agatha now, pouring more tea.

"And that's not all. I have convinced Inspector Brown to allow me to accompany him on the search. I have been in touch with Jude. He is willing, eager even, to go with me. And he has a private plane at his disposal."

Agatha was shocked. She laughed and asked, "How did you ever manage that?"

"Let's just say I twisted the inspector's arm. You see I have connections. I know the governor from school days. It never hurts to name drop, you know."

"Oh, Benedicta, you are priceless. But on a serious note, you know to be cautious, don't you?" There was fear in Agatha's voice.

"Of course, and this time, we are going to find and bring back my sister. I am sure of it."

Chapter Eighteen

As the plane landed in a small airport on the edge of Denver and taxied to a smooth stop, Benedicta tried to collect her thoughts while gathering her bag and purse. *We must find Brie, and soon. Time is running out.* Stumbling down the steps of the single engine plane and stepping on firm ground, Benedicta felt her confidence soar. *We are so close to finding Brie and getting her release,* thought Benedicta. *It can't come soon enough,* was the following thought.

"Come on Benedicta. Let's get a rental car and meet up with Inspector Brown and the others," said Jude, hurrying her along.

An hour later, they entered a plain but clean room in a small motel northwest of Denver. Unpacking the few things she had in her carry-all, she sat on the bed waiting. A knock on the door, Inspector Brown had arrived. He was an early bird if there ever was one.

Benedicta greeted the plain clothes detective, making introductions.

The inspector set down the ground rules immediately: "You are both to stay back as far as necessary to be safe. That is nonnegotiable, you understand? And I have met the sheriff, Sheriff Daniels. He is going to accompany us and provide for a detail of three men. We'll get more if we require them.

"Sheriff Daniels has also made it clear that he is ultimately the person in charge," said the inspector, "this is out of my jurisdiction. We can act in accordance with his directions, but he calls the shots. And he has informed me, if you all try anything risky, like going out on your own, you will get a one-way plane ticket back to Ohio. Is that clear?"

"Perfectly," agreed Benedicta, and Jude nodded his head.

"We've tracked them to a cabin up in the mountains. They're staying there, at night anyway. It is an out of the way spot, a not much traveled or populated area. Kind of a remote area. We'll go in at dawn, surprise him. It cuts down on danger to your sister."

"I appreciate that Inspector," Benedicta said, bringing coffee from the coffee pot supplied by room service. "Anything you can do to provide more safety for Brie, I am in favor of."

"And I want to urge you again, do not take any unnecessary risks," the inspector removed a pipe and tobacco from his jacket pocket, but did not light up. Instead he filled the pipe and positioned the pipe in his mouth, continuing to focus on the danger to Benedicta and Jude and Brie.

"Doing something impulsive would no doubt be unwise for the safety of your sister as well as for you two. The only way I am going forward with you in tow is if you cooperate to the full extent possible. Even at that, I have some reservations as to whether this will work."

"Yes, of course," Benedicta said. Sipping the hot coffee, Jude nodded once more.

They had planned to be at the site at 5 a.m. Dawn would be in about an hour. They had both gotten a restless night's sleep. Benedicta settled in the back seat of a van with Jude and Inspector Brown; the sheriff and one of his deputies sat up front. The sheriff was driving. Another van was following with the other two officers.

"It's up there, beyond that rise," said the sheriff. They topped the hill and saw to the left, a small wood frame cabin. The house was dark except for a faint light coming from the rear.

"Park here, we'll go the rest of the way on foot," the sheriff said over his shoulder. Then he squinted in the faint light and said, "That's funny, their truck is missing. It is supposed to be to the right of the cabin. That is where it was when the men scouted up here last night."

Struggling out of the Jeep, Benedicta felt that familiar tug of fear.

The inspector balled his hands in fists in frustration. "We've been outmaneuvered," he said.

Is this going to be a false lead? She would not panic, she told herself, and she stifled that edge of terror now so familiar. Better to stay calm, she realized.

As Benedicta walked toward the cabin, she let out a yelp.

"What is it Benedicta?" asked Jude, turning to her.

"I've twisted my ankle, I think." Wincing in pain, she hobbled a few steps forward. Jude put out his arm to steady her. With some difficulty, Benedicta followed the others up to the cabin, where they hid in the bushes.

"It doesn't look as if they are here," said the sheriff. A thorough search of the property produced no results. "It looks like they either got spooked or they have another place to stay," said Inspector Brown.

"We can't just leave here without them," Benedicta cried out, frightened once again and disturbed by the lack of progress. Her ankle hurt like mad.

"We will find them, don't you worry, sister. We're not giving up. No sirree. We'll leave a uniformed guard here. If they come back, we'll know it," said the sheriff.

"In the meantime, you can go back to the motel and get that ankle iced," said Inspector Brown

Inspector Brown dropped them off at the motel. As they were settling into sleep, the inspector called. "They have returned to the cabin. The men are waiting for us," he said.

"We'll take our rental car and meet you. Seriously, it will be quicker," said Jude. Hanging up the phone, he picked up a knapsack and a water bottle, and helped Benedicta to the door.

"This time we'll get them," he said, "just wait and see."

They hid in the bushes with the officers. There was indeed a truck in the drive next to the cabin. It was now almost 8 a.m. The sheriff and Inspector Brown arrived.

"You two wait here, we'll advance on them." said the sheriff, moving forward.

But they had been spotted. The door of the cabin swung open. A man in scruffy fatigues was half dragging a woman, her hands behind her back; they came bounding out, heading for the truck.

"Stop there," shouted the sheriff, raising his gun.

The man in fatigues roughly threw the woman into the bed of the truck and opened the door to the driver's side. The sheriff raised his weapon and fired at the ruffian. The truck backed up as the sheriff fired a second and third shot at the tires of the truck but missed.

"Quick, into the Jeep," shouted the sheriff. Inspector Brown, Benedicta and Jude squeezed into the back, while the sheriff and a deputy occupied the front seat.

The Jeep with the law enforcement officers, Benedicta and Jude, tore down the road in hot pursuit of the truck. The sheriff said in excitement, "Look there, ahead, they're veering off onto a side road, we'll follow them," The sheriff's utility vehicle followed, swerving and making the turn.

Dust flew and covered the path, obscuring any view they might have had. Tree limbs brushed and scraped against the sides of their vehicle. They could barely see out of the window, never mind seeing anything in the distance. Coughing and sputtering, they put wet handkerchiefs to their mouths and noses. The vehicle lurched forward, then barely inched along.

Out of nowhere, they hit a snag. The inspector shouted over the noise of the motor, "Be careful, watch out. Stop the Jeep. There are boulders in the road. This may be a trick." The sheriff hit the brakes and sent the vehicle screeching. They came to an abrupt stop.

"The trail leads in that direction," said the deputy. They advanced on. As the dust settled, they saw an old one-way bridge directly ahead. The bridge was mangled, mainly rusted out. They proceeded cautiously, preparing to cross the bridge,

"Wait, wait," shouted the deputy in the front seat, attempting to warn the sheriff. "I think this bridge was partially washed out by a flood up here a while ago."

"Glad you told me. I remember hearing something about that. We could have been killed. Good work," said the sheriff, nodding at the deputy.

Emerging from the Jeep, they saw that indeed a part of the bridge was gone. Benedicta pushed down the panic inching up her spine. *What if the worst had happened? What if they had crossed that bridge? They would have been sent to the water below.* Her fearful thoughts assailed her.

Impulsively, she tore from Jude's grip, heading for the edge of the cliff where she peered into the water below. She wanted to see for herself.

"Look, there," said the sheriff, pointing directly down the cliff. "There it is. There is the wreckage of a truck. Maybe it is not from our perp, but we won't know until we inspect it, will we?"

Benedicta leaned over the edge for a better view. As she did so, she tottered on the brink, in danger of falling. Fatigue and fear had caught up with her. She flailed about, her arms tearing through the air like a bird flapping in the wind. And then, it happened. She shot over the edge.

Benedicta was frantic. In midair, her legs kicking, arms grabbing for anything to hold onto, she thought, *I have come to save my sister, and now it is going to be too late, I will die as I land below.*

Benedicta fell—and plopped on a stony ledge, some thirty feet below. She landed with a thud. Surprised by the sudden impact, she realized that she was still alive. Her backside had hit the stony precipice. Her back took the brunt of the fall; there was a sharp, pulsating pain in the midsection of her spine.

She could hear the others clamoring along, as they descended the side of the cliff to reach her. Jude was there first. "Honey, speak to me. Please, oh Benedicta, I should never have brought you out here." His hands were shaking as he attempted to see if she was all right, whether she had any broken bones.

Soon enough, real help came. The second Jeep had arrived and there was a full contingency of deputies now. And they lent their help. First, they came to determine the extent of her injuries, then to hoist her on a roughly made hammock, to firmer ground.

Inspector Brown was directing things above.

"Get her into the backseat of the Jeep. Be careful. Don't jostle her so. We want her in one piece so she can get to the hospital for treatment," he said now.

Benedicta objected, "No inspector, I don't need to go to the hospital, I want to find Brie. Please, let me find her," she let out a little wail from being moved.

"No ma'am. You are on your way to the ER." His voice was firm. Benedicta could tell even in her state of mind. "You may remain until we see what is down there, then off to the hospital with you."

Meanwhile, the sheriff and the deputies made their way down the slope. Some thirty minutes later they returned, shaking their heads in disbelief.

"That is not the truck we are looking for," the sheriff said, and advanced to the vehicle where Benedicta was lying propped up on the back seat. "This may be a lucky break for your sister. I don't see how they would have survived such an accident. You either, if that ledge had not broken your fall. I certainly hope you are not seriously injured."

Benedicta breathed in a momentary sigh of relief that her sister was not in the truck or the water below. Jude got in the driver's seat of the Jeep.

"We'll continue searching the trail in the other Jeep," said the sheriff. "Why don't you all return the way you came and go to the ER? I hope you're okay, ma'am. We'll let you know if there are any further developments." The sheriff now seemed to have regained energy and taken charge once more.

Inspector Brown, Jude, and Benedicta headed toward Denver to the nearest hospital. It was close to 5 p.m. The sun was beginning to set and dark clouds were forming in the western sky. It was going to storm.

Benedicta squirmed in the backseat of the Jeep. Her back ached in one spot and sharp pains were shooting out from another spot. She grimaced. She hurt from the new injury and her ankle was throbbing. Her head was spinning. *I am just weak from not having eaten,* she told herself.

Before her lay the unknown, with uncertainty as to whether they could find her sister alive. Benedicta had undergone periods of doubt and mounting fear before, even a sense of defeat, but this was different. It was so intense, and she did not have the energy to fight. The fear engulfed her as she lay in the back of the Jeep.

We will never find Brie. That thought hit Benedicta like a blow to the side of her head. *We must find Brie, we must,* she thought at last. "I'm going to be all right. I can tell already, nothing is wrong with my back," she said to the two men sitting up front. And mercifully, she drifted off to sleep.

A storm hit the mountains that night. Benedicta and Jude were just returning from the ER. A CT scan had shown no obvious injury to her spine, merely severe bruising of the tissue of her back. The ER staff had wrapped her ankle and given her something for pain. She was feeling much better. "That pain medicine set me on my ear," Benedicta said, with a giggle.

Two more days of waiting, two days of nerve chilling worry, praying for some miracle.

Benedicta and Jude said very little as they waited. Finally, she asked, "What is going to happen to her if we don't find them, Jude?" Benedicta wanted an answer to her worst fears.

"We've come too far now. We're in the vicinity, I can just feel it," said Jude, trying to be optimistic but at the same time he had renewed hope in the search.

"But we don't know—" her voice trailed off, and she looked beseechingly at Jude.

"Oh, Benedicta, you have faith. You believe in a God of mercy. You know a God who wants to give us only good things. Our search is not going to go unrewarded. We are going to find her and alive. I believe that with all my heart."

Inspector Brown called Benedicta at the motel Thursday afternoon. "We've got something on them. He used a credit card in a town not 50 miles from here. There is a lot of wooded area out that way, the sheriff tells me. We're headed toward that region now. We'll let you know immediately if we get a trace on them, okay? Don't come back now. Just stay put until I advise you," he added quickly.

Benedicta was reluctant to remain behind, but she knew she needed to keep her ankle iced and elevated and rest her back. She felt too tired to be of help, so she agreed.

Friday there was no news. Benedicta and Jude spent the time renewing their own friendship. They ironed out the problem of Jude's marriage, and its current effect on them. Benedicta was heartened that he was putting plans in place to ask the church for an annulment of his marriage. He felt he had serious grounds to declare that there had been no marriage in the eyes of the church.

Saturday, Inspector Brown called again. "Benedicta," he said, speaking in quick spurts, "we have a lead. It is not much but it is something. There was a hair clip found up in a canyon about a two-hour drive from the town. We need you to identify if it is Brie's. It is a long shot, for sure. Will you come out here or you want me to bring it to you?"

Benedicta sucked in her breath. She wanted a lead, God she did, but she was afraid this clue might mean Brie was in even greater danger. "Of course, we'll be there shortly."

"The clip is Brie's," Benedicta said when they finally joined Inspector Brown. "I bought it for her last Christmas."

"This clip found up in the hills is the only lead we have. We've enlisted volunteers. They are preparing to scour the canyon and go up into the surrounding countryside," said Inspector Brown, folding his hands in his pockets, and taking them out again.

"I'll join in," said Jude, and looking at Benedicta he said, "Benedicta, please, would you stay here?"

"No, I think not. My ankle feels like new and my back is on the mend. I want to go look, too. It is better than remaining here."

They went up on Sunday morning: Benedicta, Jude, Inspector Brown, and the sheriff and his three deputies. All day they scrambled through briers and brush, up rock quarries, and down into valleys. No further leads.

They rested in their vehicle that night. They had a supply of food and water and were prepared for an overnight stay. The group set out on the search again the next day.

They had been searching for hours. The sun was high and hot. It was about noon. Benedicta wanted a shower and breakfast. "I would die for a cup of fresh coffee and a doughnut," she said as they came up over a rise. "What is that up ahead?" asked Benedicta.

"It looks like that is the outpost that a trapper-turned-storekeeper runs up here. He doesn't have a lot of business. There aren't many folks in these parts, but for some reason, he stays put," said Sheriff Daniels.

"I think I'll get a cup of coffee. See if he has a pot on the stove. Want one, anyone?" asked Benedicta. All were in favor.

Benedicta traipsed up the hill and entered the cool, dusky quiet of the store. It wasn't much, a few bins loaded with vegetables, a long counter lined with candies, chips and sweets, a couple of shelves of canned goods, behind which were stored cigarettes and booze. A row of sodas sat on the floor, and what looked like some farm equipment was tossed in a corner.

"Hi," said Benedicta. "Are you the owner of this establishment?" asked Benedicta, trying to connect with the storekeeper. "Have you seen a bearded scruffy looking man, redhaired, probably in fatigues, accompanied by a woman in her thirties, a brunette, thin and attractive?" she asked the storekeeper.

"Nope," he said and spat into a spittoon in the corner of the store.

Disappointed, she turned around with her box of coffees, and was ready to leave.

The storekeeper spoke again, "I did see a man of that description though, he was alone." Spitting once more, he said, "Yeah, I saw a man, kinda lookin worse fer wear, with red hair, and a bandanna over his face. He came in here yesterday to buy a month's worth of supplies. He loaded up good and proper."

"Just a minute," said Benedicta, excited, elated, and momentarily forgetting her desire for coffee, she went to get Sheriff Daniels and Inspector Brown.

The storekeeper was questioned but lent no further information until they were ready to leave, then he said, "Are you trying to find this gent?"

"Yeah," the inspector said, putting his hands in his pockets, "we're looking for this man. Got anything to tell us?"

"Well then, I think you ought rightly to know, he bought matches," he said, turning, with a broom in hand to sweep the floor.

"Do you know by chance which direction he went?" asked the sheriff.

"I think I can tell you more than that," said the storekeeper, sending a cloud of dust into the air with his broom. "I would give a guess he is a stayin' at a cabin, an abandoned farmhouse in a remote area just west of here, bout ten or fifteen miles west, I would rightly say," and scratching his head, he went back to his sweeping, remarking as he swept, "Ain't no t'other place fer a stranger round these parts."

Benedicta was dumbfounded. *It is too good to be true,* she thought to herself. She was hopeful. Right there she decided, *I want to speak with this man who has caused such havoc in my family for so long. I am sure that this kidnapper is the same man who had, in his teens, started the fire in our family's kitchen resulting in the death of my brother.*

Benedicta went to the head of the pack of volunteers as they prepared supplies for their continued search. Determined, she picked up her pack, shouldered it, and, holding her canteen of water in her hand, followed the deputies up the hill.

They'd been climbing and struggling, slipping and sliding, amid rocks and up hills for an hour. Huffing and puffing, Benedicta went on, knowing she wasn't in the best shape for this, knowing she should get more exercise. She was, though, keeping up with the group, and that was what counted. She made a mental note, *I plan to start swimming when I get back to Cincinnati, I'll bike again, do weights.*

It was a cool early morning, predawn. Each of the deputies, Sheriff Daniels, Inspector Brown, Jude and she had flashlights in hand and a walking stick to balance.

"Hush, be still," said Inspector Brown, peering into the grey black sky. "There's a cabin there, in the clearing. If they are here, we're close," he fingered the Glock in his shoulder holster.

They had scouted the mountainous terrain and canyons yesterday and found the cabin. Now they were here again, waiting.

It was chilly on an early October morning in the mountains. Benedicta had on a jacket, and she pulled it tight about her shoulders now. She slumped onto some rocks, surveying the situation. A dark plume of smoke rose from the chimney. The cabin was dark, pitch black and ominously quiet. Shadows were everywhere as dawn advanced upon them. Danger seemed to lurk behind every tree, every rock.

No one appeared to be stirring in the cabin. Could they capture him while he slept? she wondered. It had all come down to this, sitting in the dark, the officers planning their next move.

An animal howled in the distance, breaking the silence. *Probably a coyote,* she thought. Another animal, this one closer, whined. Crickets chirped, *why haven't I heard them before?* A bird began a song. Earth was awakening. Rays of glittering sun shone faintly in the sky overhead.

A glow of light appeared in the cabin. Noises, voices, cursing, followed. Glass shattered, an outline of two people pummeling each other could be seen in the window.

A scream! *It is Brie. Brie is in trouble. What is happening?* Benedicta shot to her feet, made a move forward but Inspector Brown pulled her back with a firm hand. "Listen," he whispered, "you don't want to give away our advantage, not yet. It will be safer for your sister." She relaxed back against the rock on which she had been crouching. Jude took her hand.

A second scream. This time the scream held more distress.

"You damn bitch," shouted a male voice, "I'll teach ya to try to git the better've me."

The light was getting sharper, they could now see clearly the ramshackle cabin. It was set against a hillside. A door and a window were in the rear, wood was piled up beside the door. An axe lay next to the wood. They were planning a lengthy stay by the looks of things.

A struggle could be heard and seemed to ensue inside the cabin. Moans and loud grunts, cursing and sharp screams punctured the early morning silence. "Oh God," said Benedicta, "what is happening to her?"

The men were hunched together planning strategy. Benedicta felt hopelessly alone with her worry about Brie. Jude had his arm around her shoulders and was attempting to console her. She felt bereft.

That was when it happened. Brie burst through the door and out into the grass. She had on a bra and panties and a pair of sneakers. She was running as she looked over her shoulder at her assailant. Following in pursuit was Wooley Catrell. Dressed in a pair of boxer shorts and barefoot, he tore out after Brie.

Wooley tackled Brie, taking her down. The two scuffled on the ground. Benedicta watched in horrified fascination.

"No! No! I won't do it. And you are not going to make me," screamed Brie, using a stick to thrash the air, then she began throwing rocks.

Wooley slapped her across the face, hard, then pinned her arms to her sides.

Benedicta gasped. She could see what was coming next. Wooley reached for Brie's panties. As he did so, the sheriff stood, and came forward, within earshot; he fired a warning into the air. "Hold it right there, the jig is up," shouted the sheriff. "You are under arrest for the kidnapping and attempted rape of Brie Malloy. Put your hands in the air."

Wooley, stunned, jerked his body up and off Brie and reached for his gun. There was no gun, no pocket, no trousers. Seeming confused for a moment, the perpetrator hesitated. A few feet away lay a holster holding a gun, a Glock, propped against a tree. Wooley lurched for it. He retrieved the fire-arm, and next, grabbed Brie. Holding the firearm in one hand and grabbing Brie with the other, he hoisted her to a standing position, and pinned her in front of him as a shield as he released the safety on the gun.

Brie was quick in her thinking. She raised her foot and viciously stomped, mashing his bare foot. Her shoe became the weapon. In one swift pirouette, she twisted, kicking him hard in the groin.

"Ow, damn! Ow! Ow!" Wooley doubled over, dropped the gun in his surprise and pain, and then clumsily, reached for it. Brie pounced first, seeming to fly through the air, her whole body coming to rest on top of the weapon. Quickly, lest her attacker take action before her, she managed to hold the gun in her hand. In one telling movement, she flipped over on her back, and raised herself to a sitting position, just in time to face her assailant. She sat poised, pointing the gun at Wooley.

Brie cocked the gun. "This is for all the days you've kept me tied up," she hissed. "This is for the humiliation you've caused me. This is for bringing me up here, for taking my freedom, for terrifying me." Wooley seemed to cower in front of her.

Benedicta and the others watched the drama in stunned disbelief. Now, Inspector Brown broke from the pack, came out from behind the rocks, held his own gun pointed at Wooley, and walked decisively toward the two.

"It's all over, Catrell. Lie down on the ground, hands behind your back." He looked at Brie, and said in a gentler voice, "Brie, good girl. You've managed to stand up for yourself quite nicely. Are you ok?" He advanced to the side of Brie, leaned over and took her weapon, stuffing it in his waist band, his own gun still pointed at Wooley.

"I am ever so glad to see you, Inspector," Brie said as he helped her scramble to her feet. "You came just in time. He was going to rape and kill me and go back after Benedicta. I couldn't let that happen. I wouldn't," she said.

Jude came forward and placed his jacket around Brie's bare shoulders.

The sheriff advanced and put handcuffs on Wooley, reading him his rights. "You have the right to remain silent, anything you say can and will be used against you in a court of law. You have the right to an attorney. If you can't afford one, one will be appointed for you—"

Benedicta thought for a moment. All the months of tension and fear, all the time of not knowing, all of that had come to an end here. Her anxiety dissolved within her. Yet, there was more for her, something she wanted to know.

Benedicta rushed forward. "Brie, are you all right? Oh Brie, it's over. You are safe." Benedicta put her arms around the nearly naked young woman and hugged her tightly. Wooley spat at Benedicta as she came close with the sleeve of her jacket, grimacing.

"Wooley," Benedicta addressed the captured man, and said to him, "You don't deserve leniency, but I want to know what happened to my brother. I will help you if you tell me. You were in the house the night of the fire. You know what occurred, don't you?

Wooley spat at Benedicta once again but missed her. "I'm nut tellin ya anythin, bitch," he growled.

The sheriff yanked on the handcuffs, Wooley let out a fierce yelp.

"Pay attention to the woman, speak up," said the sheriff, again yanking on the handcuffs.

"Yeah, I know all right," he said. "I shot your brother t'death. I started a fire to hide the evidence. He knew I was messin roun with the old lady. He was going t'tell, spoil it fer me. I couldn't let that happen." He shook his head and said, "I had a good thing goin."

Despite the news that Wooley had shot and killed her brother, Benedicta let out an audible sigh of relief. Her breathing quickened. She felt her whole body relax. Benedicta took a deep breath and let it out. Ben had not burned to death in the fire. Her worst fears collapsed.

"Thank you for telling me. And you came back a few nights later, did you not?"

"Yeah, ya bet your life I did. I would've had my way with ya then but the old lady surprised me. She would've found me. I had to run."

"And why have you been after us, these many years later?" She had wanted to know the answer to this question.

"I was a neighbor to your sister at the Milner Hotel. I was afraid she would recognize me. I didn't want no trouble."

Someone put a blanket around Brie and she pulled it close to her, her hand linked with Benedicta's.

The sheriff jerked forcibly on Wooley's arm and roughly led him away.

Benedicta gazed into the distance. The hills seemed to rejoice, the birds were singing just the right melody, the sun, now bright in the sky, sparkled on the countryside. She fell into Jude's arms, with a flood of emotions. She was elated, relieved, triumphant, and most of all, grateful. Benedicta turned to Brie and said, "Honey, it's all over, let's go home."

Chapter Nineteen

"Alleluia, Alleluia," sang the choir as they processed through the aisles of the church. The lights on the ceiling were set at full brightness, even as sunlight streamed through the stained glass windows.

The organ swelled in sound as it echoed throughout the church. Two servers filed past, holding aloft burning candles, another server led with the crucifix. A fourth server in the procession swung the thurible high in the air, emitting a strong cloud of incense, which filled the church with a pleasant and rich fragrance.

The deacon was next, holding high in the air the gold bound book of the Gospels. Finally, the priest processed by, striking an awesome presence in his simple gold vestments.

On Sunday noon, Benedicta, Jude, Lulu, Jake, and Brie worshipped at the Mass at St. Xavier's Church in downtown Cincinnati.

The Gospel was about the healing of the paralytic. Mathew 9: 2-9: "And just then some people came carrying a paralyzed man lying on a bed. When Jesus saw their faith, he said to the paralytic, 'Take heart son, your sins are forgiven.' Then some of the scribes said to themselves, 'This man is blaspheming.' But Jesus perceiving their thoughts said, 'why do you think evil in your hearts? For which is easier to say, 'Your sins are forgiven,' or to say, 'Stand up and walk?' But so that you may know that the Son of Man has authority on earth to forgive sins'—he then said to the paralytic—'Stand up, take your bed and go to your home.' And he stood and went to his home. When the crowds saw it, they were filled with awe, and they glorified God, who had given such authority to human beings."

Benedicta felt a kind of transformation. She had been cleansed last night, she knew, after going to confession. She embraced a deeper appreciation of her faith. The change was nothing anyone could particularly see. She did look radiant, her make-up was flawless, she had a new hairdo, a new dress, but the change was more a spiritual one.

A huge weight had been lifted from her. As the words, "your faith has saved you," were intoned, Benedicta experienced being brought to a new freedom and joy, a healing. The world looked different. Her world was different and would never be the same.

Brie was home with her again. Her painful memory of her baby brother, Ben, had been replaced by a more peaceful image. She felt close once more to Jude, who was in the process of getting an annulment of his marriage with Charlotte.

And she was overjoyed for Lulu, who had been reconciled with Jake. Jake had completed a stint in rehab, had joined a men's group in his parish, had been working on paying off his debt to his dad who had assumed his loan, and was active in the St. Vincent de Paul Society in St. Peter and Paul's Parish. He had a counselor who held him accountable, and he had had, it seemed to Lulu, and now to Benedicta, a conversion of his own.

They returned home to find Sister Anne had prepared a brunch with an egg omelet, bacon and sausage, crispy potato wedges, and buttered toast. There was also orange juice and coffee. Inspector Brown and Agatha Forest were there. Mother Margaret Mary was not among the group as Benedicta and her entourage had visited with her after Mass. Also present were Lulu and Jake, smiling at one another, caught up in their own little world, it seemed.

Jude had gone to the Marjorie P. Lee Nursing Home and picked up Lydia, who sat now in her wheelchair in the dining room, surrounded by the cheerful group. Her mom smiled and patted Brie's hand.

Benedicta made a toast to Inspector Brown, "Thank you Inspector, for all you did in getting Brie back to us," and she lifted her orange juice glass in the air.

"To Inspector," all said out loud, clinking their glasses all round.

"No, I thank you, Benedicta," said the inspector, standing up and addressing the little group. "I must admit, it was a little unusual to have a victim's family accompany me on such a dangerous assignment. It was risky and frowned upon by the police department. Yet, you all helped immensely. Your energy, your willingness to go to any lengths, spurred me on."

Still later, Brie had her own announcement. She seemed a little embarrassed as she rose from the table to face the group. "I want to thank all of you who were instrumental in my being found. I have figured out along the way, well, I have figured out I am stronger than I give myself credit for.

"I have decided," Brie cleared her throat and then continued, "I have decided to have a personal goal, a challenge, really. I am enrolling in courses at Raymond Walters College for the fall quarter. I will study medical transcription. I plan, when I am prepared, to work from home on medical records. Perhaps I will work on medical records for a hospital if I could. I would like that. It would give me something positive to do, something constructive, and I could make a bit of money besides."

There was an awkward silence for a long moment. Benedicta was stunned. Benedicta considered Brie's decision and thought: *this could work. Even though at times she hears voices and has rough patches, she could do it. More mental health clients work today than ever before. This could be a turning point for her.* Benedicta smiled at Brie. Benedicta was for once at a loss for words. Sister Anne began clapping and everyone joined in. Then there were hugs and pats on the back.

"This is such good news," exclaimed a joyous Benedicta when she had a moment with Brie.

Still later, Jude and Benedicta, alone on a bench in the cool of the evening, talked of the day's events and how they were feeling.

"In a way, I was healed when Wooley gave me the news that he had killed my brother. I was relieved, certainly, that Ben had not suffered or been burned to death in the fire. And through this whole process of attempting to keep Brie safe and then losing her and subsequently finding her, I have had to put my trust in the Lord," she said as she took Jude's hand in her own. "In many ways, I was not in control of any part of what happened. I found healing in a way I wouldn't have thought possible."

She was quiet for a few minutes, and Jude thought she was finished speaking. Then she squeezed his hand, and said, "The story of the paralytic this morning seemed as if the story was speaking to me. I was in a sense that paralytic. I was so afraid, and when the Lord said, in the Gospel, 'Your faith has saved you,' my faith was affirmed."

"Blessed be the Lord,'" Benedicta said.

And Jude finished the Biblical verse. "'For His goodness lasts forever.'"

Dear Reader,

Just a note to say a heart-felt and sincere thank you to all who read my book.

It was with love and joy that I wrote each page.

I hope you enjoyed reading the novel as much as I enjoyed writing it.

I began by wanting to include something of the spiritual, to allow for the Divine in the pages. I also wanted to say something about emotional mental illness and I hope I have done that.

Please could you write and send a review to Amazon? That would be great and so thoughtful of you. Thank you.

If anyone wants to get in touch with me for whatever reason, you may join me on my Blog on my website at: www.normajean.naiwe.com. I'll be more than happy to hear from you.

Thank you.
Jean Jeffers

About the Author:

    Jean is a passionate writer who attempts to express her love of the spiritual, to be a voice for good, and to make a statement about emotional healing for those affected by mental illness, in her first novel, *Journey Toward Healing.* Jean believes that an author needs to write with a "higher calling" and include something of meaning and substance in a spiritual way.

~~~~~~~~

Journey Toward Freedom

The air was bone-chilling, a fog had settled over the area, and a light glaze of frost covered patches of the windshield in front of her, the frost having formed in the brief moments she had sat staring into the dark night. Both the defroster and heater were not working. She had the window down partway and could hear the sounds of the night.

She sniffed the air, tried to breathe normally, and peered into the darkness, her senses aroused by something, something on the road ahead. Pushing back panic, Lulu tried to make sense of her suddenly chaotic thoughts. *What was out there? What was there to see?*

She had been driving home, along Erie Ave., and was at Erie and Ridge Road. A senior apartment complex, The Dupree House, sat on her left. After attending a meeting, she had joined some of the group for drinks. It was late. She was sleepy. Wide awake now, she surveyed the road ahead.

When the incident occurred, she was visualizing her bridesmaids' dresses for the wedding. *My wedding,* she thought peacefully. *Hard to believe Jake proposed only a year ago. A June wedding would be nice. A great time of year, June was usually not too hot. We could have the reception on the grounds here at Pinecroft.*

She pushed the defrost button again, just to make sure it was not working. *Drat! It is cold,* she thought as she shivered. She went back to thinking of the wedding. *We could have the ceremony outside. I see a white trellis covered with red roses, and a runner, a white one, marking a path between rows and rows of white folding chairs for guests. I could march down the aisle and join Jake in front of the priest.*

Do I want lavender or turquoise blue for the dresses?

Really, it would be a small wedding, probably no more than one hundred people in all attending. Where will I get my wedding dress? she asked herself now. *There is a place in Kenwood, they have inexpensive attire. I could go there.* Shivering again, she tried the defroster one more time without success.

Lulu pulled the fur trimmed collar of her coat up around her neck. A shadow of darkness greeted her when looking at the road ahead. With that, a dark-clad figure stepped into the path of her car. Lulu slammed her foot on the brakes, tires squealing. The car missed the man and swerved on the wet pavement, coming to rest after skidding to the side of the road.

What was it that darted in front of my car? Another sudden movement caught her eye, this time a second figure following closely behind the first, the metal of a gun glittered in his hand. Lulu blinked. And blinked again.

Was it a gun? She couldn't be sure. The outline of a man, a definite form, stood in the beam of her lights. He was not paying her mind. The gun in his hand was poised in midair. He pointed it, like a missile being sent, and discharged the bullets at the dark-clad figure. Three shots rang out in quick succession, breaking the stillness of the night.

Lulu gasped. Another two shots punctured the silence. The form of the first man slumped to the ground. The gunman crouched over him, pulling something from the victim's pocket. Standing, the gunman turned and seemed to see her for the first time. Despite the dim illumination from the street light, Lulu was quite certain their eyes made contact. The figure raised his arm and aimed his gun at her, slowly, ever so slowly, as if this action was just routine work. He pointed. Through the open window, he pointed. The man pulled the trigger aiming at her but nothing happened. He went to fire again, still nothing. The gun was jammed.

The pulse in her neck throbbed violently. A trickle of sweat ran down the back of her neck. Her hands began to tremble.

The gunman stood there for what seemed a long time. A lone car came to a halt at the traffic light. The gunman shifted his attention to the traffic and just turned and walked away.

Made in the USA
Middletown, DE
30 March 2023

27710525R00126